SHERLOCK HOLMES

A DEATH IN VENICE

AND OTHER CASES

SHERLOCK HOLMES

A DEATH IN VENICE

AND OTHER CASES

TED RICCARDI

JAICO PUBLISHING HOUSE
Ahmedabad Bangalore Chennai
Delhi Hyderabad Kolkata Mumbai

Published by Jaico Publishing House
A-2 Jash Chambers, 7-A Sir Phirozshah Mehta Road
Fort, Mumbai - 400 001
jaicopub@jaicobooks.com
www.jaicobooks.com

Published in arrangement with
Pegasus Books LLC
80 Broad Street, 5th Floor
New York, NY 10004

To be sold only in India, Bangladesh, Bhutan,
Pakistan, Nepal, Sri Lanka and the Maldives.

SHERLOCK HOLMES
A DEATH IN VENICE AND OTHER CASES
ISBN 978-81-8495-502-6

First Jaico Impression: 2014
Second Jaico Impression: 2015

Originally published as *Between the Thames and the Tiber*

Printed by
Trinity Academy For Corporate Training Limited, Mumbai

For my daughters and my sons

Claire and Miranda

Matthew and Nicholas

CONTENTS

PREFACE

THE READER OF MY CHRONICLES OF SHERLOCK HOLMES will have noticed inevitably that I have employed only the greatest reticence when writing of myself. This is, of course, as I deem it should be, for the public, which spends so much of its time perusing these adventures, is ever greedy for what it can learn of the great detective, and while it sometimes speculates about the life and origin of his friend, the good doctor remains, most appropriately in my sincere judgement, in the background, a useful second to the great master of detection.

An unexpected event in the not so distant past, however, leads me now to break somewhat with the rules that I imposed upon my editorship, for, though personal to me, it impinges on Holmes's work and the way in which it was carried out in the volume that follows.

In the fall of 1900, I received notice from Combs and Herriot, barristers-at-law in Cornwall, that I had fallen heir to the estate of an uncle who had just passed on. I was most surprised by this news. As the reader may recall, I had considered myself alone in this world as far as family was concerned and had little inkling that I had a surviving uncle. My elder brother and I were the only children of older parents who passed on just before I left for Afghanistan in 1878, and they rarely spoke of any of their relations. My brother died in sad circumstances in Manchester. Regrettably, I had not seen him in many years.

In subsequent talks with the executors, I learned that a Mr. Peter Tomkins, of Cornwall, was indeed my mother's younger brother, and that, except for me, he had no living issue. Mr. Tomkins, I was informed, had spent his declining years in Italy, in Rome to be precise, where he had lived quietly but lavishly before a stroke had paralysed him. He never recovered, and his final demise came as no surprise to his doctors.

I found myself suddenly the fortunate beneficiary of this gentleman, one who had been a successful tea planter in Assam and an indigo merchant in Bihar, whose private fortune thus accumulated would suffice to support me in ease for the rest of my life. It is curious that he lived in Rome for many years and not far from where Holmes and I had set up our living quarters. Neither Holmes nor I ever ran into him. He was, I gather, a recluse who lived alone except for an Indian servant who took care of his daily needs. His friends and acquaintances consisted almost entirely of the upper strata of Roman society.

I deliberately said nothing of this good fortune to my friend Sherlock Holmes, for I intended to have him share in my luck. Since half the inheritance was more than enough for me to survive, I requested the Cornwall barristers to deposit the other half in an account for Holmes, to be administered for him by his brother Mycroft. Mycroft informed Holmes of the wish of a generous donor who preferred to remain unidentified. Holmes did not pursue the matter, though I am sure he knew all along who his benefactor might be. The practical effect of this was to free Holmes from any financial worries and to allow me the leisure to accompany him wherever necessary. This arrangement continued until Mycroft's death, when Holmes received the remaining portion as part of his brother's estate.

It was this unexpected legacy then that made it possible for Holmes and me to spend long periods on the Continent, in particular in Italy, where Holmes had become as well known as he was in England. Although he was often paid handsomely for his services by rich clients, he often charged nothing for his services, particularly if his client proved to be impoverished. It also made it possible for him to concentrate on cases in which the only interest was the intellectual one of finding the solution to a difficult problem, whether or not a crime had been committed.

London, of course, and our quarters on Baker Street continued to be our home, but the sunny rooms on Via Crescenzio in Rome continued to beckon to us. In time, we became as comfortable on the banks of the Tiber as on those of the Thames.

The cases that follow contain a small sample of the many that Holmes pursued in Italy. I accompanied him in all, including "A Death in Venice," the one that made his early reputation in the limited circles of Italian criminology. This case, for reasons that should be obvious to the reader, concerns the death of one of the greatest figures of nineteenth-century Europe. Indeed, its publication even today, and after so many years, may be premature. Holmes, however, has insisted on its public appearance, to quiet the growing rumours that have become part of the daily tabloids.

The collection also includes an account of the death of Mycroft Holmes and his attempt to prevent the great conflagration that enveloped all of Europe. Had Mycroft lived just a few days longer, it would indeed be possible to argue that this conflict might have been avoided altogether. At any rate, the case provides convincing evidence that the war did not start nor have its causes in Eastern Europe but in the cruel events that took place just before Holmes returned to England, in 1894.

Holmes has also permitted me, with the greatest reluctance, to write frankly, if not in detail, about his long relationship with Lady Jennifer Maxwell. In this, I must confess that I insisted over a number of years on some mention of his respect and affection for her. It was only in recent months that he acquiesced with an "All right. May the Devil take you," and took peevishly to his violin. He has not returned to the subject since.

The title of this volume, *Between the Thames and the Tiber*, was suggested to me by an old acquaintance, an American, whom I got to know in London after my discharge from the army medical corps in Afghanistan. A writer of great fame, he was kind enough to review the manuscript in its entirety before final submission to the publishers. The reader should note that the terms "Thames" and "Tiber" are not to be taken in any strict geographical sense, but rather as symbols of the two imperial powers, one of which is our own, the other of course being the Roman, that have formed and dominated the cultures of Europe as well as many of those that lie far beyond what is now the known world.

A final word with regard to myself. The young, provincial, and amusical doctor who accompanied Sherlock Holmes to Italy soon became an astute observer of the astonishing creativity of the human spirit, particularly in the city of Rome. These changes in personal habit and interest took place largely under Holmes's tutelage. When there was no problem in detection confronting us, I would frequent the Rome Opera on an almost daily basis. Holmes often accompanied me, explaining the intricacies of both music and text. It was Holmes who removed my "tin ear," as he often put it, and permitted me to hear things that I had never heard before. My reading also changed and I found myself engrossed in such difficult works as Berlioz's treatise on orchestration edited by Richard Strauss. It was through this work that Holmes and I came to know Strauss quite well. I identified him fairly quickly as "the man in the blue coat."

I must interject a word here about Holmes's great nemesis, Professor James Moriarty. As time passed, Holmes became more and more of the view that Moriarty might still be alive, even after painstaking investigations of every credible report that he had been seen in England and in France. His belief was based mostly on the evidence provided to him by Fred

Porlock, originally a disciple of the evil professor, later his chief rival. In the end, however, Holmes came to the conclusion that it really was no concern of his whether Moriarty had ceased to exist or not. "What is important to understand, Watson, is that the battle against evil is a constant one, a struggle against one of the great powers in the universe, not the fact of a man or his life of crime. Indeed, evil is not a fact; it is a condition of the universe. Were it a mere fact, we would have done away with it. Obviously, we cannot. We are part of an infinite struggle, timeless and without end."

It is over a decade since the notes for the last of these cases were recorded. In their final composition, I have had to make a few editorial decisions that will please some and displease others. Thus, in a few places, I have quoted the speech of a character in the original language spoken, often of course in Italian, but sometimes in French or German. Some will revel in these passages, others will find them obstructive annoyances in the flow of the narrative. In my defense, I can say that Holmes has given his full support to my textual decisions. Indeed, at one point he suggested that he wished I might write these accounts entirely in French or Italian. They would thus serve him as mnemonic linguistic devices for his further language study. My knowledge of French and Italian are far too weak, however, for such a task.

In recent days, Holmes has announced that, upon the conclusion of his treatise on the motets of Orlando di Lasso, he intends to compose a treatise on crime and its relation to music. No one but he could conceive and execute such a work; no one could surpass it.

With the passage of time, Holmes has become less reticent and his intellect remains as sharp as ever. My memory has weakened, however, and I may have misstated a fact here and there. For these and other inevitable lapses, I beg the indulgence of the reader for one who is fast approaching old age. To paraphrase the great Latin poet: *de senectudine nihil nisi malum.*

JOHN H. WATSON, M.D.
April, 1931

AN AFFAIR IN RAVELLO

OF ALL THE ADVENTURES SHARED WITH ME BY MY FRIEND Sherlock Holmes, the one that follows is perhaps the most revelatory of certain elusive traits of character which, despite our deep and intimate friendship, remained well if not entirely hidden from view for as long as we knew each other. It contradicts most thoroughly the image that he assiduously cultivated of himself as a machine without emotions, a bodiless brain created solely to think. This cold façade which he put forward so convincingly, however, cracked on occasion despite his best efforts. The reader indeed may recall my observation, in the case of the three Garridebs, of the great affection that I saw move across his face when he feared that I had been fatally wounded. Despite these occasional breaks, Holmes persisted obstinately in his chosen portrayal of himself, for, even if untrue, the image frightened away fools and those who would waste his time on the trivial. In any case, let the reader know that Holmes has passed on the present manuscript with a benign smile and a laugh not devoid of irony.

I have remarked as well in past accounts that my friend's personal habits, despite his well-known disorderliness, were of the most abstemious kind, even ascetic in their nature. In that portion of his life in which many of these cases fall, tobacco was his only habitual indulgence. As to food and drink, he ate only what was necessary to keep mind and body alive and drank even less, indulging from time to time in a single peg of whiskey or a glass of wine.

In Italy, despite the wider palette of temptation afforded there, I observed little change in his habits. He still ate sparingly and thought little about the food that was presented to him, though I noted that he had acquired a taste for the strong Roman coffee and the warm crusty loaf that the servant boy brought to our table every morning at dawn. As soon as Holmes finished with that simple breakfast, he would retire for a time to consult his books, perhaps the chief area in which his natural abstemiousness had failed him.

As in London, Holmes surrounded himself with old dusty volumes, and in Rome he had found a few bookstores that were greatly to his liking. Stacks of books appeared spontaneously everywhere like large toadstools, and I dreaded the inevitable moment when I would return home to find them invading my own room.

We had found new quarters on Via Crescenzio, in the spacious residence of la signora Manfredini, a rather outlandish woman, who regularly beat her husband, a croupier in Monte Carlo, with a large broom as soon as he arrived on his monthly visits. Seeing that il signore was never seriously harmed during these encounters, we took to disregarding the commotion to which they gave rise, though the beleaguered gentleman, hoping for a place to hide, sometimes raced through our rooms with his wife in hot pursuit shouting *Disgraziato!* and other formidable insults as she rained blows with her broomstick on his tender bald head. On the last such occasion, Holmes chuckled softly, but did not bother to look up from his work.

Our lodgings consisted of three rooms on the top floor of a grey stone building recently refurbished. They were filled with light and looked out onto a verandah that ran around the entire residence. From there we could see the dome of the Church of the Val d'Aosta, and in the distance that of St. Peter's. The rooms were spacious and plainly furnished: a bed, a table and chair, and large almirahs were what our eccentric landlady had provided. Holmes made us each more comfortable by purchasing lamps, shelves for books, and rather worn but comfortable easy chairs on his wanderings in the flea market at Porta Portese. His own shelves filled immediately with tome after tome and music as well. Most of the latter was rare pieces for the violin, but some of it consisted of operatic scores by the newly popular verismo composers Puccini, Leoncavallo, Giordano, and Mascagni, for he had acquired an interest in these works, not for their music, which he strongly deprecated, but for their illustrations of the criminal motives that lurked in the dark recesses of the Italian mind.

One day, in the late afternoon, I returned to our quarters after a long walk in the Villa Borghese. I found Holmes poring over his latest acquisitions.

"A most surprising set of finds, Watson. Look, dear doctor, a group of rare works on the Orient which, being of little if any interest to the Italians, I purchased for a small fraction of what they would have cost in London."

I joined him on the floor in order to peruse the new purchases with him.

"Here, my dear fellow, is Maurice's seven volumes on the antiquities of Hindustan, an exceedingly rare work, for just a few *lire*. Note the exquisite binding. And these volumes of the *Journal of Oriental Research* given to me by the book dealer for nothing because he was tired of storing them in his crowded shop."

I picked up the largest of the tomes on the floor, a copy, bound beautifully in blue leather, of Monier-Williams's *Sanskrit-English Dictionary*.

"Holmes," I said with some annoyance, "surely this purchase was unnecessary. There are two copies of this work in our quarters in London."

"Ah, Watson, so there are indeed. Note, however, that this one is only half the bulk of the others, but has the same contents. It is a rare copy of the work printed on onionskin and thus useful for the traveler who must always pick his books carefully."

I was about to remark wryly on the improbability of his working on Sanskrit texts while traveling, but I held my tongue. Instead, I said, somewhat pointedly, "Please explain to me how and why such works find their way to Italy."

My friend looked at me with a broad smile. "You raise a most interesting question. The same query occurred to me, and I conceived of an explanation that was immediately corroborated by my book dealer. You see, Watson, many of our colonials, having spent their entire adult lives in India and elsewhere in the tropics, return after retirement to England to live their remaining years. But finding neither the dreary British climate nor the strictures of English life to their liking, they retreat to sunnier climes. Often the choice is Italy, and particularly, I gather from my learned bookseller, the coast south of Rome, in the hope that the sun and the exuberance of Italian life will bring to mind their younger days in the tropics. In this they are mistaken, of course, for it is not the sun that transmitted to them a sense of well-being, but the privilege of empire in which they participated. Nevertheless, in this mistaken hope, there has gathered, or so I am told, a small but growing number of Englishmen, who, having served in the Subcontinent and our African dominions, now live in and around the warm hills near Salerno. When the last of the family dies, the estate is disbanded, the goods sold off, the books winding up with the other family possessions in the junk shops of Rome and Naples, to my good fortune, of course."

"Most interesting," said I.

"Indeed," said Holmes, "I gather that others, rather than move entirely to Italy, have taken to a more transient existence, dividing the year between the banks of the Thames and the shores of the Mediterranean. It would be of great interest, when there is a break in the work here, to travel south to see what we might make of our compatriots settled in the Mezzogiorno."

The break that Holmes looked forward to was far longer in coming than either of us would have surmised. Indeed, it was work rather than leisure that finally took us to the Italian south. The winter had been one of constant effort for Holmes. The case of the violin forgeries in Cremona as well as the case that ended bloodily one night in Hadrian's tomb preoccupied him through the cold damp months of January and February. It was only in the middle of March, when Holmes thought himself free at last, that Inspector Grimaldi, of the Roman police, appeared in the very early morning at our quarters. He was, as usual, elegant, both in dress and demeanour, but he looked tired, as if he had not slept. Holmes offered him coffee, which he gratefully accepted.

"I am here not because of events in Rome, which have given me a sleepless night," he said, "but because I have received word from Inspector Niccolini of the Naples police. They are baffled by a case and wish to enlist your help, particularly since several of the principals seem to be British now domiciled in Italy. Because you have often mentioned your desire to travel south, I thought that this would be a good time, *anzi un momento perfetto*."

"Let us hear, dear Grimaldi, what the matter concerns," said Holmes.

"I can relate to you only what I know from Niccolini. On the face of it, it is a rather trivial matter that Niccolini alone might have resolved there in Ravello, but because the matter concerns British citizens as well as Italians, he has felt that your presence might prove useful. It is one of those mysteries that the police often refer to as *il mostro nella soffita*, the monster in the attic. This may be one of the more interesting cases of its type, though I leave that to you to judge."

Grimaldi leaned forward to sip his coffee. "*Dunque,*" he continued, "according to Niccolini, living near the town of Amalfi is an Englishwoman, who is known locally as la Signora Indiana, the Indian lady. She is so called because she is married to Sir Jaswant Singh, an Indian gentleman who is, according to reports, one of the richest men in England. Sir Jaswant owns a villa not far from the centre of Ravello, in the hills east of the town, where he and his wife spend a few months in the spring and early summer. Three weeks ago, Sir Jaswant and his wife arrived for their usual stay. But Sir Jaswant, sometime after his arrival, was suddenly called to Switzerland on business. His wife remained behind to ready the villa and await his return. Feeling safe even without her husband in their home, Lady Singh did not ask for a guard but said she would rely on the servants, who were nearby, in case she needed help. In any event, her husband left and reminded her that his factotum, Habib, would arrive with the rest of their baggage before him himself returned.

"One week ago, la Signora was awakened by what she described to Niccolini as the sound of a wounded animal, a kind of moaning accompanied by growls. She said they appeared to emanate from within the villa, perhaps from the large vacant attic. Frightened, she rang for the servants. They came promptly, but none of them had heard anything, understandably since they sleep in a small building separate from the main residence. The servants searched the house but found nothing. Habib, who had arrived the day before, appeared only later, after the search, apparently unaware of anything strange that had transpired in the house itself. The rumours of what had happened rapidly spread among the *contadini* of Ravello, Positano, and Amalfi, and those living in the surrounding villages. By the time they reached Niccolini, they had been amply embroidered. Some said that a large tiger had been sighted, others that the English lady had seen a ghost and gone mad in the night. In any case, Lady Singh insisted that a guard be hired, but only one old fearless Amalfitano, one Giuseppe Amendola, was willing to stay at the villa with la Signora.

"Two nights ago, the same sounds occurred. Lady Singh called for old Amendola, but he did not appear. She then went to the landing. From there she saw the old man lying on the floor in a pool of blood. Aroused by her screams for help, the servants rushed to their aid. They found the guard still alive, but bleeding profusely from a sharp wound on the left side of his neck. They stanched the bleeding and sent for medical help. They also notified Niccolini, who arrived that evening with several *carabinieri*. They questioned the guard, who said that he had seen nothing. He heard the strange noises, which appeared to him to have come from the top of the staircase, but saw nothing. Then in the dark, he first felt something soft then something sharp touch him just below the ear and he began to gush blood. He fell into a swoon."

"Most interesting," said Holmes happily. "No need to continue. I should be happy to meet with Niccolini as soon as possible. The singular circumstances more than justify a trip to the Mezzogiorno."

"*Benissimo*," said Grimaldi. "I shall wire your agreement and the details of your arrival to him immediately. There is a train to Naples in two hours."

"We shall be on it," said Holmes.

Grimaldi left, and Holmes and I each packed a small valise and took a cab to the train station. Grimaldi was there with our tickets and we waved to him as the train departed. Three hours later we were in Naples station sitting aboard the train south, talking to Fausto Niccolini, chief inspector of the Neapolitan police.

"A very strange business, Signore," said Niccolini, as the train departed.

"*Stranissima davvero*," said Holmes, and the conversation continued in Italian with occasional lapses into French.

"Yesterday, we searched the entire villa from top to bottom. There is nothing. No sign of entry, no hidden rooms, no sign of a wild animal. And there is no clear motive why any one should want to frighten the poor lady."

"What is the history of the house?"

"You ask that question, Mr. Holmes," said Niccolini with a smile, "*con leggerezza*, with too light a heart. History in Italy is a madness from which each Italian suffers, a labyrinth in which we walk all our lives. The villa? Well, it was built by one of Naples's first families, the Alessandrini, in the early eighteenth century. By the end of the century, it had become part of the booty of the French. It became most famous perhaps for the trees that the Alessandrini planted. Now well over a century later, the trees, mainly huge Roman pines and oaks, provide a grove incomparable in the estates of Campania. Napoleon himself stayed there on several occasions, wandering deep into the forests till he came to the cliffs and the sea. After his defeat, the villa reverted to the Alessandrini, who, in a state of near destitution, sold it some ten years ago, in 1891 to be exact, to the Anglo-Indian banker Jaswant Singh. He has used it as a retreat and hunting lodge and has spent several million *lire* on its restoration. It was not until he married, however, that he began to use it more often, and except for recent events, nothing untoward has happened. The Alessandrini were popular here, for they were, unlike so many of their class of *latifundisti*, generous to the peasantry who lived on the land, and so the house has been safe from intrusions of any kind, including *il malocchio*, the evil eye. There is no ghost of the Alessandrini."

"And where is la Signora at present?"

"She is nearby but away from the house, in a convent watched over by a few nuns. She would not stay another night in the villa. She has sent for her sister, who is to arrive from Pienza tomorrow."

"And her husband Sir Jaswant?"

"He is on his way, but will not reach here for several days."

"And the factotum?"

"He is there and awaits his master. Singh has ordered him to watch over the Lady. He is Sir Jaswant's oldest friend. He has been employed by the banker for many years, and he is completely loyal to him. He is a bit *antipatico*, a stout man, one who runs slowly and perspires a lot, but of great energy."

Niccolini leaned back in his seat as the train raced forwards and said, "I must tell you that I do not trust this Habib. I am a local policeman, Signor Holmes. I have traveled little outside this place, my native Campania. I have seen deeply, not widely. And yet, despite this limitation, I can read the human soul through the face, the eyes, the gestures. I know when a man is lying to me or when he has done something wrong. We Italians are an antique people, one with long experience and, therefore, one that has a certain intuition as well. *Il signor* Habib is lying. There is something that he knows that he refuses to reveal. Signor Holmes, I must tell you that your countrymen and their retinues who have sought to retire here have brought a certain *problematica,* a tension *per modo di dire,* shall we say, to the region. The local peasantry is at once attracted by their wealth, but repelled by their habits."

It was just after noon when we reached Amalfi, a rather squalid little town on the sea. Niccolini had arranged our accommodations in a small hotel, the Albergo Santa Croce, in nearby Ravello and far nearer to the Villa Alessandrini, he himself staying with a cousin in Amalfi, the better to learn what he could from the observations of the local population.

"I will learn much from the rumours in town," he said with a smile as he bargained for a cab to take us up the steep hill. Once arrived, we found two excellent rooms awaiting us. From the windows, we could see the Villa Alessandrini resting on the top of a hill not far from us. Peach in color, its olive groves and its magnificent green forest extended behind it upwards into the Apennine Mountains and down towards the sea below. The gardens in front were English, no doubt created by Lady Singh. They were in full bloom, filled with masses of wildflowers, and in the fields to the left thousands of red poppies seemed to dance in the air.

"Come, Watson, let us see what the villa holds."

Holmes lost no time. A rocky foot path led from the hotel to the villa, about a half mile away. As we approached, I saw Niccolini wave to us.

"*Benvenuti,*" he said halfmockingly. "You may examine the villa at your leisure. I hope that your luck is better than ours."

He sat under one of the great trees, writing in a small notebook.

"Habib will guide you," he said with the merest irony in his voice.

We nodded to him and walked to the entrance, where Sir Jaswant's servant awaited us. Habib was as described to us, a fat man, with a disheveled appearance, somewhat obsequious in behaviour. His eyes darted constantly as if he were permanently on guard. I disliked him immediately.

"Where shall we begin?" he asked.

"The house is very large and there is no need to go through the whole building at once. I would like to see Lady Singh's quarters and the place where the guard was attacked," said Holmes. Habib nodded in assent.

If the villa on the outside was a delight to the eye, the mood on the inside was one of unrelieved gloom. Sir Jaswant's vaunted millions had barely begun the changes necessary to a happier atmosphere. The baroque ceilings of the great halls and public rooms were covered with a century of soot and dust, the walls burdened with portraits of the Alessandrini in the style of the Neapolitan painter Ildebrando Rosa. Little light entered through the windows, for the surrounding trees blocked it. The feeling was one of unrelieved foreboding.

We followed Habib to the second floor. Just at the top of the stairs he pointed out the place where old Amendola had been attacked. The blood had been thoroughly cleaned. Holmes studied the spots that remained with his glass, but said nothing. His gaze took in every detail.

The Singhs' own quarters were sumptuous indeed, and were presumably the result of Lady Singh's efforts to redeem the villa from its past. Here there was light, and the Alessandrini were banished from the walls. Holmes paid little attention to the rooms themselves but examined carefully the large windows, the veranda on the north side of the house, and the branches of the trees that grew close by.

"The house has been swept clean since the incident in question," he said pointedly to Habib. "A pity."

"We did as we were told by Lady Singh," said Habib in reply.

"No matter, I have already seen enough. Let us go to the roof. Is there a way?"

"Yes," said Habib, "follow me."

There were four stories to the villa. The highest was uninhabited and was filled with old Renaissance furniture and other dust-covered remnants. At first Holmes paid closest attention to the windows, then to a door that led out to a small porch. He spent several minutes in thought as he studied the door and its relation to the stairwell, walking back and forth between the two, his finger tips together. Then he got down on all fours, like a bloodhound, looking for what we could neither see nor yet divine. He arose expressionless and then went outside, and while Habib and I waited on the veranda, he climbed to the roof. I watched him as he stared intently below, gradually adjusting his gaze until it arrived at the roof itself and the trees that grew nearby, particularly those that were higher than the villa itself. As he re-entered, he took one last look at the trees.

"Very well, then, I have seen enough," he said. "While there is still time, let us question the old guard."

We descended to the ground floor. There waiting for us was Amendola, the old man who had been attacked by whatever it was that had come into the house.

He spoke quickly in his local dialect, Cylinder, as they called it. Holmes questioned him with Niccolini's help.

"*Ajja paura,*" he said, "*non ajja mai avudd 'na paura cumma ghesta*"

"He says that he is afraid and that he was never as frightened as when he felt the presence of this creature."

Amendola pointed to the bandage over his wound.

"Ask him," said Holmes, "if he has any idea as to what it was."

Once started, the poor man could only babble on without stopping. Holmes recorded his very words in order to examine them thoroughly later.

"*Nullo saccio, era 'bbastanza grande, cumma se fosse nu cane, o forse na specie da 'attu, o magara na gatta da muntagna. Da golora neru, o forsa brunnu. capedda' morbida, cumma nu ucedd. M'a morso achi, e poi s'e na scapadda.*" (I don't know, it was fairly big, like a dog, or maybe a cat, or maybe a mountain cat. Black, or maybe brown. Soft fur, like bird feathers maybe. It bit me here, and then ran away.)

"Io su nadu qui, ajju passadu la vida mia indera da rachhenna, ma vi digo che io non va chhiu da sola fuora la sera, eppura la famiglia resta a casa e non va fuora. Chistu paes non e cumma era primu. E non sara mai cumma era. Adessu, lu Diavolu se stessu s'e messu fra noi e Diu. Sima tudda disgraziad', non sima mangha cristian'. Lu malocch' e benuda cu' ghista genda schifosa indian'. Bisogna che se na andassa da chi. So' cumma i zingara." (I was born here, I have passed my entire life here, but I tell you that I no longer go out at night, and my family also stays home and doesn't go out. This place is no longer the way it was. And it will never be the way it was. The devil has put himself between us and God. We are all unfortunates, we are not even Christians any more. The evil eye has come with these Indian people. They have to go away from here. They're like the Gypsies.")

Amendola suddenly became silent. Holmes thanked him for his words and then said: "Despite your fears, I intend to visit the forest tonight. Will you come with me?"

"No, mai. Se matt cumma tuda sti ingles." (No, never. You are crazy like all these English.")

The conversation ended abruptly when the old man said he wanted to answer no further questions, Holmes and I took our leave and together with Niccolini began the walk back to the hotel. I noted that Habib left without a word.

It was by now late afternoon. As we entered, Niccolini was handed a note by the door man.

"Some troubling news," he said. "I have learned in the market in Amalfi that among the baggage brought by Habib was a large box that apparently contained something live, either a large bird of prey, or perhaps a large dog. And a message from Grimaldi that Sir Jaswant did not go to Switzerland at all, but after receiving an urgent message from Habib, went to the French-Italian border where the police were ready to seize a large black box. I gather that the local French *douanes* submitted to temptation and allowed the box through, as did the Italians for presumably the same fee. Because of his position and power, neither police demanded to know from Singh what was in the crate but let it pass. Habib then arrived with the box and without further incident."

Holmes smiled and said, "Troubling, but helpful, *caro* Niccolini, I think that the thought that Habib may be covering up for his master has occurred to all of us. But let us now visit Lady Singh herself."

The convent lay about a mile down the long hill from Ravello, off the main road and down a dirt path. It appeared more Moorish than Italian in appearance, perhaps originally an old fort. The nuns were of a pious meditative order and found the presence of three men most difficult until they discovered that we wished to see Lady Singh. We were not allowed beyond the gate and were asked to wait outside in the garden, where the lady appeared almost immediately. She was a tall woman, handsome rather than beautiful, of considerable dignity, whose anxious expression spoke eloquently of the tension under which she had been since the terrible incidents at her villa had begun. She greeted us with warmth, however, obviously trying to control her fears as she spoke.

"Welcome, Mr. Holmes and Dr. Watson. I am greatly relieved that you have chosen to come. Mr. Holmes, I have heard much about you from my sister, Lady Maxwell."

I saw a look of surprise move over Holmes's face.

"I did not know that she was your sister. Indeed, I have often wondered how she fared after the terrible incidents in Calcutta."

"She is well, and will be here shortly. She has left England and is residing in the Val d'Orcia near Pienza, just a few hours from Rome. But she will explain all to you herself. Tell me Mr. Holmes, have you discovered what the monster is?"

"No, my lady, but I have several theories. Perhaps you could relate to me your experience, however distasteful that may be."

"I have told all to the police, but it may help if I repeat what I remember," she began. "Sir Jaswant and I arrived here three weeks ago. We began our usual schedule, staying at the *albergo* while the house was readied for us. My husband in retrospect seemed preoccupied with his bank. About a week after our arrival, he informed me that Habib had wired saying that questions had arisen in Switzerland and that he would have to go to Zurich. I was disappointed of course, but I was buoyed by his belief that it would be a short trip. Nothing occurred until a week after his departure. Habib arrived with more of our belongings a few days after Jaswant left and told me that my husband would be further delayed. I was again disappointed but glad to see Habib and the safe arrival of our belongings."

"It was just over a week ago when I heard the terrible sounds. It must have been around three in the morning when they began, low growls, moans if you will, coming from some unknown place. At first I thought they were the growls of a dog or a cat, but they soon took on the eerie sound of something I had not heard before. Terrified, I rang the bell. No one came at first. I screamed in terror, and finally the servants came. Habib was nowhere to be found. When he appeared a while later, he said that he had fallen into a deep sleep and had heard nothing.

"It was then that I insisted on a separate guard in the house. Habib made a rapid search through the house but found nothing. I went back to my room but could not sleep. I heard nothing more except rustling in the trees, which I took to be the early morning breeze.

"At daybreak, I left the house and asked the servants to make a complete search. In the afternoon, Habib reported that nothing had been found and that in all likelihood it was a stray animal and that he was convinced that the house was safe. I insisted on my stipulation that a guard be hired. The old man Amendola was employed. I felt relieved that day and laughed at my own fear. It was, after all, only another monster in the attic. But that night the growls occurred again, and when I rushed to the landing I saw Amendola bleeding badly. Poor man, he was almost unconscious when the servants rushed in and saved him. Habib this time was immediately present, terrified himself it looked. He scoured the place but found nothing."

Holmes listened intently. She spoke without guile, but filled with dread, to me very bravely under the circumstances.

"Your account differs almost not at all with that of the others with whom we have spoken. But, tell me, is there anyone who might wish you and your husband ill and want you to abandon your beautiful villa?"

"I know of no one, Mr. Holmes. Everything has been peaceful and the local population more than generous with our eccentricities. Two years ago, my husband told me that he was having difficulty with the bank and that he would have to spend more time in Europe. He has been deeply preoccupied ever since, even though he has admitted to me that the bank has never been in better circumstances."

"And you have no idea what preoccupies him at this point?"

"No, I do not. We have grown apart these last few years. I make no secret of it, and we were hoping to grow closer while here."

"I assume that you did not meet in India."

Lady Singh smiled. "No, I have never been, and my husband is hardly Indian, having lived so long in England. My sister, Lady Maxwell, is responsible for our meeting. Upon her return from India and its disastrous toll on her, she decided to live in Italy. One of the things that she inherited from her husband was a large tract of land near Pienza in the Val d'Orcia. It was an unfortunate purchase by his father for he found that he had been duped and that he had acquired a mud swamp infested with malarial mosquitoes. He himself contracted the disease, and it is our belief that his premature death was caused in part by the infection. The only good thing was the old villa which, with some repairs, could be made entirely livable.

"After her return from India, my sister decided to take it on and redeem it first from disease and then dedicate it to the longer goal of farming and horticulture. In searching for the suitable experts, she met in Florence one Jaswant Singh, who told her of his early experience as a medical researcher in malaria before he became a banker. It was through him that she found the help to redeem the land, which is now a thriving enterprise, and a husband for her sister. I shall let her fill in the story for you since you already know each other. Perhaps we might all meet tonight. Jenny is due to arrive in an hour at the hotel in Positano, and will come to the convent. Perhaps we could all meet at your *albergo* since the evening views are so lovely."

We took our leave of Lady Singh and returned to our rooms. On the way back, Holmes was filled with talk of Jennifer Maxwell.

"A woman of the greatest intelligence and beauty, Watson, someone who has impressed even me, who has little time for the more tender emotions."

On one of the rare occasions that I had observed, he seemed happy to jest about himself and the attitudes that he had publicly displayed for so long.

"I am most anxious to meet her, Holmes," said I.

"But please, Watson, keep your well-known charms hidden. You have benefited from our adventures with the acquisition of at least one wife."

"All right," said I joining his laugh, "tonight at least I shall be an old doorstop."

"Good, dear doctor, so be it. And Watson, pack your revolver, as I shall mine. It will be an evening of danger as well as good company."

Two hours later, we received word that Lady Singh and her sister awaited us in the garden. As we descended, we could see the sisters sitting on the veranda. I followed Holmes's quick step.

"Lady Maxwell, I presume?" said Holmes.

"Indeed," she replied with a laugh. "Mr. Roger Lytton-Smith, I presume?" she asked, "or is it really Mr. Sherlock Holmes?"

"It is he, with no disguise whatever this time. And Dr. Watson," said Holmes, looking in my direction, "the chronicler, nay, the inventor of the great detective."

And so it began, a long conversation in which Holmes did his best to concentrate on the case at hand, until his interest in Lady Maxwell took charge.

"Have you any idea what the wild beast is that has invaded the villa?" she asked.

"Let us say that I have several ideas, none of which is certain. I need more evidence, which I expect to come quickly."

The conversations stretched over an hour. I am not privy to Holmes's, for he and Lady Maxwell early on began to stroll alone together in the garden. My words with Lady Singh, as I recall, were stilted and hers not particularly memorable. We were reduced to pleasantries and then a polite silence.

As darkness fell, Holmes returned to us and said that he would walk Lady Maxwell back to the hotel and that he and I should meet at our quarters. I was surprised that Holmes would wish to walk the lady home in the dark considering the incidents that had taken place. I nodded to him, however, and accompanying Lady Singh back to her hotel in a cab, I rode back to our hotel.

By eleven, Holmes had not returned and I grew concerned. I noted belatedly that I had not seen him or Lady Maxwell on the road when I accompanied Lady Singh to her hotel. This fed my fears that something had happened. It being a short distance to the hotel and the cab driver Salvatore having retired for the night, I decided to walk down the road to see if I would meet Holmes on his return.

It was dark, but I could see the lights from Positano as I walked down the steep hill. For some reason, I began to feel uneasy and I remember shivering in the mist. I clutched my revolver to make sure that it was there. That was the last conscious thought I had, for I suddenly felt something almost feathery touch my ear. A sharp pain in the neck followed and I went into a dead faint.

I know nothing of what intervened for the next thing of which I was aware was that I had awakened in a hospital room in Positano. I tried to move, but my neck caused me unbearable pain.

"Do not try to move, Watson," said Holmes in his familiar voice. "You are out of any danger, but I must say you gave us quite a fright. And had I kept to the business at hand, it would not have happened. Too long a talk with a beautiful woman."

He was pale and fatigued and I could see nothing but relief in his eyes.

"What happened, Holmes? The last thing I remember is a prick like pain in the neck and then . . . I must have lost consciousness."

"You did indeed, Watson, and did not see your assailant in the dark. But I did."

"And what was it?"

"All in due time. You have been here for almost three days, in and out of consciousness. At times I feared the worst, for the attack on you was far more serious than that on old Amendola. Take rest for a short while longer, dear Watson. I shall tell all when we reach our quarters. I have arranged a special cab to take us back."

It was late morning the following day when, with the consent of the doctors in Positano, I was allowed to leave the hospital. I was as weak as a kitten and was grateful for Holmes' strong shoulder as he almost carried me to and from the cab. At the hotel, new quarters on the ground floor awaited us. Once ensconced in a comfortable rocking chair and given a hot cup of tea, I began to feel considerably better. My impatience to hear what had happened must have filled my expression, for without my saying a word Holmes began his intense account of what had transpired.

"Let us return to the moment when I left you to walk Lady Maxwell back to the hotel," he began. "In order to have a bit more time with her, I suggested that rather than take the road back that we walk down the path through the olive groves. You may have wondered why you did not see us from the cab you had taken. But we heard you pass and continued on our chosen path. It took us far longer than I thought it would, for the groves were fenced off into small plots and every few feet we had to jump a fence or scale a wall. We reached the hotel around ten thirty. It was then that I realised that you might come in search of me, but I dallied a bit longer with the lady, finally leaving her around eleven, precisely the time that I judge you to have left our hotel."

"Quite right, Holmes, it was exactly eleven by my watch."

"In a few minutes I heard your step and then a groan. It was your voice in pain that I heard and I cursed my own weakness and inattention. I ran towards you and saw you there bleeding on the road when suddenly I was grAbbéd from the rear and thrown down. I wrestled the creature to the ground—my baritsu is still serviceable despite the passing years—and found myself staring into the malignant face of an almost naked but hideous dwarf. He tried to throw me, but neither of us could best the other. His grip around my chest was so great that I could barely breathe. Finally, he tired and I knocked him out with a blow to the head. I raced to you. You were unconscious and bleeding steadily, but fortunately slowly, from a small but sharp puncture in the neck. I stanched it with a piece of my shirt and carried you down to the hotel. There, with a quick explanation, I left you with Lady Maxwell and her sister, who sent for the doctors. I raced back up the hill in the hope that I had sufficiently injured the beast for him to be there still. But it was not to be. He had recovered and was gone. I decided then that in the dark a search was almost impossible. There was one place to look, however, and I went there: to Habib's quarters. As I approached his hut, I heard the growling that must have terrified Lady Singh. With revolver in hand, I threw open the door. There sat a very calm Habib, with the dwarf collared, the leash in Habib's firm hand."

"Please come in, Mr. Holmes. You have nothing to fear. He is well chained. I am sorry that you broke into our little secret, and I pray that Dr. Watson will recover."

"As to Watson, I do not know. He is a strong man, however. You have much to answer for, dear Habib, and I am about to inform Niccolini of the latest happenings.

"Before you do, Mr. Holmes, I would ask you to hear me out. I will tell you what I know, but I cannot tell you more than that And what I tell you will show no disloyalty to Sir Jaswant, my benefactor, who is due to arrive tomorrow. This creature has been the charge of Jaswant for many years, ever since one of his earliest voyages. He found him on a ship to America, a starving stowaway on a large steamer. Jaswant fed him thinking that he would keep him alive until the boat docked and he would follow his own fate. He appeared to be of great intelligence and resourcefulness, and Sir Jaswant took a liking to him. The creature was dumb except for a few words of some language known only to him. When the boat docked in Baltimore, I believe it was, Sir Jaswant thought it was the end of the matter, however enamoured he had become of his newly found pet. A month later, however, in some obscure place in America, the creature somehow found him. Jaswant had no idea how he had spent the month, but decided to keep him, completely hidden if possible. He gave him the name Pepe and it is that name to which he answers.

"It was only after Sir Jaswant's success in London that Pepe's existence became difficult. When his marriage to Lady Singh approached, he decided that Pepe could no longer live in London, where a special house had been kept for him. I, an old friend of

Jaswant's, was hired solely to take care of Pepe. Sir Jaswant decided that if he purchased a large villa outside of England Pepe might be happy there. And so we find ourselves here, dear Mr. Holmes, near the villa bought for Pepe to live in, our lives brought together by the existence of this strange but human creature. At first, it worked and Pepe stayed, alone and happy, roaming the trees, never even glimpsed by the local people. But one day, I could not find him. I searched everywhere. Three weeks later, Sir Jaswant notified me that Pepe had somehow returned to England.

"It was then that the problems began. Pepe attacked several people in London, fortunately none of whom died. Sir Jaswant, without making himself known, paid handsomely to keep these events secret. But Pepe's temper, and his cruelty, have grown more unpredictable despite the kindness with which he has been treated. Indeed, his misbehaviour has increased since Sir Jaswant's marriage to Lady Singh."

"As Habib talked, Watson, I observed the creature. He was about three and a half feet tall, but perfectly formed to human proportions, except for his hands and feet, which were tiny. He was extremely well muscled, with smooth yellow skin, almost gold in color. He had a full head of dark, dirty hair and a countenance made horrific by a great sullen powerlessness that issued forth from his dark eyes Indeed, I at first found it difficult to meet his gaze until I realised that his eyes hid the mind of a child.

"And that is his weapon of attack?" I asked, pointing to what looked like a fly whisk that lay next to Pepe.

"Yes, he makes them regularly. He uses it to kill small animals for food. The feathers he takes from birds. The sound and the feel of them calm the victim just before the sharp blade-like part of the weapon is used."

Within the feathers, I found attached a white object, whittled out of bone with an extremely sharp point, so sharp that even a touch of the point penetrated the skin.

"A small dab of poison on the end of this and the victim's quick death is assured."

"Yes," said Habib, "but luckily Pepe has limited access to such things."

"I left Habib, confident that he would not allow Pepe to escape, at least for the moment. I returned to the hotel in Positano to find our two lady friends anxious about my return. The doctors were guarded about your prognosis, but towards morning you took a turn for the better. They suggested two more days in hospital for rest before you ventured out. I then asked that the ladies leave Positano for Pienza, Lady Maxwell's residence, where they would be safe. I said nothing about what Habib had told me. They left in the morning, and I promised Lady Maxwell that you and I might call on her someday soon after our return to Rome.

"I then went to the Villa Alessandrini to await the arrival of Sir Jaswant Singh. Habib and Niccolini were already there. I told Niccolini of the events of the night and of your condition. A look of anger passed over his face.

"You have brought a monster to our region," he said to Habib. "The law will not be easy with you."

"Please listen to Sir Jaswant before you make your decisions," said Habib. "Something has gone wrong with our plans."

Within an hour, a phaeton drew up to the villa, and Sir Jaswant, one of Britain's most powerful men, alighted. He was a tall man, about fifty, lithe and graceful in his movements. He boasted a dark black beard, and his head had been shaved clean.

"My deep apologies, gentlemen, for the grief that has been caused here. I hope that we can make amends for what has happened."

He motioned us to the sitting room, where we sat and discussed what was to be done. He argued eloquently for his point of view, and finally convinced Niccolini, who was the most recalcitrant.

"In essence, I affirm," said the banker, "that if the Italian authorities bring no criminal charge against Pepe, Habib, me or my family, that I will take Pepe to a home for the criminally violent and insane, near the Franco-Swiss border, where he will reside permanently at my expense. He will never enter either England or Italy again. The reason for my tardy arrival is due to the complicated arrangements I was forced to make with the authorities at the borders. At first they refused to allow Pepe's entry, but now there is no difficulty. In addition, since my wife's experience has been so painful, I am prepared to deed the Villa Alessandrini to the citizens of Ravello to house an orphanage for the town and surrounding villages. My wife and her sister are only dimly aware of Pepe's existence and I wish that it remain so. Amendola has indicated to Habib that a sufficient emolument will seal his lips and calm his fears."

"Sir Jaswant," said Niccolini, "the attacks on Amendola and Watson are criminal offenses in Italy, and it is difficult for me to overlook them. However, if Watson also agrees, then I will go no further with the matter."

"I cannot speak for Watson. He is fully conscious now and capable of deciding on his own. You must ask him," said Holmes.

It was a short time after that the assembled gentlemen visited me at our hotel. After listening to Sir Jaswant's entreaties, I agreed to the arrangements and directed that during my convalescence Holmes be empowered to speak for me.

The following morning Sir Jaswant and Habib left for Berne with their strange baggage. Holmes and I remained in Ravello for another week and then returned to Rome. He had much to say about the "the small human being," as he referred to him.

"Pepe is from some distant shore of the Indian Ocean, the Andaman Channel or perhaps even Australia, dear Watson, and while I was willing to accommodate Sir Jaswant in the matter, I am sure that our small human friend appeared in his life long before his sea journey to America. He indeed may appear again. In the end, it may not matter at all, however."

Shortly thereafter, Holmes left for Pienza, where he remained for several weeks. It was the beginning of a deep relationship with Lady Maxwell that lasted well over a decade, until her tragic death in a riding accident on the road to Montepulciano. Holmes was with her when she died. In so far as one can, he has recovered from this great bereavement and has moved on. One of his consolations has been the lines of Goethe:

> Aber abseits, wer ist's?
> Im Gebusch verliert sich
> sein Pfad;
> hinter ihm schlagen
> die Sträuche zusammen,
> das Gras steht wieder auf,
> die Öde verschlingt ihn.

A CASE OF CRIMINAL MADNESS

IT WAS IN THE SPRING OF 1901 THAT SHERLOCK HOLMES received formal notice that he had been elected to the *Accademia dei Lincei*, one of the oldest and most prestigious of the scientific academies of Europe. He beamed with pride, unable to conceal his pleasure, as he handed the ornate letter of appointment over to me.

"My compliments, old boy, you certainly are deserving of it."

"Without doubt, Watson," he said self-mockingly, "and you will note that the letter states that I am one of only three Englishmen to receive the honour since it was bestowed upon Newton himself."

"The letter says that you are to deliver a lecture at the *Accademia* within the next three months," said I, running my fingers over the embossed letters.

"Yes," he said. "I have already chosen the topic: The Master Criminal."

Holmes worked furiously on the paper, and delivered it to great acclaim in Rome, in October of that year. In a short time, it became justly famous for its brilliant analysis of the criminal mind. In it, Holmes argued that crime of the common kind is almost entirely the result of the influence of society. The common pickpocket, the petty burgler, the swindler, even the angry murderer, are all part of the intricate social web in which we live. They are simply the prisoners of society and the victims of its many cruelties.

The master criminal, however, differs considerably. He is mentally free of social influences, often transcends their bonds, and with a logic impenetrable to the ordinary observer, creates continual havoc, thereby reducing an unsuspecting society to fear and trembling, one without the will to fight. The master criminal, often born to privilege, can cause catastrophes well beyond those that are normally considered to be at the limits of human evil. Indeed, it is no wonder, wrote Holmes, with great insight, that crime and politics go hand in hand. What, after all, is the tyrant but a criminal politician gone insane?

"The criminal genius is a rare bird, however," said Homes one afternoon as he read through the piles of congratulatory letters that reached our flat every day. "In fact," he said with a smile, "my paper has so annoyed the world's criminal geniuses—there are but five who are left—that three have already made fatal errors, of which I have taken full advantage to put them behind bars. The two who remain are a rather odd couple who will pool their resources in order to do me in—"

With these last words scarcely out of his mouth, Holmes leaped into the air, throwing a large white envelope across the room with all the strength he could muster.

"What is it, Holmes?" I asked in fear.

"You know the poison called upas? The deadliest gift one human being can give to another? The faint sweet odor reminiscent of cardamom is the immediate clue. That letter you see lying there could kill everyone living within a kilometre of our sitting room had I opened it and allowed its contents to circulate in the air. It is not alive, Watson, but we must treat it as if it were some dangerous animal. Luckily, I know it well."

Holmes put on a thick pair of gloves and placed the offending envelope in a container that he had lined with lead for use in cases such as this one. He twisted the lid as tight as he could, and put it behind a set of Scott's novels where it would remain until he could dispose of it.

"There now, Watson. Enough of these letters for a while. God only knows what horrors may still lurk in them. Perhaps I shall ask Lestrade to give them over to the laboratory at Scotland Yard for preliminary examination. I hope they can do it without killing us all," he murmured as he lit his pipe.

"But what do we do for the long run?" I asked with concern. "Surely, the two remaining geniuses as you call them will eventually do you in. We must take some precautions for your safety."

"Quite so, my dear fellow. That poisoned epistle shows clearly that they will not stop until they have destroyed me—and you as well."

I smiled. "Let them try, then. And who are they?

Holmes puffed slowly on his pipe. "A singular duo, Watson, of the greatest criminal intelligence, but distorted for reasons only partially known to me as yet, though I have some evidence that they prepared under Moriarty himself. Protected by their highly placed acolytes, they move wherever they wish in Europe, amassing untold wealth and power. Their chief theatre of operations has been France until recently, but now they have begun to shift here to London. I am sure the poisoned envelope was meant not only as a declaration of war, but also as an announcement to me of their arrival in the high society of London. One of their underlings has twice served as a colonial officer on the island of Macassar, and has a specialized knowledge of tropical poisons."

"And where are they from, these criminals? And what do they call themselves?"

"They are by name René and Jeanne Rouxmont."

"And what are their special interests in crime?"

"Almost everything. They have amassed the world's largest collections of paintings, particularly Renaissance Italian painting of the Caravaggio school. All of this is now stored in one of their large Medici palaces near Florence, the most splendid of which has become their latest abode. They were present at my talk at the *Accademia* and were infuriated by my remarks. I must say in all modesty, old boy, that it is possible that I am the reason for their change to London."

"Curious," said I, "but I don't recall any reference to them in your paper."

"I could not refer to them directly, Watson, since they were seated in the front row, very elegantly and appropriately attired and accompanied by a veritable retinue of criminal admirers. They are a talented and vicious lot. Remember too that there exists always the problem of evidence sufficient to convict. Without such evidence, any attempt to expose them is met with incredulity by the police as well as the demi-monde in which they live. They are, to say the least, an odd couple, but their oddity only adds to their unbounded appetites. It is true too that at this fin de siècle period what they are matters not in the least. It is what they do that must be addressed, for it is an ever widening nightmare for all of those who should be unfortunate enough to come within their purview."

Holmes went over to his scrapbooks where he kept files on all the criminal horrors referred to in print.

"Here, Watson, is one of the few photographs of them that exists," he said, handing me one of his scrapbooks.

I saw a woman who towered over her companion and who looked twice his age.

"They are most odd," I said, "and rather unattractive to boot."

"Indeed," he said. "She is tall and thin, frighteningly pale, her face puckered with wrinkles caused by a powerful acid thrown at her in childhood by an angry relation. The image of her that I carry around with me is not that of a human being but of a high-backed chair, one with wooden arms and legs and tattered upholstery at the top. He, on the other hand, is more human, but in appearance only. He is a rather stout man of half her height. In real life he has a broad face, pinkish in color, half bald, the only clue to his brain being his cruel grey eyes. He is an excellent shot and carries a weapon at all times, but uses it only in moments of crisis. As with all master criminals, the Rouxmonts require that the crime itself be committed by one of their henchmen. They themselves are the leaders of the gang. They plan and conceive, but do not execute. In this way, they maintain the appearance as well as a certain distance from their foul deeds. As chief disciples, they of course revere the memory of the late Professor James Moriarty."

Holmes became silent for a moment as he paced back and forth, his pipe firmly between his teeth.

"Their weaknesses? There are two. They are brilliant in conception but irregular, even lax, in the execution of their crimes. To put it bluntly, they do not prepare well. Second, they believe erroneously in their own invincibility. Another blunder. They remind one of a playwright, who writes the play and delivers it to the director, who hires the actors to perform it. Having conceived of the play, the odd couple then purchase tickets, so to speak, and sit in the audience watching it as if it is the work of others. It is only at the very end of the chain that they have created that they become active again. At this juncture they evaluate the loot and take their share, which I have been told sometimes reaches a staggering ninety per cent. To defeat them I have a plan, of which you will be the chief executor. After me, of course."

"And what is it, Holmes?"

"First, you must announce my retirement. Preposterous, you say? Not at all, dear Watson. The time will come when we both think of retirement as a necessity. Even at this early moment, however, it is plausible that I remove myself from the fray. We must make it completely believable if I am to succeed in destroying this strange couple. Do you recall that small cottage in Sussex where we stayed for a few weeks? I think it might be the perfect spot in which to disappear for a time. As I recall, it is isolated but not far from an old Norman ruin still inhabited by friendly people. Let us go there this afternoon and see if it is available to us. I shall reveal to you more of my plans once we are on the train. Come along, old fellow. In time you will see your friend disappear into a number of disguises."

That afternoon we investigated the cottage. The owner, Major Potter, told us that it had been vacant for some months, and that he welcomed our interest. We found it still to our liking, and upon our return to Baker Street, I called The Times and announced Holmes's retirement and the end of his active pursuit of the world's criminals. He would place such endeavors in the capable hands of Inspectors Lestrade and Gregson and the other brave men of Scotland Yard. Later, he stated emphatically in public interviews that he wished only to keep bees and pursue his interests in other subjects, the chief of which would be the motets of Orlando di Lasso. He refused to comment when asked about his memoirs.

A short time later, Holmes moved to the cottage in Sussex. I accompanied him. The world largely ignored the move, but it was vaguely understood from published reports that he would divide his retirement between London and somewhere in Sussex, where he would spend the greater portion of his time. Both the Foreign Office and Scotland Yard posted unobtrusive guards at Baker Street, and I felt largely free of any danger, somewhat foolishly perhaps. A guard was also posted at the cottage. Except for an occasional suspicious incident and near misses such as falling flower pots and runaway horses in the city, we felt safe and scarcely aware of the guard that protected us in our daily lives.

Holmes spent much of his time in the country, cultivating his bees and playing the violin. The suspicious incidents, he assured me, the work of the Rouxmonts, would last only a few weeks. Once they no longer occurred he would begin to put in place the last part of his plan. He counseled patience on my part and said that he was sure that the Rouxmonts would show their hand in time for him to thwart them.

And so, for a precious while, the world at large forgot Sherlock Holmes, convinced that he was no longer active in the world of crime. The underworld of London and Rome no longer had to fear him. Indeed, I gathered from Lestrade that the younger criminals now active had never heard of him, even though his retirement had commenced only a few months before.

I visited Holmes often, and the two of us took our long walks together through the still, thick forests of Sussex. Holmes usually had a list of periodicals that he required, and I did my best to find them when I returned to the city. It was through them and reports from Scotland Yard that he kept in touch with the world in which he had lived and worked for so long. Far too often for my nerves, however, he still returned to London, solving several cases that baffled the police, but only Lestrade was made aware of these activities. Holmes's so-called "retirement" continued without untoward incident, and his mind was sharper than ever.

On our walks, he spoke of his plans for the Rouxmonts, but did not reveal them to me until he had been in Sussex for almost six months. During that time he often disappeared for long periods. He refused to let me know what he had been doing or where he had been.

"Patience," he proclaimed softly, continuing in the same low voice. "The time has come, old boy, for us to act. I have just learned from one of my many sources that the Rouxmonts are on their way to Italy, after waiting for a time to see if I were about to re-enter the world of crime. I am told that their henchmen are gorging themselves on the recently discovered treasures of Sybaris, a city justly famous as one of the richest of the ancient world. It is their intention to remove all of Sybaris that can be moved and sell it to the highest bidder. The Rouxmont gang have been working tirelessly to have the site closed. 'Closed' not by the Italian government but by the Rouxmonts themselves, of course. One of the odd couple, René, has got himself appointed as assistant superintendent of the excavation. At night, the odd couple unleash their archaeological ants that dig as fast as they can and carry their loot to a small village somewhere in Lucania where it is packed carefully for sale. You can imagine the joyful greed now passing through the hearts of the richest of Europe and America as the rumours grow. The prize? Sybaris, the ancient centre of world hedonism, now for sale down to the last sherd.

"From Italy, they will transport their booty by ship to the Moroccan coast. There they will meet with their prospective buyers, Americans presumably, who have succeeded in having one of their own henchmen appointed as head of the American legation in Tangiers. Once inside the legation, it being the diplomatic equivalent of an embassy, the treasure is beyond our reach."

Holmes spoke in a matter-of-fact manner, but I could feel his enthusiasm as he continued.

"After you return to Baker Street today, you are not to visit Sussex again. I have hired two actors to replace us. They will travel regularly as we have between London and our cottage. They are quite good at impersonations and might fool even Mrs. Hudson. Look out there, old boy, and tell me what you see," he said, pointing to the window.

I did as he asked and saw to my amazement Holmes and me strolling slowly towards the house, apparently conversing in our voices as well.

"I'm not sure who we are, Holmes. They are very good indeed."

"I would have you meet them, but we haven't the time. Here are your instructions in this small envelope. Memorise them, and then destroy the paper as soon as you reach Baker Street. Tomorrow morning at eight, you must be on the train from London to Rome. You will travel in the costume of an English monk, by name Friar Odoric. Your disguise is in this valise. Everything you will need for the trip is in there. Talk to no one, concentrate on your Latin prayers. I assume that you can still mumble convincingly."

"And where will you be?" I asked.

"Not far away, old fellow, at least for the time being. Do not concern yourself. If I am correct, the gang will not notice you. Do not forget: they want me, not you, but are content for the moment for me to be a retired bee keeper in Sussex. Take the valise, Watson, and return to Baker Street. Quickly, old boy, your double is about to enter the room. If all goes well, humanity will be rid of the odd couple just as we meet again."

I returned to Baker Street as Holmes had instructed. His note was terse and to the point:

> *Meet me 23 May I Sassi 24 at 12 noon. Come armed. Inform Grimaldi.*

I was puzzled by the note, particularly by the phrase "I Sassi," but I found it quickly in one of Holmes's indices: the phrase means "The Rocks" and refers to some ancient caves carved in the side of a cliff in the town of Matera in Italy. A strange place for us to meet, but there it was. I must say that I was more than a little unnerved by the note. Why such an out-of-the-way place? Surely, the odd couple must have had a strong reason to travel so far from London. Then I recalled Holmes's reference to the ancient city of Sybaris and the Rouxmonts' desire to pillage it.

That morning I left on schedule. I met Grimaldi in Rome, informed him of what was about to transpire and left for Matera. The train went through Potenza, the capital of Lucania. From there, the ride to Matera was magnificent, passing through miles of vigorous yellow wheat in the fields.

Beyond them the rugged mountains of southern Italy loomed in the distance. It was just before noon on 23 May. I was on schedule.

I walked the short distance to the railroad hotel, hoping to see Holmes before our scheduled meeting. But I had learned that once a plan of his was accepted, unless there was a large enough reason, it should not be changed. Holmes was fond of saying that his precautions were so carefully executed that change could be suicidal.

I continued in the role of an English friar, and inquired in my poor French as to where number 24 would be among I Sassi. The woman behind the desk gave me a small map and I was off.

Lo sasso 24 was not far. Once I arrived there, I saw what made the place so justly famous. I Sassi consisted of a gigantic cliff in the side of which there were innumerable caves, carved either by men or nature, I could not tell which. Number 24 had a large wooden door which swung open for me as I arrived. An old crone stood there babbling in the local dialect which sounded nothing like the language that I was accustomed to hearing in Rome.

"Benga inda, caru fradu miu, lamigo sta inda la casa ncoppa," she said pulling at my frock. I followed her up the stairs. In the dark I could make out a familiar figure.

"Well done, Watson, you are on schedule. Come, we haven't a moment to lose. We are to meet Grimaldi within the hour."

Holmes too was dressed as a monk. "This disguise is one of the most effective I know. I have been within a few feet of the odd couple as they ate in a local *trattoria*, and they took no notice of me—that is, until I identified myself to them. They were astonished to learn that I knew their plans down to the last detail. Let us go, old boy, to our meeting with the odd couple."

Once outside, Holmes hailed a cab and we were on our way, he said, to the village of Marsico Vetere. It was in this remote village that the Rouxmonts had decided to receive the great treasure removed the night before from the site of Sybaris, and it was in this remote corner of Italy that Holmes had spent his absence from Sussex.

The dirt road went east, and in about twenty minutes we arrived at the edge of the village where our coach could go no further. The village of Marsico sat on a low hill. The walk was steep, however, and as we approached I saw that much of the town was in ruins. Holmes indicated to me that a strong earthquake had struck a few months before. It was empty now of its inhabitants. The central piazza and the church were rubble and only the low buildings remained standing. Holmes took me to what had been his abode for the last few months, a small stone house indistinguishable from the others except for the garden of flowers at its front.

"Watch that you do not step on the flowers, Watson, they are my pride and joy."

The house was totally empty except for a few chairs and a small table. As I closed the door behind us, I caught a glimpse of our elegant friend, Grimaldi.

"They are on their way, Holmes. They have hidden the treasure in the next house. They are on schedule and hope to be in Lecce by early tomorrow morning when they set sail for Tunis. We have to stop them—either here or in Lecce."

"We are three against their five."

"Reinforcements should be here within the hour," said Grimaldi.

"Then let me change into the peasant clothes I borrowed from the owner of this house. This disguise won't fool them for very long, but I will not need much time if all goes as planned."

Holmes went out and sat on an old bench and lit his Italian pipe. Grimaldi and I sat waiting as the first signs of dusk hit the village. It was just at sunset when we heard the sound of horses and the wheels of a large coach. They had arrived.

Grimaldi and I peered through the window. Holmes had not moved. He was still sitting on the bench, staring intently at the trail that we had ascended.

Three men dismounted from their horses. One of them opened the door to the coach. The odd couple jumped out and quickly examined their surroundings, like two wild animals sniffing the air after too long a confinement. They climbed the hill together. By now we could hear their voices.

"Where have you put it all?" asked René.

"There, in the largest house," said his henchman, "the one next to where the farmer is sitting. He is known as old man Battaglia, the only resident who has returned after the earthquake. He's no trouble. We have kept him happy with a few liras."

"Peters, you are far more of a fool than I thought you were," said Jeanne, "but we have come prepared."

She turned and addressed the old man.

"Hello, Holmes," she said, "we expected more of you than a mere ambush. Call off your men, including anyone in the house. You have your men and their guns, but we have this, enough to kill all of us."

She reached into her purse and produced a large white envelope and tore it open.

"Come now, my dear Jeanne. We are only three against your five. If released in the air, the powder will kill you and your gang as well. I venture to say the obvious," said Holmes, taking the pipe from his mouth, "that you have hardly come to this remote part of the world to commit suicide. As in all of your plans, you have left a few loose ends to make your lives more interesting: a little risk to prove your criminal courage, your master criminality, shall we say? Even you have to justify your existence. Killing me and Watson would destroy that last opportunity to test your invincibility with opponents you deem worthy. Come, let me show you your booty. It is all there, in good order, every artifact, every last piece of pottery. Your henchmen have done a commendable job."

The two walked over to the other house, opened the door, squealed with delight at what they saw, and returned to Holmes.

"Thank you for guarding the treasure. And you who are still in Signor Battaglia's house, please join us."

Grimaldi and I came out of the house and stood near Holmes. Jeanne Rouxmont moved not at all as she spoke. She was speaking to three men whom she considered to be already dead.

"'Tis a pity, dear Sherlock, that we cannot take you and your friends with us. But you are on the wrong side. There is nothing to be done."

"Perhaps not, dear *René et Jeanne*, one never knows what will happen in this unpredictable world of ours."

As he spoke, Holmes suddenly began to jump up and down furiously on his flowers, destroying the neat beds that he had planted with infinite care. René pointed his gun at Holmes, but it was too late.

"Quick, inside both of you," cried Holmes.

A strange noise, of countless transparent wings, filled my ears. As I peered through the window I saw that the odd couple and their three henchmen were covered with dark swarms of the great wasp that lives in the soil of Lucania. The huge wasps brought them screaming first to their knees and then to the ground.

I looked in terror at the unmoving bodies among the flowers.

"Holmes," I cried, "they are all dead."

"Unfortunately, Watson, they are dead, for which I am truly sorry. My plan for them worked out in every particular. It is the angry riposte of a very tired bee keeper. These bees are a rare Australian species that have survived in the remote areas of Lucania. The breed emits a deadly acid that destroys the skin. I should dub it Vespe Lucaniane, a poor joke, no doubt. Grimaldi, I trust that your men are on their way and can dispose of—ah, our coachman has waited for us. Come, Watson old boy, I feel the need to return to England, where we shall find, perhaps, that things are a bit easier."

Holmes and I returned to Matera that night. In the morning we were well on our way back to Rome. Holmes barely spoke until we arrived in London. It was there that I heard him utter quietly as if to himself the immortal words of the great poet:

Così si fa il contrapasso.

THE DEATH OF MYCROFT HOLMES

In the fateful summer of 1914, Mycroft Holmes, the brother of my friend Sherlock Holmes, older than he by almost eight years, passed away quietly at the Diogenes Club in London, the eccentric institution which had been his tranquil abode for over thirty years. He was in his seventy-third year and had shown no sign of illness. There was little doubt, however, in the minds of those who knew him that his extreme corpulence had contributed to his untimely end.

The news of his death was conveyed by the heartbroken Sidgwick, Mycroft's lifelong assistant and confidant. Sidgwick had found him lifeless in his chair, facing towards the window. His clear blue eyes were fully open, and Sidgwick proffered that their intense gaze recorded the deep concentration in which he had been immersed for days. To him at least, Mycroft, under the great strain of an intractable problem, appeared to have died of a sudden massive stroke, for he had uttered neither a word for help nor a cry of pain.

"A great loss, Watson," said Holmes as we left for the club. "Mycroft's role in the affairs of our Government will never be told in full now that he is gone, but I can assure you that it was great, so great that we shall soon see in coming days the inevitable deterioration of Government, particularly of the Foreign Office."

Holmes spoke in a matter-of-fact way. He had as yet displayed no emotion with regard to his brother's death. Only his eyes occasionally showed the fraternal sorrow that he concealed beneath a cloak of calm and resignation.

Once we arrived, Holmes quickly identified the body and notified those few who had been Mycroft's friends of the quiet funeral that would follow. Mycroft had stipulated the most modest of services in his will, one to take place in Yorkshire, far from the Government in London. So esteemed was he in Whitehall, however, that the crowd of ministers and diplomats that came to pay its respects not only filled the small church but also mobbed the narrow village lanes on that humid rainy day.

In the fortnight immediately following the funeral, as executor of his brother's small estate, Holmes took possession of Mycroft's papers. These were few, for Mycroft did not keep extensive records. His brain was far too large for that. He simply committed to memory what he wished to preserve and burned the rest. The long story of his role in the British Government and his negotiations with foreign powers, therefore, died with him.

Mycroft had often told Holmes that his disdain for note keeping was part of his physical laziness.

"On some days, my dear Sherlock, I lack even the energy to pull open a drawer in my desk. The brain, however, remains active. What better solution, then, could there be than to commit to memory the papers to which I must refer in the future?"

Holmes smiled as he recalled his brother's words. "There was one inconsistency in my brother's habits, however," he said.

"And what was that?" I asked.

"He kept a day book of his thoughts on current problems, often speculating in it on possible solutions. When the book was full, he destroyed it after committing to memory what he wished. Sometimes he procrastinated indefinitely before he burned it. He left the latest one on his desk untouched. It contains, amidst a jumble of thoughts and scribblings, a rather disquieting note: 'Branko Vrukonovic Die Tote Stadt in London. Extreme danger to us. Must warn Sherlock of impending catastrophe. . . .' Here the writing grows weak and turns into an old man's illegible scribble."

"And who is Vrukonovic?" I asked.

"I have no idea," said Holmes. "I have looked through the entire diary and, allowing for Mycroft's bizarre and often recherché reasoning, I remain puzzled. Die Tote Stadt, if memory serves, is the name of an old anarchist group."

He interrupted himself to hand me the book.

"Take a look yourself. There is nothing that would illumine the name Vrukonovic, but there are other things perhaps hidden from our gaze at the moment."

I leafed quickly through the diary. Except for the single entry that Holmes had indicated, there appeared to be little of relevance to my unpractised eye.

"And what other things are there?"

"Look more carefully, Watson, particularly at the second-to-the-last page."

I did as Holmes directed and saw a thin piece of wire about six inches in length and perhaps an eighth of an inch in width. It had been doubled over and curved so that it looked like a small pair of tongs. I noticed too that the wire had been traced onto the page in pencil.

"But surely, my dear Holmes, this has little to do with anything. It looks as though Mycroft may have been playing with a paper fastener."

"It is indeed a paper clip, Watson, but I doubt if it is a mere irrelevancy. Mycroft did nothing without a reason. No, the wire and the drawing may be part of an attempt to arrive at a solution to whatever he was investigating. For us, it must remain an indispensable clew. The wire is not of British manufacture. Notice also, Watson, that there are striations at different points scratched onto the surface of the inside. Let us have the glass, Watson."

I handed him his magnifying glass. He studied the inside of the wire for several minutes and then said: "What I can read, Watson, are numbers and letters but no words. They are quite small, no doubt done by a skilled craftsman, probably a jeweler. Take them down as follows. Reading from the right tong towards the curve: 1G 2J NilR 3C; in the curve RH; and then on the second tong outwards towards its end: 4P 5B NilR 6G 7B.

I handed Holmes what I had written. "A difficult one, Holmes."

"No doubt, Watson, and a very short message, so cryptic that we may not be able to decipher it. But let us reason it out. Sometimes we may know more than we think. This is a message that may originate with Die Tote Stadt. Let us see what we can find out about them. Watson, please hand me the "D" volume from our criminal indexes."

I did so, and he quickly leafed through it and read; "Die Tote Stadt: a clandestine group bent on assassination, sabotage, and other anarchist acts. Seven members of mixed nationality forced to leave England. One Gordonov incarcerated. Others still at large; presumably have re-grouped in Europe, probably Italy. Their names: Gabrinowich; Cabez; Jetic; Branko; Vrukonovic; and the leader, Prinzip."

Holmes paused for a moment. Then glancing at the inside of the wire again he said: "How interesting, Watson. Seven men with seven names. And the first letter of each name corresponds to a letter on the wire."

The door bell rang, and we could hear Mrs. Hudson open the front door.

"Ah, good," said Holmes looking at his watch, "it is Sidgwick, if I am not mistaken. I asked him to come at this hour."

I had never met Sidgwick before. He was a small man, frail, almost entirely grey in color except for his dark eyes which showed certain, if not monumental, intelligence. Despite his thin frame, he resembled Mycroft Holmes in his facial expression. He had been with his master and mentor for many years, and it was quite natural that he had borrowed some of his mannerisms. He sat absolutely still.

"How are you bearing up, dear Sidgwick?" asked Holmes quietly.

"It is most difficult, Mr. Holmes, most difficult. I knew that his health was not the best, but as you know he took no notice . . . only the problem at hand."

"And what can you tell us of the last problem at hand, if anything?"

"Mycroft kept it to himself. He seemed to relish playing with it, improvising answers, testing hypotheses. I only know this because on occasion I heard him mumble something to himself or shout "no, no, no" when he thought I was out of earshot. I can tell you only that he had mentioned a certain Vrukonovic, asking me to arrange meetings with him."

"Indeed, my dear Sidgwick. The name Vrukonovic is among the few clews we have from Mycroft's diary. Who is he?"

"It is a long story, my dear Holmes. For years, he was a member of a group known as Die Tote Stadt, or the Dead City, a secret group bent on creating mayhem in London and elsewhere."

"I knew of them for a time," said Holmes. "They could have done infinite damage here and in Europe but they seemed to have dissolved . . . seven desperate men from as many countries threatening havoc. Somehow Mycroft penetrated their organization, perhaps through this Vrukonovic."

"Quite right. Indeed, and I tell you this in all confidence, it was Mycroft who destroyed their horrific plans with the help of members of our secret cadres. Vrukonovic was the key, for he had so come under Mycroft's spell that he agreed to turn informer. Once that had happened, it was only a matter of time before the gang was chased out of England. It was recently however that Vrukonovic, after a period of absence, perhaps as much as two years, reappeared, claiming that the Dead City had regrouped and was up to new acts of madness, the nature of which they had managed to keep well under cover. He spoke only to Mycroft at first, and appeared only at night. One evening, while Mycroft was asleep, he asked for me and I went to the back door of the Diogenes Club. There he handed me a piece of wire turned and curved in the middle. 'Give it to Mycroft, he will solve it,' he said in a frightened voice."

"When was this?" asked Holmes.

"The night before Mycroft's demise."

"Is this the wire?" asked Holmes, removing it from the notebook.

"Quite," said Sidgwick, "indeed it is. Mycroft was clutching it tightly when I found him. It was I who put it in his diary."

"And what of Vrukonovic himself? Where is he?"

"Curiously, enough, he came to the funeral service. He handed me a note which said: "Now Mycroft's brother."

"Interesting," said Holmes, "and how do we find this Vrukonovic?"

"Since Mycroft's death, I have met with him three times in secret. He claims that the gang still does not suspect his role as our agent. He is most insistent that the Dead City is up to some terrible deeds and that he must discuss them with you. In turn, I have told him that I would speak to you first. In the past, his information has been most reliable, but he has told me nothing of what he considers to be their latest plans. Provided that it is at night, I can arrange a meeting."

"Then do so immediately. We must assume that Mycroft's final ruminations had some real import, and that the word brother in his message to you meant me of course. And we must judge, ourselves, Vrukonovic's bona fides."

Sidgwick left, and I sat silently watching as Holmes's expression became graver.

"You know, Watson, it was unusual for Mycroft to be as concerned about something as dangerous as this without his discussing it with me. He was, of course, a bit of a gambler, and perhaps wished to solve the matter himself, but one must wonder at his wider motives, if there were any. And of course he may have solved the mystery just before his death. Perhaps, just perhaps, he had decided that nothing should be done."

It was not until the following afternoon that we received word that a meeting had been arranged with Vrukonovic to take place that night. Sidgwick appeared at dusk and we took a cab to Russell Square. There we followed Sidgwick a brief distance on Bedford Street, where he knocked. A wizened hag appeared and directed us to the top floor.

As we climbed the stairs, I heard a key turn above us. A door opened and a middle-aged man of about fifty, dressed in a white undershirt and baggy trousers, appeared in the dim hall light and ushered us into his quarters.

"I am Vrukonovic," he said in English.

Sidgwick introduced us as our host pointed to some worn and rather filthy armchairs. I glanced around as we exchanged preliminaries. There appeared to be one small room, dusty, filled with warm, stale air trapped by a closed window over which a filthy shade had been drawn. It was quite dark therefore, a small lamp providing the only light. The room was cluttered, and there were a few photographs. Vrukonovic spoke quickly in a soft voice, as if he had spent his entire life trying not to be overheard. He was a short man, but slender and lean, of considerable strength, I judged.

"Forgive my circumstances," he said, "the vicissitudes of life have brought me to a most difficult moment. I have lived through better. Were it not for Sidgwick and your late esteemed brother I would not have survived at all these last few years."

"You have chosen," said Holmes, "a most difficult path to follow. The life of a spy is not only dangerous but rarely lucrative. What brought you to the Dead City?"

He laughed, showing badly damaged teeth.

"The desire for revenge," he said, "as it brought us all. Turk, Serb, Hungarian, Italian, and Russian—we have joined in a brotherhood of revenge."

His accent was heavy and foreign, but I did not recognize it.

"When I was thirteen, my family was annihilated by the Austrian army in an attack on the poor of Zagreb. I cannot tell you of the grief and horror that I had to live through when I found their bodies in the charred embers of our small house, my mother, father, two sisters, and a young brother of five. My one older sister was carried off by the Austrians. I never saw her again alive. I was left with no one except a friend who brought me into contact with revolutionary groups which were filled with persons who had experienced the same kind of atrocity. One of these groups became the organization known in German as Die Tote Stadt, the dead city being in my case Zagreb, a city butchered by every European army. But from the point of view of the membership, the dead city was any city of suffering, it was for every member the city that he had suffered in—Istanbul, Belgrade, Budapest, Naples, Kiev. It is for us the world itself. As I grew up within the cadres of this group, its members treated me as an equal, and I learned of their unprecedented success among the many anarchist movements of Europe. Their hand had reached into America where they were responsible for killing two presidents, McKinley and Garfield. You cannot imagine the joy that passed through our group when word of these successful executions reached us. I had become part of a sacred order destined, we thought, to change the world and rid it of its parasites."

"And then?" Holmes asked quietly.

"And then, Mr. Holmes, the leader of our group, Gordonov, was captured in London and arrested. He is now in prison. I was spotted and followed for a long time until it was clear to the remaining leaders that the group would have to leave England and regroup in another country. They chose Italy, in particular a village near the city of Trieste, the home of one of the leaders, who assured the membership that they would be safe and could move quickly throughout Europe, where the group had decided to become very active.

"I was apprehended and brought to Mycroft Holmes for questioning. I was no match for this gentleman, for his eyes saw right through me, and I told him all, just what I am telling you now. Mycroft convinced me that I should continue as a member of the Dead City but report to him any plans that interfered with British interests. He vowed that I would be well paid, and that I could rest assured that I would have as much protection as could be afforded to me. If I did not accede to his wishes, he made it abundantly clear that I would languish in an English gaol for the rest of my life. I of course agreed. I left for Trieste where I explained to our leadership that I was willing to remain in London to see if we could free Gordonov. Since that time, I have traveled back and forth, reporting secretly to Mycroft Holmes on the plans of the Dead City and negotiating with him the release of Attile Gordonov. Gordonov remains in jail, and I am under intense surveillance. On my last trip to Trieste, the group seemed wary of me, and a new policy of secrecy within the group makes it difficult for me to know what the plans are."

Holmes took the piece of wire from his pocket.

"What is the meaning of this?" he asked.

"I myself do not know. It was given to me by Prinzip, who is in charge until Gordonov's return. I was told to deliver it somehow to Gordonov. But I gave it to your brother instead. It may mean something to the leadership of Die Tote Stadt, but I myself do not know." Holmes took it back, fingering it gently.

"I understand, Vrukonovic, the great danger in which you have been placed. We are all in your debt, and I shall see to it that you have safer quarters immediately, outside of London, I think."

We left and returned home in the dark. By then it was past ten, and Holmes had said nothing along the way. Sidgwick took his leave with a wave of the hand and we parted.

When we entered our quarters, I saw that Holmes's face was somber and deeply perturbed. He removed his coat and settled on the couch.

"A most enigmatic clew, this piece of wire. Let me have Mycroft's day book once again, Watson."

I handed him the book and watched as he leafed through it.

"Note, Watson, the drawing, a tracing no doubt. Note however that something is added in the drawing: a swiggle of a line that crosses the two parts of the wire. The letters Nil are at one end of the swiggle and at the other end there is the letter R."

"Surely the letters do not refer to the Nile River?"

"Far fetched, but not impossible. The Khedive is not an obvious target for this group. Let us sleep on it, Watson. Maybe some rest will suggest a solution."

It must have been around three in the morning when I heard a loud knock at the door. I arose, but before I could put on my robe, I heard Holmes say in a clear voice,

"Watson, Lestrade has just arrived. Vrukonovic has been murdered."

I went out in my pajamas and greeted Lestrade.

"Quickly, Watson, get your clothes on, we haven't a moment to lose. I misjudged this badly," said Holmes.

I dressed in haste, and the three of us without a word hopped into a cab. Holmes gave the man the Bedford Street address. A distraught landlady showed us to the room. Vrukonovic was seated in the chair that he had occupied when we had met. His hands were now tied behind his back and he had been badly beaten and shot through the left eye. The room bore the signs of a great struggle.

"An execution," said Holmes.

"Indeed," said I, "within the last two hours is my guess."

"How did you learn of this, Lestrade?"

"The landlady let someone enter around eleven. He was a large muscular man, and he pushed his way in, and frightened her, but she did nothing. He had been there several times before so she gave his rudeness little thought. She said she thought he was an Austrian named Karl Ritter. At around two, she heard an argument, in German, and a shot. She ran out to find help, and while she was gone, the killer escaped. The bobby who eventually appeared notified Scotland Yard. The bobby said that two gentlemen had appeared earlier. From the description, I judged that it might be Holmes and Watson. Hence, I stopped at Baker Street before coming here."

As Lestrade spoke, Holmes began his search of the room. So thorough was the search that he did not finish until it was nearly dawn. I saw him take two photographs from the table that had served Vrukonovic as a desk. As he put them in his coat pocket, he snapped his fingers and the trace of a smile went across his face.

"Let us depart, Watson. I have done what can be done. And Lestrade, have the contents of the room packed and sealed until we can give them a thorough scrutiny. They will provide ample evidence for conviction of the gang, if we get that far. And Lestrade, have Gordonov released immediately. We must follow him to his gang. If you have difficulty with the prison authorities, tell them that I shall go to Mr. Gladstone himself, with whom I am on excellent terms. And Lestrade, please have Gordonov followed. If you do not have a good man available, get Shinwell Johnston to do it."

Holmes remained deep in thought on our way home, but once we reached Baker Street he began to tell me what he had deduced.

"It is obvious, my dear doctor, that Vrukonovic was executed. But by whom? His own gang or some agent from police abroad assigned to wipe out members of the gang? I suspect the latter, though we may never know for sure. The executioner was a large powerful man who was able to subdue Vrukonovic, a well-built man himself. He was known to the dead man, smoked Turkish cigarettes, and drank straight gin, judging from what was left on the table before them. But now we have only one way of locating the gang, and that is by following Gordonov in the hope that he may lead us to them. Let us get a bit of rest, Watson, before Shinwell or Lestrade arrives."

I remember slipping into my bed just as the first rays of the sun began to come over the roof of the building across the street. I was asleep at once. The next thing I knew was that I was shaken awake by my friend.

"Wake up, Watson, it is almost four in the afternoon. And Shinwell is here with his report."

Shinwell almost ran in, and spoke in a breathless voice. "From Scotland Yard jail, Gordonov went immediately to the nearest telegraph office where he sent a message to Trieste. A reply came almost immediately. When he left, the telegrapher allowed me to see them. The first one was "Where?" the reply "On schedule, Trieste." I caught up with him at Victoria where he purchased a ticket for that city. The train leaves in two hours.

"He may not make it to his destination, for Bobby saw the Austrian police agent Ritter buy a ticket for the same train. Ritter is presumably the one who killed Vrukonovic."

"Watson, pack a valise quickly. We shall be on that train to Trieste. Shinwell, purchase a ticket for yourself as well. You will be accompanying us. Pack your weapons, Watson. We shall be among desperate company."

Within the hour we were aboard the first of two trains that would take us to Trieste. Holmes was silent, deep in thought. Shinwell made one short visit to us reporting that Gordonov was safely aboard in the next car and that Karl Ritter had also boarded.

It was night and we were about to retire when the door of our compartment opened. A large, tall man in a long black coat entered and sat opposite us. He lit a Turkish cigarette.

"I believe we have met before," he said, directing his remark toward Holmes with barely concealed animosity. "My name is Karl Ritter."

"When we last met, your name was Heinrich Kurtz, of the Austrian secret police and the Archduke's chief body guard and myrmidon." said Holmes coldly.

"You have a strong memory, Holmes, though your characterization of me is not as complimentary as one could wish. However, let that rest. This time our governments have common interests, interests in stopping Die Tote Stadt and its gang of filthy criminals. But neither of us knows enough—we must combine our efforts. Otherwise we shall fail."

Kurtz looked at Holmes and said without expression, "I want the piece of wire."

Ignoring the Austrian's words, Holmes reached into his inner pocket and pulled out an envelope out of which he took the two photographs that he had taken from Vrukonovic's room.

"The wire, Herr Kurtz, is concerned with events still in the future. Let us for a moment consider the past. These belonged to the late Vrukonovic, your most recent victim. But he was playing a complicated game. Do you still hunt, Herr Kurtz?"

Kurtz took the photographs as they passed through my hands. They were of a much younger Kurtz and two others, a man and a woman, in what appeared to be a hunting camp. The woman was quite beautiful.

"Ah," said Kurtz, "Prinzip and his wife, the younger sister of Vrukonovic. So you remember that night."

"Indeed I do."

Holmes turned to me. "Another of those horrible events that leads only to even greater disasters. Let me tell you, and recollect for Herr Kurtz the early circumstances that led to our present meeting on this train.

"It was January, 1893. If you recall, Watson, at that precise time I was about to leave India to return to England. I had foiled Anton Furer but he had escaped. As I was about to leave the Nepalese jungle, I received word that the Austrian archduke Ferdinand and his camp were only a few miles away and that the Maharajah wished me to join the party. Reluctantly, I did, arriving by elephant in a few hours at the camp.

"It was by far the most lavish camp I had as yet seen. The gentleman seated opposite us was in charge. Indeed it was he who introduced me to the Archduke himself, an immediately repellent character, who was drunk already in the late morning. There was a large contingent of Austrian soldiers, a full complement of personal servants to His Majesty, and the usual women's camp, made even larger by a number of native women supplied by the Maharajah for the Archduke's seemingly inexhaustible appetites."

Kurtz said nothing as Holmes spoke, silently smoking cigarette after cigarette.

"One evening, just before dusk, the Archduke was heard to call out at the top of his lungs in anger. His wrath was directed toward his chief valet, a young man named Prinzip. Prinzip had readied the wrong boots for His Majesty and was punished then and there in front of the assembled crowd. He was tied to a tree and severely flogged by the Archduke and by the gentleman seated opposite us. Prinzip screamed as no man I had ever heard. Then his wife, who had refused the prince's advances, was tied to a tree next to him. They were covered with fresh goatskins and honey to attract the wild of the jungle. The Archduke climbed gleefully into his machan to await what predators might come. 'Let us see what I decide to do—kill another tiger or watch it eat,' he said with a laugh."

"The honey had by now attracted swarms of ants and flies and other insects which began to torture Prinzip and his wife. At the same time, the Archduke's dinner and drink were brought to him by a number of trembling servants, one of whom he kicked off the ladder and who fell, breaking his leg. I remained a witness to this scene, helpless to do anything.

"The hours passed, and by now Prinzip and his wife were almost in a faint from the torture to which they had been exposed. Then, around eight, I saw a large tiger enter suspiciously and quietly into the cleared area in front of the trees. It moved very close to the two prisoners. The Archduke did not move but stared down, his gun nowhere to be seen. The crowd of attendants was silent, frozen. The tiger began licking the honey off Prinzip's back. The man was shaking with fear. I quietly took my gun, stepped out of the circle, and with one shot felled the tiger. Then, I shot one warning shot at the Archduke and ordered him out of the machan or I would shoot him dead.

"Bewildered and drunk, the Archduke struggled down. His minions were about to grab me when I was surrounded by a group of the Maharajah's men, who escorted me a short distance away. The Maharajah then ordered Prinzip and his wife to be treated and freed, and they were brought to where I was. In minutes, the three of us were on elephants, our destination the Indian border. Faced with a dead European or an angry potentate, the shrewd Maharajah chose the latter, making it clear that the Archduke was expected to leave his territory as soon as possible. Furious, the Archduke ordered his party to pack and leave.

"We escaped to India, where I parted company with the Prinzips, who disappeared from my view until I saw their photographs at Vrukonovic's flat. I gather that in the face of the Maharajah's sovereign authority and his superior military might the humiliated Archduke made a fast retreat out of Nepal and headed to the Viceroy's palace in Delhi, the incidents described here never coming to public notice. Later, I received a personal handwritten note from the Maharajah, complimenting me for my help in avoiding needless bloodshed.

"I leave the past to you, Holmes. It is the wire that interests me."

"I give it to you with great pleasure, Herr Kurtz."

Kurtz took it and greedily perused it. "What does it mean?" he asked.

"I suggest that you submit it for analysis to your experts in Vienna. Waste no time. And Kurtz, at the earliest opportunity, get word to the Archduke that he should stay within the protected walls of his palace until Die Tote Stadt is apprehended. I can assure you that although we may have thought that an assassination attempt might take place against the Emperor, the Kaiser, or the Czar, the chosen victim is the Archduke, of this I have no doubt."

Kurtz rose stiffly and left.

"The attack dog returns to his master," said Holmes.

"Now what, Holmes?" I asked.

"My guess is, Watson, that Gordonov is already off the train at some previously agreed stop before Trieste and that all we have to do now is await the assassination attempt, which we shall attend."

Holmes's words I found puzzling.

"How indeed do you know that?"

"Just before we left London, Watson, I deciphered the message. It is quite simple: the wire itself stands for a curved road on which the Archduke is supposed to travel. The letters are the initials of the assassins and their positions along the route. The groups of assassins are placed mostly at the curve in the road. You will remember that the letters RH remained undeciphered. They stand for Rat Haus, or City Hall in German. A building located right in the curve. Thus, the Archduke is expected to cross a river that begins with Nil, and that is the Nilichka. He is to be greeted by local dignitaries at the Rat Haus and then proceed. At the curve, before or after he enters the Rat Haus, his limousine must slow down. It is there, then, near the Rat Haus, that the attempt will be made. There is only one city on the Archduke's tour that meets all these requirements."

"And which is that?"

"The sleepy city of Sarajevo."

In Trieste, Holmes wired Sidgwick who informed us that the best information of the British Government was that the Archduke would visit Sarajevo on 28 June, and that he would enter the Rat Haus at approximately three p.m. He would be accompanied by his wife and an armed bodyguard which was thought sufficient to ward off any attempt on his life. The Foreign Office also had information that the Archduke, when told of the possible assassination plot somewhere along his route, refused to change it, declaring that he was safe among his people.

After a week in Trieste, Holmes and I journeyed to Vienna and then to Sarajevo. After a walk along the road the Archduke would travel, we settled into a small inn near the central square run by a Frau Dreisschok, a rather slatternly woman of indeterminate age and features, since her disheveled hair fell in long thick locks over her face. There we waited. Holmes had talks with the local police, who arranged for us to be at the Rat Haus as the Archduke entered.

And so, on that fatal afternoon, Holmes and I took our places in the large crowd that had assembled to greet the Archduke and his wife, Sophie. Somewhere in that great mass, standing nearby, was the assassin, Prinzip, his accomplice Jetic, and perhaps his sister. Holmes kept staring through the endless people, hoping to recognize Prinzip after so many years.

The news passed through the crowd that the royal limousine was well on its way. In minutes we heard its motor and then saw the ornate automobile, its flags flying around the faces of its royal occupants. For a moment, Holmes's glance caught that of the Archduke and a look of puzzlement and fear crossed the Duke's face. He stood up as the car slowed. Holmes stood frozen, staring in disdain at the Austrian.

At that moment, a man and a woman came forth from the back of the crowd and pointed their guns at the royal vehicle. Shots were heard, and the Archduke fell over the side of his car as if from a tree. His wife slumped in her seat, fatally wounded. Kurtz, who was sitting in the front seat, tried to protect his master, but it was too late. He received a bullet directly to the head. I rushed to the vehicle to do what I could, but it was clear to me that the Archduke and Kurtz were dead. Sophie was alive for only a few minutes before she succumbed to the attackers' bullets.

The crowd began to go mad and Holmes motioned that we should leave quickly. We barely made it back to our rooms when we heard the police firing into what had become an unruly mob. That evening we learned that Prinzip and his wife had been apprehended and were to be tried for murder.

It was several days before we returned to London. We consulted several times with the Viennese police, Holmes revealing all that he then knew There is no need to recount the events that took place in the aftermath of the assassination, for we are living through them now.

"Well, Watson, without Mycroft, the Foreign Office has behaved as incompetently as one might have feared," said Holmes handing me the paper. "We shall be at war soon. Those who have a lust for blood shall have a surfeit of it this time."

Holmes took his violin from its case and began tuning it slowly. It was late July, a month after the Archduke's death, and Holmes's prediction was soon to become true. For my good friend, there was to be no respite. He responded to his country's needs with courage and determination. He had no illusions, however, about the dreadful events that were to begin shortly.

THE CASE OF THE PLANGENT COLONEL

IT WAS ON AN UNUSUALLY WARM DAY IN LATE APRIL of 1898 that the incidents alluded to below first came to notice. Holmes had left a note saying that a minor matter had taken him to Castel Gondolfo and that he would return in the afternoon. Having no special tasks to which to attend, I determined to put my solitude to good use by taking a long morning stroll in the Villa Borghese. I spent the better part of an hour in the museum with Canova's celebrated statue of Madame Recamier, and after my walk, I sat on a bench in the cool shade of the Roman pines, studying, with great pleasure, the wide variety of Romans who passed by. I then took a light meal at one of my favorite *trattorie* on Via Palestrina, and reached our quarters shortly before two.

The city was already quiet with the siesta, that afternoon restorative nap which characterises so strongly the life of the Italian. I too felt that sweet lethargy to which the Roman air, coupled with a few glasses of cool frascati, inevitably leads one. As I began the climb to our quarters, I was suddenly met on the first landing by a young woman hurriedly running down the staircase. She addressed me instantly in English.

"Please forgive me, but might you be Mr. Sherlock Holmes?"

"I am not," I answered, "but I know him well. Is he not there?"

"The landlady let me knock on his door, but there was no answer."

"Hallo, Watson, and whom have we here?" said a voice suddenly from below.

I turned to see Holmes, a smile on his face, obviously satisfied with his trip.

"This young woman is looking for you, Holmes."

"Then let us make the climb together. I trust that la signora Manfredini will prepare a cup of tea for us."

The young woman smiled with relief, turned on the stair, and led the way up. I directed her to our sitting room where we began our conversation.

"I take it that you are English?" Holmes inquired.

"Yes," she said, "from London."

As she took her tea from our landlady, I observed her for a moment. Young, perhaps no more than twenty-two or twenty-three, almost pretty, she was dressed in a dark blue dress, a straw Italian bonnet over her chestnut hair. There was a look of strength and determination in her green eyes, but she appeared to be quite tense, her fingers moving nervously on her lap and then fingering a silver locket that she wore around her neck.

"I come to you with a matter of the greatest concern to me, Mr. Holmes. I must speak to you in all candor. I trust that this gentleman is as trustworthy as—"

"I myself am. Quite correct. This is my colleague, Dr. Watson. You may speak before him as you would to me. You are a pianist, I see?"

I could sense her wonder as Holmes began to ply his tricks.

"Indeed, I am, but how could you know that?"

"It is simplicity itself. I noted as you took your seat that your bag contains a common edition of some music. Noting the letters—ven protruding from the top, I assumed the name of Beethoven. Judging from the thickness of the volume and its well-worn look, I was sure that it was a volume of his sonatas, obviously among the commonplaces of the pianist's trade. Add to that your posture, which speaks eloquently of hours at the piano, and your well-developed hands and fingers."

"It is with reason that you have the reputation that you have," she said admiringly.

"But there is more, dear lady. You have been practising with great assiduity a particular piece—the piano concerto in D minor of Anton Rubinstein."

At this a look of disbelief crossed her face, and she became almost angry as she answered, "That is unfair, Mr. Holmes. You are correct, of course, but I feel now that someone has told you of me and that you are engaged in some kind of deception, to what end I do not know."

"Forgive me," said Holmes, with a smile, "I can assure you that I have not spoken to anyone about you—I do not even know your name—and that so obvious are the clues to me that I often forget how mysterious their explanation may be to the untrained eye. Among other things, I am a student of the human hand. Because of its wide use in our work and activity, it can be even more important in revealing a life than the face itself. Thus while la Signora Manfredini was pouring your tea, I observed your hands as they moved unconsciously on your lap and then stretched as you toyed with your locket. Noting the span between the fingers, particularly between thumb and forefinger, I surmised what was almost assuredly a D minor chord. The rhythm and repetitions brought me to the melody and cadence of the Rubinstein piece, now the rage in Europe among pianists. But tell me what I do not know, to wit your name, and why you are here."

The young woman appeared relieved by Holmes's explanation, and said: "You are most amazing, Mr. Holmes. I shall not forget easily these illustrations of your methods. I hope they can be used to help me. My name is Alice Morel, and I am indeed a musician. I have trained at the Royal Conservatory in London, and was selected to take part in the piano competition soon to take place here in Rome under the auspices of the *Accademia di Santa Cecilia*."

"A singular honor," said Holmes. "And a rather nerve-wracking one, I would imagine."

"It is, Mr. Holmes. It means all-day practise, little sleep, and the anxious feeling that comes over one when one knows that the leading pianists of the world are the judges.

Rubinstein himself is coming. Winning means a year's study with him. And rumours are rife that Busoni and Theodor Leszhitisky will also attend."

"I see," said Holmes. "But, while the excitement must be great, there is something else that is producing a certain agitation in you. What is it?"

"Let me tell you how it came about. I won the preliminary competition in London two months ago, and was told to prepare for my immediate departure for Italy. Once arrived, I was to spend the next three months in preparation for the competition, which is to take place at the end of this coming August. It was made clear to me by our director that my performance would mean much to the national honour since whatever our accomplishments abroad we were not known in Europe or America as a musical nation."

"'Tis true indeed, we English are not considered musical, a not unjust opinion of us in some ways, but not totally true on the other hand. Pray continue, Miss Morel."

"On my arrival in Rome I was met by the British vice consul, Mr. Herbert Spenser, who helped me settle in and also to find a suitable piano on which to practise. Through the officials at the Academy he helped me find a flat on Via Ezio, off the Via Crescenzio. According to the notice, the flat was fully furnished, and I was told that it was the property of a Colonel Santoro, a military man of some note in Italy and recently retired. He seemed kind and friendly in our first meeting and showed me through the flat. Despite the disappointment in Italy at its armies' defeat at Adowa, Santoro was one of its few heroes, and he showed me many photographs of himself and his various medals. "The flat was furnished with heavy wooden furniture from the Carpathians, somewhere in Hungary or Austria, I think, hardly to my taste, but I did not complain. Indeed, when I saw what was in the study I was overjoyed. It was a large concert grand piano, originally given to his daughter, he said, but hardly used. The piano, a Vulsin from Graz in Austria, was all I could ask for. I touched the keys and I heard the sweetest tone emanate from it. Mr. Anzio, the music publisher, had supplied it instead of offering it to some foreign potentate. Mr. Spenser had done very well by me, and I thanked him and the Colonel profusely for their help. It was precisely then that Mr. Spenser gave me this locket as a good-luck charm."

"A Maria Theresa *thaler*, if I am not mistaken," said Holmes. "May I see it?"

She handed the locket over, and Holmes examined it closely while Miss Morel continued her tale.

"With this start in my Italian adventure, I was filled with optimism and practised long and hard each day, knowing that if my work continued at that level, I surely should have a chance at first place in the competition. Then my luck began to change."

Tears formed in her eyes, and she drew a handkerchief from her bag. She kept her composure, however, and Holmes conforted her with a soft, "Pray continue, Miss Morel, we are ready to help you."

"Forgive me, Mr. Holmes; it has been a nightmare that perhaps only a musician could understand."

"Indeed," said Holmes, "I am well aware of the strictures that the musical life puts upon one. I am a violinist of sorts and know well the tensions of such a career."

Miss Morel smiled wanly at us, and continued her account.

"The first thing was the piano. About ten days ago, after a long hard practise one morning, I went out to walk in a nearby square not far from the Tiber. I returned after but an hour and sat down at the piano eagerly without even removing my coat. Suddenly my valued friend had changed. The piano had gone badly out of tune and half of the keys in the middle register were stuck. Perplexed, I lifted the lid to see what was wrong. Like most pianists, Mr. Holmes, I know little beyond the basics of piano construction. I could see nothing amiss. The rest of the day was spent finding a piano tuner. Colonel Santoro found one who finally came that evening and restored the sound of the piano. He attributed the problem to a change in temperature and left.

"For two days, I played constantly, always fearful that if I ventured out, I would find the piano again in unplayable condition. But one day, I returned after a visit to the Academy to find two strings broken. The tuner came, and replaced them, saying that the strings appeared to have been cut by someone."

Holmes listened with increasing interest to the young woman's story. His expression became more serious as she spoke. He leaned forward and returned the locket to her. As he did so, he wiped his hands with a handkerchief.

"Pray, continue, Miss Morel," he said quietly.

"After the tuner left, I sat down to play, but after a few minutes, I was interrupted by a knock at the door. I opened and found an older woman standing there, elegantly dressed, accompanied by a much younger man.

"'Scusi,'" she said in Italian, *'sono la Signora Santoro e quest'è il mio avocato, Giorgio.'"*

"I understood what she said, but impressed upon her as intelligibly as I could that I spoke little Italian. She then continued haltingly in English. I invited them in and the signora explained to me why they had come: She and the Colonel no longer lived as husband and wife but were separated, though not divorced, however, since divorce was not possible in Italy. A court had awarded her the flat. The Colonel was allowed to live in it but was not permitted to rent it to anyone. She told me that I would be served and asked to appear in court as a witness to the Colonel's breach of their agreement. She went to great lengths, and so did her lawyer, to explain to me that they bore me no ill will but that I would have to move immediately, the sooner the better. She also asked to see the piano that the colonel had given to me for practise. She became quietly furious as she walked around it. She then stormed out, shouting that the piano too was hers. The lawyer handed me what appeared to be a summons and left.

"When they had gone, I realized that circumstances were conspiring to make the practise necessary for the competition almost impossible. To add to the matter, and even worse, an hour or so later, the Colonel appeared at the door. No sooner had he entered than he was down on his knees, pleading with me, crying and sobbing, saying, if

I understood correctly, that he would be ruined if I testified in court against him.

"'Please,' he cried, tears running profusely down his cheeks, 'leave as quickly as possible. I will help you.'

"I told him that I would certainly not testify against him in court and that I would be resident there for only a few more weeks. He agreed, though not without many more tears, to allow me to stay a while longer. I realised, however, that I might have made a grave error. He left, and I tried to compose myself. Exhausted, I decided to retire early."

Holmes filled Miss Morel's cup and asked her to continue.

"The following day was even worse. I arose and dressed and walked into the living room. There I found the Colonel sound asleep on the floor near the window. I must have uttered a cry, for he suddenly awoke and again began his soulful wailing. He asked my forgiveness for his intrusion into my privacy, but he was there because his wife had arranged it so that he could not return to his lodging. He complained bitterly about the fact that he was a war hero but in spite of that, he had to live in the gutter.

"Still quite frightened by his unexpected presence, I ordered him to go, which he did, not again without tearfully beseeching me on his knees to leave at once.

"When he had gone, I went to the study. I sat down at the piano and sensed that something was terribly wrong again. I opened the lid and saw that the keys had been damaged and several hammers broken. The piano was now unplayable and perhaps it never would be playable again."

As Miss Morel's story progressed, the expression on Holmes's face moved from one of amused benevolence to one of deeper concern.

"Please continue, Miss Morel," he said gravely. Your story is far more interesting and the circumstances more dangerous than I would have thought at first."

"There is little left to tell . . . except that I found these in one corner of the room."

She took from her bag three piano hammers and gave them to Holmes.

"I found these behind the door to the study as I was leaving. They are badly damaged," she said.

"Broken, the felt partially removed. Miss Morel, I very much want to help you, but you must take my immediate advice not to return to your flat. La signora Manfredini has several empty rooms here. I suggest that you take one and move another piano in. In the meantime, there is not a moment to lose. I would like to visit your flat before any more time passes. And if you trust us, we will arrange for one of Mrs. Manfredini's maids to pack your things."

Miss Morel readily assented to the scheme. She seemed completely relieved that she would not have to return to her flat, and quickly handed the keys over to Holmes. As we left, she was engaged with Signora Manfredini over which room to take. Maria, a strong servant girl from the Abruzzi, left with us.

"One final matter, Miss Morel. How might we find Colonel Santoro?"

"Mr. Spenser knows him quite well. He should be able to help you," she replied.

The trip along the Via Crescenzio was a short one. The spring rains had muddied the streets, however, and the continuous travel of countless coaches had created deep ruts. It was over an hour later when our cab turned into the Via Ezio and we entered the foyer of *numero* 27, and then *interno dodici*, or flat number 12.

"Keep the maid with you here, Watson. I wish to take a preliminary look myself, to make sure that nothing untoward has happened."

I held back with the maid as Holmes entered. In the half light, I saw that we had entered a large and well-furnished flat. Nothing seemed out of order until I noticed what appeared to be a human figure in military attire, resting on its knees, its arms as if in abject supplication to some unseen deity, its head attached to a long wire hanging from the ceiling. The figure appeared dead, motionless, except for a slight spin from the long wire. Holmes rushed over to cut the body down. As he did so, he laughed.

"Clever, Watson, eh?"

I rushed over in the hope that some life might be left in the man.

"Don't touch, Watson. It's not quite what you think it is."

He grinned, as he pointed to two pillows stuffed inside the soldier's uniform, which had given the whole the thick look of a rather stout human figure. The wire was hooked onto the back of the coat collar just below where a large ball of white wool acted as a head. A military cap hid most of the latter.

Holmes went into the bedroom. There the piano that Miss Morel had played so lovingly had had its legs removed and was sitting on the floor, the legs in the corner.

"Good lord, Holmes," I said, "this is an insanity."

"Quite, my dear Watson, and a bit of a mystery as well."

While we still had light, Holmes quickly looked over the flat.

"For what it's worth, Watson, the wire from which the figure hangs is the low A string plus a piece of the C tied to it. The pillows are from the bedroom, and the uniform, if I judge correctly from the epaulettes, that of a colonel in the Italian army. Let us leave it in place."

"Poor Miss Morel. This was meant to scare her out of her wits," said I, thinking of our innocent client.

"Indeed, this would have shaken her a bit. I think it was put there more for the Colonel's benefit than for Miss Morel's. It is an ominous warning," replied Holmes.

Holmes glanced about the room and then asked, "Watson, are you feeling sufficiently strong to help me put the legs back on the piano and place it upright?

"Of course. It should be easy enough."

"Then let us bring the legs over and see what we can manage."

With great effort we moved the piano onto its straight side, put two legs in place and while Holmes held it up at its narrow end, I screwed in the last leg. Holmes let it down with a bit of a grunt.

"Now let us see what this instrument is about," he said, lifting the lid.

"A beautifully made instrument," said I. "Why on earth would one want to destroy it?"

"When we learn that, dear Watson, we will have solved our little mystery. . . . Ah, here we go. Most interesting."

Holmes had taken out a rule and measured the side of the case.

"Fully three inches deeper . . ." he muttered to himself. As he spoke, he crawled under the instrument to examine the sound board.

"There are deep holes drilled into the case, where screws have been removed," he said as he stood up.

Holmes moved his hand and fingers over the sound board.

"A fine dust, Watson. Most interesting. Come, let us go and visit La Casa Sanzio, the supplier of pianos to all of Italy. And there is time to stop at our embassy to meet Mr. Spenser."

As we left, I saw Holmes looking at a photograph on Santoro's desk.

"Three people—Miss Morel, Colonel Santoro, and presumably Mr. Herbert Spenser. Odd, is it not, dear Watson, that our Englishman has the same name as an illustrious personage? Hasn't that occurred before?"

"Indeed," said I, "there was Mr. Arthur Wellesley, who passed himself off as the son of Wellington. Terrible fellow, that one."

Holmes said nothing as he wiped the dust off his hands with a handkerchief, and we were off. Our route took us to the British Embassy to meet our vice consul. Holmes was in and out in seconds.

"As I suspected, Watson, there is no Herbert Spenser at the Embassy. The post has not been filled for several months.

Mr. 'Spenser,' whoever he is, is a liar and a fraud. We shall catch up with him soon, I hope."

I sat quietly as Holmes reflected. I knew nothing of the Sanzio establishment, which was involved not only in supplying pianos but also was one of Europe's leading music publishers.

"The case is a remarkable one, Holmes," I said finally. "I must say that I am more than a bit mystified. The mock death of the colonel, the destroyed piano . . . to what end?"

"I have some ideas, old fellow, but I too am still in the dark."

Holmes was silent and then began to hum a tune to himself, something I did not recognize.

"Puccini, Watson, from the third act of *La Bohème*."

"Never heard of him," I retorted.

Holmes smiled. As we approached the Sanzio establishment, he broke his silence.

"Without Sanzio, Watson, there would be almost no music in Italy, especially new music. Leoncavallo, Puccini, Mascagni, and many others must give credit to Amilcare Sanzio for his support and interest in their work."

"I know nothing of Italian opera, my dear Holmes," said I. "I am, dear fellow, a musical ignoramus. A tin ear, as they say."

"Then you will learn while we are here. By the by, old fellow, I am sure now that this case has nothing to do with opera, music in general, or pianos, for that matter, except incidentally. Ah, but here we are *da* Sanzio. Come along, we are about to meet one of the great publishers of Europe."

The Sanzio establishment, I noted, was located in an ornate palazzo, not far from the Piazza Venezia. Arrigo Sanzio, a tall, handsome man of about fifty, greeted us warmly in Italian, but once he realized that I knew little of his language, he spoke to me in French.

"Forgive me, please, *dottore*, but we Italians know almost no English."

"And we English are quite stubborn about foreign languages. French is the only language we know."

"Except for the languages of our colonies," said Holmes sardonically.

"We Italians are late in building an empire, *caro dottore*, but someday perhaps we shall establish a new order in the Mediterranean and bring back the glory of ancient Rome. *Ma, basta*, you are here because of Miss Morel and her piano."

"Yes, indeed, but most importantly, I have some questions that you may be able to answer for us," said Holmes.

"*Dica, signore*," said Sanzio.

"Miss Morel was given a Vulsin, I think, a piano presumably made in Austria. I confess to ignorance of the Vulsin piano. Could you enlighten us as to the history of the company?"

"The Vulsin, *caro ingeniere*, is, as Miss Morel has put it, a fine instrument. I would go further, however, and describe it as the best piano ever made. The company is new and makes very few, no more than twenty or thirty each year, and we must fight to get our share. The company is now owned by Colonel Santoro's wife, the Baroness Horvath, of Budapest.

She has turned the small company founded by her father into a musical giant. Our competitors sometimes offer outlandish prices. This year, I have received an order for twenty grand pianos all destined for Egypt, and I am happy to say that the director of the Vulsin factory has agreed. We have almost all of them now."

"Isn't that rather odd?" asked Holmes incredulously. "Who on earth ordered twenty pianos?"

Sanzio smiled. "The Khedive himself. Ever since the success of Verdi's *Aida*, the Khedive has decided to make Cairo the foremost musical city of the world. Unfortunately, Signor Holmes, by mistake, one of the pianos was given to Miss Morel as a practise piano. I am told by my tuner that the piano has been severely damaged, perhaps by one of our rivals, or by one of hers. In any case, you need not worry, I have sent Miss Morel an excellent piano for her use. For her trouble, I have given it to her gratis, for as long as she needs it. The piano is a Blüthner, designed and played by Liszt himself."

"That is most kind of you. Tell me, Signore, by what route do your Vulsin pianos go to Cairo?" asked Holmes.

"To Lecce via rail, and then to Cairo on a ship provided by the Egyptian government."

"And are they inspected before they leave here?" asked Holmes.

"I oversee the final inspection. If I am absent from Rome, they are sealed by your vice consul, Herbert Spenser. He is very knowledgeable about music and represents your government in Cairo. He has been very kind in his services to us."

"And where is he now? I should like to meet him," said Holmes.

"He is in Lecce with the first part of the shipment for the Khedive. Fifteen grand pianos, all Vulsins, constructed to the highest standards and now the premier piano of Europe. When he returns I shall introduce you."

"Thank you Mr. Sanzio," said Holmes. "I have one last request."

"*Dica*," said Sanzio.

"Where are the other five pianos destined for Egypt?"

"They are here in this building, on the floor below." Sanzio replied.

"Would you allow me to examine them?"

"Examine? But of course. What are you looking for, Mr. Holmes?"

"Let us say I am interested in the workmanship of the Vulsin factory."

Sanzio snapped his fingers and instantly a small boy of about ten years appeared.

"This is Pasqualino," said Sanzio. "He will take you to the room of instruments. It is late, Mr. Holmes, and I have many things to attend to."

"Thank you for you patience, Signore. I shall be quick."

Holmes and I followed the boy down the stairs into the basement. Though the light was not strong we could follow Pasqualino to the pianos that were to be shipped to Egypt. Holmes lost no time. In a few seconds he was on the floor, moving from under one piano to another. I heard him give out an occasional chuckle and every so often a self-satisfied, full-bodied laugh.

"All right Watson, jot this down will you? Vulsin serial numbers: 178 to 1803."

"What are these numbers. Holmes?" I asked.

"They will tell us which of these pianos has been altered in order to hold a special treasure for the Khedive. My examination was cursory, but I can tell you, Watson, one of the pianos carries a very large number of ten-pound notes. They are excellent counterfeit, and in Egypt no one will recognize the difference, or care for that matter. The remaining pianos will carry bags of Austrian Maria Teresa silver *thaler*, coinage highly prized by the Ethiopian soldiers who defeated the Italian Army at Adowa. And finally, dear Watson, you see the oversized grands in the corner there? They contain the latest examples of the Salzburg rifle, now the most accurate weapon of its kind available in Europe."

"Good Lord, Holmes," said I. "The pianos alone are worth a small fortune. What would be the worth of the cargo?"

"I would say old boy, well over two, possibly three million. Enough to fight a long-drawn-out war. The pianos are loaded with their cargo in Austria, where they are manufactured at the Vulsin factory just beyond the Italian border. They are shipped here to Rome by freight train, then sealed in metal cases, whence they are shipped to Lecce and are placed on the Egyptian steamer that takes them to Egypt. Once they leave Rome they are not opened again; hence their cargo is safe. Safer than any other mode of transportation. The disguise, Watson, I judge to be completely successful.

The question for us is where and by whom these instruments are turned into mere containers. These pianos hold a large fortune, enough to supply more than one sizable army with its needs for at least a year of fighting."

Holmes stood still for a moment.

"Listen, Watson, a noise. Did you hear it?"

"Yes, it came from behind the basement door there, a groan—"

Holmes strode over to the door and I pulled out my revolver. Slowly he turned the knob.

As the door opened, a man bound and gagged, resting on his haunches, fell forward before us, dead.

"This time the real thing," said Holmes.

We removed the gag and the rope and sent a quaking Pasqualino to summon Sanzio.

"He's dead, Holmes, but—"

"Santoro, no doubt," said Holmes.

Sanzio turned pale when he entered. "*Mio amico è morto. Chi l'ha ucciso?* Who killed him?"

"I have my suspicions, but only time will tell. Note that his position is that of a beheading, Watson, just before the executioner strikes. I suspect that we may find out who the attacker was after we find Mr. Herbert Spenser, and la Signora Santoro. Please call *Ispettore* Grimaldi," he continued. "We shall await his arrival."

Santoro's body lay stiff on the floor, and I covered it with my coat. He had been dead for several hours and the sound that had alerted us to his presence was, perhaps, an involuntary gasp.

"He is just as much a suppliant as a victim, Holmes. I suppose we must tell Grimaldi to go after Spenser," I said.

"Indeed, and Santoro's wife. A well-organized attempt to smuggle all this contraband has fallen apart with Santoro's death."

Grimaldi was there within the hour. "So. At last Santoro himself, a war hero," said Grimaldi, marking his words with deep irony, "one who works for a gang of criminals, all of whom served in Ethiopia."

"What do you know about them?" asked Holmes.

"Very little," said Grimaldi. "I know that Santoro and his wife became arms suppliers after the loss at Adowa. This we learned by accident, for one of their shipments was intercepted in Brindisi. It came into the port on the backs of donkeys from the hills of Basilicata, the guns wrapped in thick sheepskins. In the dark, all escaped, but one of our men swore that Santoro was there. He showed a rifle that he had found. It bore Santoro's military insignia. All signs pointed to him, but because of his prestige as a war hero and the political influence of his wife, he was exonerated. We have an idea of what he was up to, but we never discovered how he managed to do what he did. Until now, my dear Holmes," he said dryly, "if I am not mistaken. The gang too has broken up. I suspect that your good citizen Spenser is part of the reason for the gang's breakup."

Holmes beamed. "*Se monumentum quœris, circumspice*," he said. "The piano, my dear Grimaldi, is the latest means by which the Santoro gang shipped whatever they wanted to, concealed from all eyes by the deceptive irrelevance to war of this great instrument. A splendid example of what I have referred to as the Dupin Principle: should you wish to hide something, leave it in partial or full view. Examine the pianos at the end there, and you will see pianos that are empty inside. In them, even the metal frame and the pin block have been removed, in order to lessen their weight and to allow for more to be stored. But they still bear the unmistakable form of the piano. Fill one of these cases with counterfeit bills and you have a fortune neatly hidden. Strap it closed and you have a foolproof disguise. Should the odd customs official raise questions, a small emolument coupled with a threat, and you silence the only ones who could open them."

"Then," said Grimaldi, "I trust that we no longer must chase Lucanian donkeys in the dark."

"You need not," said Holmes with a smile. "I think we should go after Mr. Spenser even though he is no musician. He pretends to be the vice consul, but he is not, we can be sure of that. What started out as the Santoros and Mr. Spenser in a unified company in league with the Khedive and some other African potentates, are now Mr. Spenser and Mrs. Santoro against the dead Colonel. Come, Watson, it is getting late. Will the illustrious *signori*, Grimaldi and Sanzio, join us at the Campo dei Fior, at La Carbonara, to be precise, in the next hour?"

It was at a very late hour that a courier delivered a note for Holmes as we sat in a small café discussing the case. It read:

Dear Sherlock Holmes,

Sorry to have escaped again, old boy. Please keep trying. It amuses me. I am happy that Santoro is now out of the picture.

He should still be in a closet in Sanzio's basement. A fool who thought he could steal from us.

And by the by, I send you best wishes from Alice Morel, who is here beside me as my new bride, now totally free of the burden of that awful instrument. (Signed)

Charles Darwin, Jr.

(Aboard the Beagle)

"Good Lord, Holmes, can it be—that a young woman of her abilities would run off with a total charlatan like Spenser?"

Holmes smiled ruefully.

"Darwin, old fellow. He has changed his name again. To paraphrase the Sage of Königsberg," he said, with a smile, 'two things fill me with wonder: the starry heavens above, and the idiocies below.' I trust that Mr. Darwin is not very far away."

Grimaldi smiled and held up his glass.

"To innocence—and madness," he said.

PORLOCK'S DEMISE

Among the members of the criminal gang with whom the late professor James Moriarty surrounded himself, none was more formidable than the man who ventured forth under the nom de plume of Fred Porlock. The reader may recall my brief references to him in "The Valley of Fear," one of the longer accounts that I have dedicated to the exploits of Sherlock Holmes.

Porlock was Moriarty's right hand. More than Sondberg, the cruel and avaricious murderer, and Vitsle, the extortionist, Porlock showed not only the sinister intelligence required to survive in a world inhabited by such villains, but a contorted spirit surpassed only by that of Moriarty himself. In comparison, even the highly touted Sebastian Moran was no more than a common ruffian.

Unlike such loyal but obsequious minions, however, Porlock maneuvered his position so deftly that he became essential to Moriarty's success. It was he who transformed the theoretical crimes conceived by the Master into the ever increasing number of disasters that baffled all but my dear friend. It was, as Holmes was wont to say, Porlock's genius that enabled the evil professor to realize his ambition of criminal supremacy in Britain, if not in all of Europe. Indeed, so fine was Porlock's touch in concealing his teacher's presence, that some sincerely came to believe Moriarty to be a figment of Holmes's overworked imagination. It was as if Moriarty's invisibility increased as his power grew each day.

And yet, as Holmes was wont to remark on occasion, Porlock too had his weaknesses, the chief of which was his moral ambivalence toward crime. A large part of him desired to be a man like other men. Despite the riches which came his way, he considered the world of crime beneath him, at best a quagmire of fraud and misery, and he both despised and admired Moriarty for having bestowed upon him his career of ill-gotten wealth, but wealth nevertheless.

I laid eyes on Porlock only once in all the years Holmes knew him. It was in early December of 1891 on a snowy morning towards the beginning of the month that I met Holmes at the Rosetta Stone in the British Museum. He had arranged to examine a recently acquired papyrus which contained the earliest Greek treatise on poisons and their antidotes. We were about to follow the attendant to the reading room when Holmes turned and said, "This, my dear friend, is the wizard to the king."

Holmes bowed in a mocking sort of way to a gentleman who suddenly stood next to him.

"And this, no doubt, the learned chronicler of the great master detective," said Porlock quietly. Neither of us proffered our hand, and Holmes did not attempt to cover the momentary awkwardness. He merely said, "Please wait for me here, old boy, I shan't be but a moment."

A few minutes later, he returned alone, a sombre expression on his face.

"Come, Watson, we haven't a moment to lose."

"Where to?" I asked as we hopped into a cab.

"Home," he said quietly.

Holmes made it a point now never to discuss his work when we were in a public conveyance, and "home" as it turned out, required a walk back of several blocks so that our cabby, if interrogated, could only give a destination other than Baker Street.

As we entered our quarters, my friend became even more pensive. He went to his room, opened the window, and returned to the sitting room. He sat on the sofa without removing his coat and closed his eyes.

I took the opportunity to mull over the little I had seen of Porlock. He was not impressive physically. He wore a grey fedora, wet and stained from the dirty rain now so common in London. A dark blue woollen coat, frayed badly at the sleeves, covered his frame. His shoes and trousers were spattered with mud, and a muffler hid most of his face. What I could see of it was pale and unshaven. I had the impression of someone who was employed in a printer's shop or perhaps a clerk in an old book store. He was also indistinguishable from the great lot of human kind who toiled ceaselessly reading at the long tables of the museum.

"A rather strange bird, that Porlock," said I when I saw Holmes's eyes open.

"Far stranger than you might think if you knew him as I do, and my knowledge of him is quite fragmentary. He was about to tell me something of the greatest importance when a young boy, perhaps eleven or twelve, walked into the room. Porlock bolted like a rabbit. He clearly thought that he was in grave danger. The boy did not follow him but walked out into the hall. That is when I returned to you. Porlock is probably quite correct in that he feels endangered—most assuredly by Moriarty himself. Like all the vile characters around Moriarty, he is a victim as well as the beneficiary of the great master of crime. Born into a dirt-poor family in Liverpool fifty years ago, he ran from home at the age of eight, and survived in the street until he was by great luck picked up by a wealthy Scotsman who took him home and saw to his education. These contrasting experiences—the gutter and the castle—immediately set up in his mind an ambivalence that has penetrated and vitiated every move he makes.

"You seem to know quite a bit about him."

"Not as much as I would like. Look at it this way, old boy. A youngster, no more than a child really, is forced into crime to survive, his body encrusted with coal dust and the dirt of our most neglected city. He is taken in by a wealthy man, who gives him a new life. Then at the university his mathematical talents are immediately recognized by Professor Moriarty and a new life begins for the young student. He becomes Moriarty's assistant, then the custodian of Moriarty's wealth, unaware until later of its criminal origins.

Later, he is surprised but not displeased at Moriarty's revelations, and throws his lot in totally with the great genius. At present his is the brain through which Moriarty's ideas are consummated."

"Really, Holmes, I can't believe that Moriarty has given over so much to such a nondescript character," said I.

"Nonsense, my dear fellow, do not be deceived. I have entered a room more than once and have not recognized Porlock until he informed me of who he was. That rather inconsequential figure that you saw today is only one of several roles he has created for himself. He is like a slightly battered book that fills the dusty space on the shelf, a pair of old slippers forgotten in the corner of a closet, an old lampshade waiting to be discarded. He is there but unnoticed, especially to the untrained eye. He is Dupin's purloined letter, in plain view but hidden by the obvious. His greatest pleasure is to appear at the scene of one of his crimes and to go unnoticed. You would be surprised, as I have been, to see the old scholar in the frayed blue coat appear as a bon vivant, a gourmet, a womaniser, a notorious gambler, an aristocrat of great wealth and culture, a patron of the arts, and one of London's most generous philanthropists; the list is endless. Whatever the problem, he is loyal to the members of the gang, who look to him to save them from the law. I will leave to another time his skill with Lestrade and Hopkins, so extraordinary it is that neither of them are aware of his existence."

Holmes smiled as he uttered the last few words, and lit his pipe.

"He does sound more than human, Holmes. Surely you exaggerate."

"Watson, you know I neither guess nor do I make much of little. I am sincere when I tell you that Porlock's gifts are extraordinary."

"How long have you known him? And how did you meet him?"

"That, of course, is difficult to say. He communicated with me first by letter and an occasional coded message. The Birlstone case was the first. After that, he intervened in two more, giving me enough to go on to stop Moriarty—to his great annoyance, I might add."

Holmes stood up, checked the open window, and continued.

"Indeed, perhaps the answer to your second question as to how I came to know him should be reversed. It was rather the other way around—he found me. It was when I first suspected Moriarty's existence and began to see the outline of his diabolical schemes. Here Porlock's ambivalences came to the fore, and he began warning me of those plots that he wished to foil or at least postpone. In one secret conversation, he made it clear to me that he thought Moriarty had gone too far and his judgement had become impaired. He also saw quite soon that I was as formidable as my adversary. I think then that he began to hedge his bets, so to speak, giving me only the most meagre of clues that were necessary to stop the genial professor, nothing ever more than that. So far, he has managed well. If Moriarty learns of his messages to me, however, his revenge will be swift and unforgiving."

"It sounds to me, my dear Holmes, that he sees himself as Moriarty's successor."

"Yes, indubitably, and possibly as successor to Sherlock Holmes as well. Who, after all, is the evil professor without the great detective? It all needs constant scrutiny, Watson. I suspect that Moriarty is up to no good, and that there will be a message from Porlock before dawn. Through our windows, no doubt."

I said nothing for a moment, trying to digest what Holmes had said, particularly his last statement. But I could not resist another question.

"But Holmes, what keeps them together? From your earlier descriptions of Moriarty I can construct only a rather ascetic, intelligent man, gone astray, even mad, because of his desire for power over his fellows."

"If we wish to understand what brought them together and what keeps them at one in their depredations, then paradoxically it is that their desires differ. This allows them to cooperate and revel each in the other's success. More and more Moriarty is interested in naked power. In the last year he has established a new cell in his organisation, one for acts of terror and espionage. Does he still add to his art collection, one of the best in the world? Of course! But he enjoys even more now the assassination of a prime minister in the Balkans, the kidnapping of the children of a rich sheik, the mysterious fire that destroys a steamship, or profits from a famine in India, anything to which he can contribute even a modicum of his chaotic machinations. None of this has any interest for Porlock."

I looked at my watch. It was just past midnight. Holmes lay on the couch, his eyes closed. I left him and retired to my room. I had hoped for sleep, but none came. As I lay in the dark, Holmes's disquisition on Moriarty and Porlock ran through my mind. What impressed me was Holmes's tranquility as he spoke of such frightening things; and my respect for my friend's quiet bravery only grew as I contemplated the wanton destruction that his adversaries might carry out without his intervention.

I must have gone into a half sleep, a restless doze, when I heard what seemed to be the flapping of wings. I looked at my half-open window and saw a pigeon attempting to enter. I opened the window a few more inches, and the bird flew in. I called Holmes, who came immediately.

"Good, Watson, the bird comes from Porlock, with no doubt an important message contained in the cartouche on its leg."

Holmes grasped the bird gently, removed the cylinder, opened it and read:

> *Dear Holmes: I am sure now that he knows that I am in touch with you. It is only a matter of time before he repays me for my treachery. He is hard on my heels and will soon be on yours as well. I leave with you a message that I know contains his newest schemes. It was sent to Moran only and not to me as has been the case in the past; hence my concern. Moran carelessly left it on his desk and I was able to copy it before he returned. I have not been able to decipher it. I hope you can. It is the strangest of Moriarty's coded messages, perhaps the*

most difficult. I heard him giggle to himself as he dubbed it the Moriarty Enigma.

I know neither the time nor the place of the crimes he intends. I know only that they have the greatest significance for the future of Great Britain. In any case I leave London for the Continent where I shall wait until you put the good professor in the jail that he deserves. I shall be at the usual place for the next few days should you need to get in touch.

The professor is the cleverest of men and I wish you quick success. I do not know whether we will ever meet again, and I wish you the best in your lonely struggle. Do not forget to send Cher Ami flying back to me.

Porlock

P.S. I have my son (the young boy you saw at the Museum) with me, which makes everything more difficult but unavoidable.

Holmes stared at the letter.

"Difficult, Watson, in fact most difficult," he said somberly.

I looked at the message and read:

Moran: cipher BD
Concert Moribundus et finalis: May 2, 1901
Concert Master: Ivor Novello
Covent Garden
Salut: Blind Tom plays Sousa; Chaminade valse grande brillante; Black Tom plays Elgar's enigma infra; old

curiosity hotel Little Nelles; poppin bobbin; Savant idiot. Yradier mon cher ami; d'amour.

"Pure nonsense, Holmes. Porlock is pulling your leg," I said impatiently.

"I'm afraid not, old fellow, or rather nonsense on the surface, but below it a meaning. We must crack it."

Holmes went to his desk, mumbling to himself. I stood at his elbow hoping to help him, but both the message and its meaning were lost on me.

"Moriarty at his best, Watson. This code is known in the trade as a polyvalent semantic cipher. Its very nature makes it impossible to decode with precision, it being a series of associations made by the maker. It is originally the creation of the Italian mathematician Cardano, a scientist well known for his puzzles. Here it is in the form of a garbled musical program. Now either Moriarty has included the cipher within the message, or Moran has the dictionary, so to speak, that dissolves the enigma. For us, we are confronted with the problem of Moriarty's choices. Without the key, we are forced to move toward the optimal solution without any certainty. In our case, the only certainty is the date of 2 May, that is, tomorrow. And of course the presence of Ivor Novello. Which means that at best we have twenty-four hours to dissolve the puzzle and act accordingly. Wait, Watson. Let me see . . ." He stared intently at the coded message.

"Here we are, old boy. Buried in the references to salon music and musicians (here Moriarty shows his limitations) are some obvious clues: Sousa suggests the military and the last three letters of his name—usa—surely refer to the United States. Target one. Ah, note here, Watson, the g b initial letters of grande valse, i.e., Grande Bretagne. Target two. And finally, infra, the last three letters referring to France. Target three."

"Good Lord, Holmes, I am impressed. But which targets, and when and where?"

"Let us see, Watson. If memory serves, Blind Tom is the name of an idiot savant musician of the southern state of North Carolina, divinely gifted by nature musically, but unable to perform the simplest mental operations beyond the piano; but who is Black Tom? And what of military importance is there in the Carolinas? Here we have a choice between two toms: one black, one blind. Which is significant? Note the choice between Elgar and Chaminade. Finally, we have the choice of old curiosity shop and Little Nelles. And a dead poppin. Papen! Franz von Papen, the rogue spy, ready to do anything for money, especially the large sums available in Washington. I was fooled by the notice in *The Times* a week ago that he was in Paris for negotiations with the French government, but up to no good behind the scenes. Little Knells, refers to a small hotel in Paris on Rue de Nesles near the Pont Neuf. I have stayed there on occasion. It is so designed that one can disappear within its rooms of false partitions, hidden doorways and every conceivable tromp l'oeil painting. It is run by a blind Italian Jew by the name of Piperno, who has done more to save the persecuted of Europe than anyone else I know, but whose so-called blindness does not fool me. It is there that Porlock is hiding, and it is there that we shall rendezvous with him in the hope that Moriarty has not yet done him in. It is certain that he knows more than he has told us."

Holmes looked at his watch. It was the middle of the night.

"Come, Watson, if we leave now we shall just make the train to Southampton in time for the ship to Calais. Pack as little as possible for both of us. In the meantime, I shall send a message to Lestrade to warn him of possible trouble in London, and to Inspector Muldoon in New York to warn him that America is about to be attacked by international miscreants, though more than that we cannot say."

The trip to Paris was uneventful. Holmes maintained a silence the whole way.

"Soon, Watson," he said quietly as we climbed into our cab, "we shall know if Moriarty has removed Porlock from this world as he fully intends to do."

"And the boy?"

"A mystery, Watson. Perhaps he is the son of Porlock, who appears to use him as a scout. You remember seeing him in the Museum. Perhaps Porlock has also fed the boy all that he knows and has prepared to use him in some way against Moriarty. A cruel misuse of the boy, obviously."

The trip seemed to energise Holmes, and when we arrived at the hotel, he jumped down quickly and rushed in.

My knowledge of Paris was limited, but I knew that we were somewhere on the Left Bank near the Pont Neuf on a street called Rue Bonaparte. The Hotel de Nesles lay at the end of a narrow alley just off the main street. One might easily have missed it, tucked away as it was in its own corner.

Holmes motioned to me to enter quickly. In speaking to the proprietor, he had learned that Porlock and his son were staying there but were leaving the following morning.

"Now, Watson, watch your step, old man, for you are in for a few surprises."

Holmes walked ahead of me and I soon lost him. I tried to retrace my steps but could not. I had lost my way and seemed to have stumbled into a dark closet. Its door closed in on me.

"This way, Watson. Sorry, dear fellow, but you will get the feel of it rather quickly. Take this key. You may put it in any lock and you will be given a simple way out the back door, where you will find yourself on the street behind the hotel. You can only re-enter by walking round to Rue Bonaparte."

"Amazing, Holmes. What a strange place . . ."

"The owner, Watson, was formerly the owner of the largest amusement park in France. It was one of the earliest halls of mirrors. This is his last creation: moveable partitions, tromp l'oeil effects, dozens of distorting mirrors, wall paper that goes over doors and windows and changes every few hours. Quite clever."

As Holmes spoke, the wall in front of us moved suddenly, and, as if by magic, there was Porlock sitting comfortably in a chair near what appeared to be a window, the boy next to him.

Porlock handed Holmes a note. "To you from Moriarty," he said. Holmes opened it and read:

My Dear Holmes:

You have done well with my message. At least with the unimportant parts. Porlock will fill you in with the details.

There is very little that you can do. I shall ask you to meet me upon my return, if you survive the next hour or so. I hope you do, for there is much that is unfinished between us.

Moriarty

"Where has he gone?" Holmes asked.

Porlock looked at his watch. "Moriarty has arrived in the United States. He has met secretly with Herr Reinhardt, who will take him to Black Tom."

"And who is Black Tom?" I inquired.

"Black Tom is a place, not a person. It consists of a narrow pier that juts out into the ocean near Jersey City. It was, until a few minutes ago, the largest munitions storage site in the world."

As Holmes and I stood there, I was assailed suddenly by the smell of smoke. Dark billowing clouds poured into the corridor. Signor Piperno, his clothes on fire, appeared and screamed at us to leave immediately. A fire had started in the kitchen and the front half of the hotel was in flames.

Porlock and the boy returned to their room, but Holmes pointed to a closer exit and we found ourselves outside, blackened by the smoke but unhurt. We watched helplessly as the hotel, the flimsiest edifice of dry wood and paper, burned away in minutes.

The Paris Fire Department contained the flames but could do nothing to save the hotel. In its burning rubble, they found the charred remains of Porlock, but the boy was gone. There was no sign of Piperno or other guests.

Holmes suggested that we speak to the head of the French *Sûreté* before returning to London. It was in speaking to Monsieur. Beauchard that we learned that a gigantic explosion had taken place in Jersey City, not far from New York, where the largest number of explosives had been stored for shipment to Britain. The place was known locally as Black Tom. It was notable, also, said Beauchard that the explosion in America coincided exactly with the destruction of the Hotel Demesnes, and an attempt to kill the well-known composer Sir Edward Elgar.

Holmes thanked Inspector Beauchard, and we left.

"Moriarty wins this round, hands down," he said ruefully. "Porlock, Holmes, Watson, and the boy . . . Elgar, and finally Black Tom."

I could see the anger and frustration that he felt pass across his face.

"Come along, old boy, we have a lot to do to stop him. It will be difficult, Watson; we have lost Porlock, no mean ally. Let us return to London and lick our wounds. One day, I shall force Moriarty into the light of day, where he will surely perish. There's a cab," he said as he waved his arm. "Let us return soon to this beautiful city."

A DEATH IN VENICE

HOLMES HAD AWAKENED EARLY THAT MORNING IN an uncharacteristically jovial mood. It was a few minutes before six when I heard him bustling about just as the first dull silver light of the London dawn began to come through my window. He hummed an old Scottish tune, which he punctuated with mutterings to himself and an occasional quiet chuckle.

It was a raw grey December day outside, and as I peered sleepily through the curtains, I saw that a mixture of snow and icy rain had already clogged the London streets. Despite the great temptation to linger on a morning such as this, I jumped out of bed, curious as to why Holmes appeared to be so unusually cheerful.

We breakfasted at seven. The conversation was lively, mainly about political events of the past week. When he had finished his tea, he took immediately to his violin while I went over to my desk and immersed myself in some business matters that I had neglected for too long a time.

Holmes addressed me as he began to bow. His spirits were high, he explained, because the violin had gone well the day before, and, with my acquiescence of course, he wished to continue to devote again the fresh hours of the morning to intense practise. I told him that I had no objection whatsoever, and that I would be most happy with this, particularly since my work was entirely routine.

He began with some difficult exercises, then moved to a series of pieces by Paganini, which he played over and over again for the next several hours, slowly at first, then at a more rapid tempo. There was a rare joy in his playing, and, as I sat at my desk, I was delighted at the enthusiasm with which he attacked the instrument.

Towards the end of his practise, however, I noticed a gradual change in his expression. His face darkened and his playing took on that peculiar mournful tone so familiar to me, one that I immediately associated with his frequent bouts of melancholia. He now played portions of the slow movement of the Mendelssohn E-minor concerto. His tone and expression were so beautiful, however, that I looked up from my work to listen. Halfway through he stopped, quietly placed the violin in its case, closed the cover, and moved to his chair, where he sat in his meditative pose, his eyes closed, his hands extended in front of his face, the tips of his fingers touching, the thumbs pulling gently at his tightly pursed lips.

"That was most beautiful, Holmes. I have never heard you play so well."

"I thank you for the compliment, my dear Watson, but with all due respect to your extraordinary gifts as a medical practitioner, I am compelled by the rules of elementary honesty to say that your musical judgement is insufficiently developed for me to take any comfort in your generous words of praise, however well intentioned they may be. In truth, the Paganini pieces were fairly disastrous, *ein Umstern*, as the Germans would say. As to the Mendelssohn, the merest tyro can play it with a bit of concentration. No, Watson, the violin is one of the sources of the black malady that often overwhelms me, not its cure. It is, in fact, one of the reasons why I chose to become a consulting detective."

Holmes reference to my somewhat inexperienced ear failed to offend me, for I had, after so many years, grown accustomed to his cutting words and had learned to ignore them. I continued to prod him about the violin.

"But surely you could have chosen a career as a musician had you wished."

"No, Watson. A certain talent is present, no doubt, from the French blood inherited from my maternal ancestors, the Vernets. But I became aware early on that I had just enough of this talent to play well but not, unfortunately, supremely well. It has always been my judgement that one's life should be devoted to what one can do at the very limits of one's capabilities, the determination of which should occupy the better part of one's youth. It was during the early period of my life that I came to know that I could not reach the highest peaks of musicianship, no matter how much a strong inner desire suggested such a possibility. In music, the hands, the brain, the will, all must be at one. My character I judged to be other. Rather than a single talent, mine was a group of talents that, skillfully employed, could be put to a supreme use: the struggle against the criminal. And so, I abandoned any notion of a life of music and devoted myself to the exploitation to the fullest of my greatest talents: observation and deduction. Thus, I created, almost single-handedly, the profession of consulting detective."

"But surely, Holmes, you could have been mistaken about your musicianship. It is a road not taken, its end unknown. Who knows, had you tried, you might one day have become the greatest of living virtuosi."

"I make few errors, Watson. In my line of work, I can ill afford them. I will admit, however, that youth can often mistake its path and that judgement of one's own gifts is at best a difficult one. My original determination, however, may be confirmed once again by experiences in the future. Indeed, our next client may provide us with the occasion."

"And who might that be?" I asked.

"I am expecting a distinguished guest this morning, Watson, who may need our services. You will recognize him instantly. It is through individuals like him, who have reached the highest rung of artistry possible, that one can evaluate, or re-evaluate one's talents whatever they might be."

"Very well, Holmes, I look forward to meeting him. I trust you plan to keep his identity secret until he appears—for drama's sake no doubt."

"Precisely, old boy. Now go about your business until Mrs. Hudson announces his arrival."

It was impossible for me to concentrate on my picayune business matters now that Holmes had alluded to a special visitor. As we waited, I mused for a moment, reviewing mentally those cases that I had shared with him during the early days of our friendship. Our most recent case had come to us a few months earlier from the Andaman Islands, and I entitled it "The Sign of Four" in my chronicles. This adventure also provided for me a wonderful woman, Miss Mary Morstan, who was to become my bride in a few months.

As I stared into space, Holmes's face broke into my reverie. After my marriage, I thought, we would see far less of each other, since the happiness of my domestic life and a growing medical practise would give me little time to look in upon my dear friend. I would follow his exploits as well as I could through the London press. In that way I would learn of his whereabouts. Sadly, I thought, his adventures would remain quite unknown to me.

"Perhaps, Watson," he broke in, "in the interest of adding to your already voluminous files about me, you should have an account of my recent journey to France. It was a visit to Montpellier to do research on a host of new poisons that have entered the criminal market. There was no adventure in this, the journey being free of those lurid elements which you continue to relate in your popular accounts of my comings and goings, and it may not serve your purposes. Here, however, are the results of my research, dedicated to you, my dear friend, soon to depart for the land of domestic bliss."

His voice was free of the usual sarcasm that accompanied his words when he uttered such sentimental thoughts. He leaned forward in his chair and handed me a substantial tome entitled "Poisons and Their Criminal Uses. A Monograph Submitted to the *Sûretè* of France by Sherlock Holmes."

I was deeply touched by his gift and he saw my eyes mist over.

"Do not worry, Watson, I shall be here, and I promise you that I shall take no one new into our quarters. You are free therefore to come and go as you please. And I hope you will find the free time to come. I have already told Mrs. Hudson of the arrangement and she concurs. While we await our visitor, perhaps I should explain to you the reasoning that took me to France."

I wiped my eyes, and muttered a hoarse, "Go on, old boy."

"Very well, then, here is the case, or rather the reasons for my visit to France. It was to write a book about poisons, the one you hold in your hand."

He did not move from his chair, but sat motionless. For a moment, and for but a moment, I could almost see his great brain as it scrutinized events and characters, thus bringing forth the detailed observations and deductions that led him to his inevitable conclusions.

"After we disposed of Jonathan Small, you will recall that I had little to occupy my time, and so I decided to spend a month in the south of France. There, in a cottage that belongs to a distant cousin, I continued some of the chemical researches that had been delayed because of my active professional life. My interest was in a number of poisons that I felt must be described in detail if criminal investigations were to be more successful.

"You have recorded already my constant dabblings with poisons and other toxins, and my knowledge of what you have termed sensational literature, by which phrase I assume you meant the history of crime. My historical knowledge, together with the recent results of my many experiments, I finally put down in this monograph published in France through the good offices of a friend in the *Sûretè*. Written under my name, it caused a bit of an uproar within criminological circles since it pointed to the increasing use of obscure but deadly poisons as a more and more common weapon of inducing death. I chose to publish the work in France, because my historical researches had traced the use of poison in modern Europe back to the late-seventeenth-century Poison Affair at the French court, in which several notables were involved. The poisons used by Marie Madeleine d'Aubray, marquise de Brunvillers, and by Catherine La Voisin, to dispatch many at the court of Louis the Fourteenth, were nearly all new at the time and the more difficult to detect because of their very recent appearance in Europe. The line between medicine and poison is a fine one, Watson, and my monograph showed how murder had been made easier by the recent increase in the number of substances now available from our colonies in India and Africa. The most common of these were of course the various strychnine poisons that were made from the seeds of the strychnos nux vomica, a plant native to India. These and others mimic many diseases and if given over long periods of time produce long suffering and, finally, death."

I recalled as he spoke that he remained in France for about eight weeks before his return to London only two days before. His stay in Paris was far longer than he had planned, due largely to the publication of the monograph, and he did not arrive in London until almost the end of January.

"Two days ago, while you were out, dear Watson, I was informed by Mrs. Hudson that a monk, probably of the Roman Church, wished to see me. He had appeared suddenly and unannounced. She had gathered from his broken English that it was a matter of the gravest urgency, and judging by his excited gestures, she felt that I had best see him at once. I, unfortunately, was not here either, and so our prospective client left, saying that he would return at the same time the following day." And so he had, for there was a sudden knock at our door, unmistakably that of our landlady, and Holmes nodded, asking that she show our guest in immediately.

When he entered, I was a bit taken aback, for I recognized him instantly. Still tall, though slightly bent and much older now than I remembered, there was no mistaking the dramatic figure, the powerful face, the aquiline nose, the famous moles on the cheeks, and the long snow-white hair that reached his shoulders. He wore the long black frock of the monk, and a black velvet cape over his tall frame.

"Welcome, Monsieur Abbé," said Holmes in French, "I am rarely honoured by so distinguished a visitor. And this is my colleague, Dr. Watson. I think you will find the chair near the window the most comfortable. Please sit down."

"I need your immediate help, Monsieur Holmes," said the monk, continuing in French.

"I am at your service, Monsieur Liszt. I assume that you have learned of me through—"

"The King of Bohemia, my good friend, and most recently through friends in the French *Sûretè*, where you are held in the highest esteem. The King has often recounted to me—and to very few others—the successful outcome of your intervention in his affairs, an intervention that saved his marriage and throne. And now I turn to you for help, not for myself, at least not directly, but for my daughter, Cosima, more than anyone, and for her husband, who has been my close friend for many years."

Holmes paused briefly to light his pipe. He looked at me directly as he said, "You know as well as I, Watson, that one does not have to be an avid follower of music and musicians to know of whom Monsieur Liszt speaking."

Indeed, I thought to myself, even an unmusical person such as I knew of those of whom he spoke. Liszt, his daughter Cosima, and her husband, the German composer Wagner, were the subject of constant gossip and the object of endless attacks by pamphleteers and the lower forms of the press, both in Germany and the rest of Europe. Holmes himself kept a large file on musicians, one in which Wagner and his circle figured prominently.

Addressing our guest, Holmes said, "Please continue, Monsieur Liszt. If I believe that I can be of help, I shall be so gladly."

His guest paused for a moment, struggling with his choice of words.

"Then let me explain, Monsieur Holmes. I believe Richard Wagner is in great danger, and I fear for his life. We have known each other for many years. We first met in Paris over forty years ago, and while we have had careers that often placed us far apart, we have never lost touch. Since he married my daughter Cosima in 1870, his children are now my grandchildren, and I have made it part of my life to visit with his family as often as my work permits. I was not a good father, Monsieur Holmes, neither to Cosima, nor to her brothers and sisters. My habits are well known, but, seasoned by age perhaps, I have attempted to make amends, at least to Cosima, by spending time with little Siegfried and his sisters, the Wagner children. I adore them and wish them every happiness.

"But Wagner himself, as long as I have known him," he continued, "has possessed a very difficult character. A person of strange moods and abrupt changes in character, one never knew whether he would be jovial or morose. Plagued all his life by financial worries, seeing enemies everywhere, his creative genius always found itself subject to his powerful but destructive emotions. Because he is so difficult, I at first opposed Cosima's association with him. I preferred frankly the less talented but steadier Hans von Bülow. Even after she left him to live with Wagner, I opposed their marriage, and I advised von Bülow not to grant a divorce. But after I saw Cosima and realized how happy she was with Richard, I finally relented. She told me that she had made her life very complicated by marrying Wagner, but he was the joy of her life, just as Hans, her first husband, was her life's sorrow, and her children her life's work. Richard, himself, never seemed happier than after their marriage."

"Within this happiness," said Holmes," there must be something that you find troubling, Monsieur Liszt, otherwise you would not be here. Please tell me what it is."

"I shall explain, Monsieur Holmes. In brief, it is this: for no apparent reason, Wagner's health has deteriorated rapidly in the last several years, so rapidly that I have begun to suspect an external cause. Considering his enormous success as a composer and the familial happiness that he shares with his wife and children, there is no reason for this decline and for the number of maladies with which he has been afflicted. He was a vigorous man in his youth, and except for his youthful excesses, he has been a man of abstemious habits. He is, through the influence of Schopenhauer, a kind of Buddhist, *un bouddhiste allemand*, as they say, who has led the quiet life of a composer."

"Then there is," Holmes interjected, "as I have long suspected, no truth behind all the rumours and wild tales associated with him—and about you, Monsieur Abbé, I might add."

The Abbé laughed. "Monsieur Holmes, the public desires this kind of tale. It is what fills the concert halls and pays our way. The public does not understand artistic creation in the slightest. It cannot comprehend in the least what effort and time is involved just to produce a finished score, let alone conceive it. We are not all Mozarts. Even the shortest of my *études* has taken hours not just to compose, but merely to write out clearly for the printer. The years of hard labor that go into the creation of works such as *Lohengrin* or even of some of my more modest efforts, such as *Les Préludes*, leave little time for the wild life. We lead, Monsieur Holmes, the most bourgeois of lives in order to generate the passion necessary to create the music of the future, as Wagner himself has characterized it."

Holmes watched Liszt carefully as he stood up and paced across the room. His face, that of a true Magyar, showed the greatest concern.

"I have spent several months with the Wagners over the last year, Monsieur Holmes, and I have seen the steady decline of my friend Richard. His nights are sleepless. He cannot find rest, he is tormented by fierce dreams, spasms of the muscles, deep pain through his joints and severe nocturnal hallucinations. He has all but given up composing. I have just left them. They are in Venice, a place that Wagner finds congenial. Richard is ill, very ill, and he does not follow his doctors' orders. I was alarmed at how he looked at Christmas. It was then that I thought that something was very wrong, that there might be an external cause."

"Like poison. And that is why you came to me?" asked Holmes.

"Precisely, Monsieur Holmes. I say this with no knowledge whatsoever of his condition, only a certain intuition that comes when we are disturbed by the unexpected perception of our close friends and relations. The doctors have not been able to diagnose his various maladies to my satisfaction. If I am correct in my suspicions, then we must intervene. According to the French security forces, you know more about poison and its effects than anyone alive. According to the King of Bohemia, you are the best consulting detective in the world. I believe that you are the right man to investigate the matter. And, if I am wrong, we will have lost nothing."

"Monsieur Abbé, I shall be happy to, but I shall need to have direct access to Herr Wagner and his family. And since I am not a physician, I request that my colleague, Dr. Watson, accompany me. His experience should be of great aid to us."

"That can be easily arranged. Fortunately, Monsieur Holmes, Cosima and her husband have expressed the desire to improve their own English as well as that of their children by having two English speakers live with them for a time. On my recommendation, those persons could be you."

"This would mean a trip to Venice."

"The family is at present occupying large quarters in one of the old palaces off the Grand Canal, the Palazzo Vendramin. There is more than adequate room for you, and you would lack for nothing. In addition, I am willing to pay you whatever you wish, including your expenses. I am not the King of Bohemia, Monsieur Holmes, but I assure you that I can afford to pay you whatever fair sum you require."

"I accept your offer, Monsieur Abbé. Nothing keeps me in London at present, and since I have never visited Venice, nor Italy, for that matter, I shall be happy to leave as soon as possible. I see one very large problem: Wagner, if memory of my files serves, is a person with many enemies. Despite his bourgeois life, as you put it, he has managed to offend so many people that even the first task, the narrowing of the range of suspects, will be a formidable one. There have been many enemies, like Meyerbeer, for instance."

"Meyerbeer was one of Wagner's many stupidities. Meyerbeer never hurt anyone, least of all Wagner, and, poor man, he is dead these many years. But you are right. Wagner's enemies are legion. I myself, however, do not know anyone who would go so far as to kill him. I must, therefore, have your judgement of his condition as soon as possible. If I am correct in my suspicion, then we must protect him by finding the culprit."

"You shall have my judgement about Herr Wagner's condition within a day of my arrival in Venice. As to identifying the culprit—that will be a more difficult matter, but not an impossible one. All crimes are preceded by similar ones, Monsieur Abbé, and I have learned that there is nothing really new under the sun. The history of crime, if well known, can provide us with much useful information. Already, I can think of three cases that bear interesting similarities to this one."

"No doubt," said Liszt, "one of them is the case of Mozart and Salieri."

"A most interesting case, that one, but Salieri's guilt is the concoction of the Russian poet Pushkin, who, I suspect, may know who the real culprit was. That Mozart was poisoned is clear to me. That Salieri did not murder him is also most obvious, but more of that at another time."

"Then I shall telegraph my daughter at once, informing her that I have discovered two wonderful young Englishmen who will be delighted to stay with them for a time in order to aid them in their study of the English language. And what names shall I give them?"

"Since I shall need to examine him, I shall also go in the guise of a physician. Tell Frau Wagner," Holmes said with some amusement, "that a Dr. John Watson of London is prepared to spend several months with them in Italy. He will be accompanied by his friend, Anthony Hopkins, also a physician."

As I listened, the two made their final arrangements, and Holmes bade the great pianist good-bye. The Abbé bowed gracefully and, like some enormous falcon readying itself to take flight, swiftly turned and left the room. Holmes began at once to make the preliminary preparations for our extended trip to Italy.

"Do you really think it will come to pass?" I asked.

"I can assure you that it will. Liszt is in earnest and will stop at nothing to catch the poisoner. And neither will we."

The following morning we received a note from Liszt saying that the Wagners would be delighted to receive us and that we should proceed to Venice as soon as possible. He had reserved two berths on the Orient Express and notified the Wagners directly that we would be arriving in Venice by train on the morning of seven February.

Holmes paused for a moment t to light his pipe, and I took the opportunity to interject with a certain merriment, "I am amused that you are traveling under my name."

"It was an immediate choice, safe and convenient, old boy. Neither my exploits nor your chronicles of them are as yet widely known on the Continent, and should either of our names have appeared in Europe at this early date, it was still unlikely that the Wagners would have been cognizant of either. Because of his revolutionary past and his contact with police and their agents, however, there exists a remote chance that Wagner might have heard my name. Yours would have been unknown to the police of any country, and is, unlike mine, a common one. By using your name, I have the advantage of speaking convincingly about Dr. Watson's career without having to invent an imaginary past for myself. And so, I shall begin by holding my left arm rather stiffly, this due to a Jezail bullet received in the shoulder in the campaign in Afghanistan that shattered, if I remember correctly, the clavicle and the subclavian artery."

"Well done, Holmes, if I may say so myself." He had, as he spoke, suddenly assumed my posture, and though we looked not at all alike, I had the feeling that part of me at least had suddenly appeared across the room, so convincing was his portrayal.

Holmes smiled and let out a puff of smoke.

"The Orient Express," he continued, "leaves London early in the morning and arrives in Venice the following evening, with stops in Paris and Milan. I shall use the uninterrupted time between Paris and Milan to review carefully what I know of Wagner and his career. I have fished out my folder on musicians. You may want to read through it as well. His is, on the surface at least, an extraordinarily complex life, for he is not only a composer, but a political revolutionary as well. In 1848 he participated, with Bakunin, the Russian anarchist, in the famous Dresden uprising. As a result he was banished from most of the German states by the authorities and was forced to take up residence in Switzerland—in Zurich, among other places. He still feels forced to wander a good deal. Until Ludwig of Bavaria provided him with adequate support he had no peace. It was only in this way that in the latter part of his life he has found the measure of tranquillity that he requires for his work. Despite his success, a life of travel has become a habit, and he often longs for the climate of the south, particularly that of Italy, where at one time or other he has lived in Palermo, Naples, Siena, and now Venice. His life has been filled with friendships, love affairs, and sworn enemies. There is no end of possible suspects, no end to motives, real or imagined, for the killing of Wagner, if indeed that is what is happening. His marriage to Cosima in itself has only added to the number of his enemies, including her former husband, von Bülow, who, despite his ardent support of Wagner's music, must bear him a deep and continuing grudge.

"To add immeasurably to the problem, we are required to chase our quarry in Italy—in Venice in particular—where poison has, over the last five hundred years, become so perfected as a weapon of murder that only those who are perpetrators of a crime are aware of its success. My monograph has barely touched the Italian industry, which is worthy of several monographs in itself. The case of Cardinal Tosca was a later example of this kind of skill. But even in my early experience at the time, the murder of churchman is a far simpler affair to resolve than the murder of artists. And so, if it is poison in the case of Wagner, it could come from almost anyone associated with him, from a dissatisfied servant to a rival composer. As to the means of administering the poison, that would also have a wide variety of possibilities. Wagner has suffered a variety of ailments, is known to take large doses of medication carelessly, and therefore may indeed be poisoning himself."

After this review of the situation, Holmes decided to put the matter out of mind until we had met Wagner and examined him. The train ride was uneventful. We were delayed by snow at the Simplon Pass for several hours, but the engineer easily made up some of the time once we had arrived in the Italian plain. After the stop in Milan, the train proceeded to Venice, where we descended at about nine in the morning. Our only travel companion had been a young Turkish diplomat, who was returning to Istanbul. We bade good-bye to him and alighted from the train.

I at first saw no one in the crowd whom I recognized, but as it thinned out, I saw the unmistakable figure of Frau Cosima Wagner, standing there with her children and a servant, waiting.

"Madame Wagner, I believe? I am John Watson, and this is my colleague, Anthony Hopkins."

Frau Wagner greeted us in French, and with a smile, extended her hand and proceeded to introduce her children one by one who, each in turn, curtseyed and said in stilted English, "Welcome to Venice and to our house, Dr. John and Dr. Anthony." To which the young boy, Siegfried, added: "My father could not come. He is composing his music."

We walked quickly from the station to a waiting phaeton that brought us in minutes to the canal. There we boarded a gondola and began the ride to the great palazzo that served as the Wagner home. Holmes and I immediately abandoned all hope of seeing the Italian sun that day. It was as cold and damp as London, and the mist was impenetrable. We saw little at first, but when we reached the Grand Canal we perceived enough to understand why Venice was justly famous. There, arising like fantasies in the fog, were the bridges, the palazzi, and the churches, as if floating just above the water.

"If Wagner has lived in straitened circumstances in the past," said Holmes in English, "his present life shows no sign of it."

The Wagner quarters in the old Venetian palace were sumptuous. We entered a large ornate vestibule and from there the servants led us to our quarters. We rested for a short time, and then, late in the afternoon, summoned by our hosts, we descended the central staircase and entered the large drawing room where tea was served daily to guests and friends. As we entered, Richard Wagner himself sat at the far end of the room, a smile on his face as he talked to his children. As soon as they saw us, they rushed towards us and pulled us to their father.

"Look, Papa, here are our new Englishmen, Herr Doktors John and Anthony."

"Welcome to our home," he said. "I trust you have found your quarters to your liking."

"Indeed, they are splendid and we are most honored to be your guests."

"Forgive me for not rising, but I have had painful spasms in my legs and elsewhere for the last half hour, and it is difficult for me to stand."

It was in these very first few moments that Holmes and I independently concluded that Liszt's intuition had to be taken with the greatest seriousness. Wagner was not in good health, and as we observed him carefully, it appeared quite likely that one of the great composers of the century may have indeed been deliberately poisoned, possibly over many years. It also appeared at first glance that the poison had done by this time a good deal of its work, that in all probability one of the poisons was arsenic, and that he did not have long to live. Even without examining him closely, we judged that there was much damage to the liver and other internal organs, damage that was probably irreversible, and that the only hope was if we could find the source of the poison immediately.

As the evening wore on, I kept on observing him. He was a very short man with a head too large for his body. This disproportion gave him a dwarf-like appearance at times. His hair was thin, his eyes sunken, his skin jaundiced and grey, and his abdomen horribly swollen. He breathed with difficulty, and often closed his eyes and abandoned the conversation.

That evening the many guests eventually left and only Holmes and I and a family friend, one Paul Joukovsky, a painter, remained. Despite the late hour, Wagner's mood suddenly improved. He rose slowly, and with surprising vigour, walked over to Holmes and, taking his arm for support, led him to the room where the family dined in private.

As they walked, the composer said, in heavily accented French, "I know you and Anthony are here to help us practise our English, but I understand that you are also a physician. I need your medical advice as well, for as you can see, I am very ill, far more ill than I want Cosima to know."

Holmes told him quietly that we were available to him at any time.

As we entered the dining hall, a servant announced the arrival of Monsieur Liszt, who entered almost immediately. Wagner greeted him with affection but motioned Holmes and me to sit to his left, Joukovsky to his right, and Cosima and the children at the other end. Liszt sat with his daughter. The conversation flowed without cease, and while all tried to speak in English, it was not long before everyone was speaking German, the only language that everyone at the table, including Holmes, shared.

I took careful note of Wagner's hair, which appeared to be extremely dry and brittle. His skin was grey, his eyes dilated, and there was a thin black line that ran around his lips.

Holmes noticed that Wagner had worn white gloves until they had arrived at table, and when he removed them Holmes noted that his hands were covered with red patches. His fingernails were broken, and the skin on his fingers appeared rough, to have been scrubbed hard, as if he had tried to wash some stains away vigorously.

"How long have you mixed your own ink?" asked Holmes.

"How on earth did you know that?" replied Wagner in surprise.

"No matter. As a doctor, I must pay attention to details."

"Yes, I have always done so. It has been one of my peculiar habits, Dr. Watson. I rule my own paper and write the first drafts of my compositions myself. It is only when they are completed to my satisfaction that I send them to a copyist who prepares the version for printing. The ink is wonderful.

It has a sweet taste at first, but then it leaves me with the taste of sour milk in my mouth."

At the end of the meal, we returned to the drawing room, where Liszt sat at the great Erard and played almost without stop for two hours. He began with the Chopin *Fantaisie-Polonaise*, following it with several etudes by the same composer.

Then, at Cosima's request, Liszt played his own transcriptions of Wagner's operas, those of *Tristan und Isolde* and *Tannhäuser.* He followed this with some of his arrangements of the songs of Schubert and Schumann. The last, a song called *Widmung*, or Dedication, left Wagner and his wife in tears.

Then, again at Cosima's request, Herr Wagner stood up and announced that, if Herr Liszt were willing to accompany him, he would sing parts of his last opera, *Parsifal.* Liszt agreed without hesitation, and so they began.

I sat across the room staring at these three people—Wagner, Liszt, and Madame Wagner, transfixed by the music. Later that evening Holmes told me that it was then that he knew that the violin would forever remain nothing more than an avocation, for the realisation came that he could never venture into the celestial realms of music that we were fortunate to enter that night. Liszt, whom I had heard in performance in London, outdid himself by the sheer beauty of his playing. And despite his infirmities, Wagner sang beautifully and strongly. Who, after all, could have sung Parsifal more convincingly than he?

When it was over, there was a silence, then quiet words of praise from Cosima, Joukovsky, and the two doctors. Herr

Wagner announced that he was exhausted and wished to retire. He left on Cosima's arm, and after a few moments we all went to our rooms.

Our work had only begun, however. Shortly after we entered our quarters, there was a knock. It was Liszt. Holmes bade him enter and said quietly, "Your suspicions are correct. Unless I am sadly misled by his symptoms, Wagner has been poisoned. The effects of small repeated doses of arsenic are obvious, but I suspect the use of at least three others. I am afraid also that the damage has been done and that he may not live much longer."

I told Liszt that to make absolutely sure we would have to perform certain tests.

Liszt flung his hands up in despair. "Richard will agree to no tests. I had hoped that I was wrong. Are you sure?" he asked.

"Not completely, but all the signs are there. Who is the doctor?"

"A man named Kurz," said Liszt, "but he is away and will not return for several weeks."

"Then there is nothing to be done except for Hopkins here to examine him thoroughly. And for us to find the source of the poison immediately."

"I shall aid you in any way I can."

"Who else, besides those of us who attended dinner this evening, lives here?"

"Just the servants, whom you have met. They are people I have known for many years. They are simple folk with no grievances."

"And Joukovsky?"

"Beyond reproach. He is devoted to both Cosima and Richard. And besides, he is a very recent acquaintance."

"Then the source is outside, but the poison enters and is administered to him."

"But how?"

"I have one idea, but it is only a possibility. Before I pursue it, I must explore the house. I must be able to do it without interruption or fear of discovery. I also wish to disclose what I know to Herr Wagner himself. Perhaps he knows who would hate him enough to kill him."

Liszt's face grew grave for a moment. Then he replied: "You may proceed as you like with your inspection. I shall tell Cosima. On the other point, however, I think that it would be useless. Richard is very unbalanced when it comes to his enemies, and he will try to fill your head with irrational accusations. He began to create enemies in his youth, and he has never ceased doing so. In his early days, he was a rude, excitable Saxon, and he attacked people in fits of anger if he did not get what he wished. Sometimes he attacked them in print, signing the articles with a pseudonym. He also borrowed money from countless people and never returned it. He seduced the wives of his friends, insulted the most powerful musicians in Europe like Spontini and Meyerbeer, and has never ceased to show contempt for anyone to whom he took a dislike. Were you to tell him that he was the victim of someone's poison, you would do no good and would ruin Cosima's life, since he would confide in her immediately. Please, Monsieur Holmes, I implore you, on this point, please follow my advice. If, as you think, Richard does not have long to live, let him die in peace without the knowledge that his life has been taken from him. I want to know who the culprit is, and I want that person punished if possible, but I prefer to let my friend die in whatever peace is available to someone like him. When you discover who the poisoner is, then we can decide what to do."

Holmes agreed reluctantly to Liszt's wishes, for he wished to question Herr Wagner in a thorough manner. He then told him that he wished to examine as much of the household as he could and that he would need about three hours.

"And when would you like to perform your investigation?"

"There is no time like the present, as they say, Monsieur Liszt. If you will stand guard, I shall hurry through the public rooms, but I shall need time in Wagner's study. Should he awaken, you must prevent him from entering."

"That will be difficult but I shall try. Perhaps Hopkins can distract him should he awake. Perhaps he can offer an examination to Richard."

Leaving Liszt and me on a bench in a dark corner of the hall, Holmes began his investigations. The least important would be the kitchen, for if he was sure of anything by now, it was that Wagner was not eating poisoned food. The murderer harbored no anger toward the rest of the family, since they appeared to be in very good health. No, the murderer appeared to be interested in Wagner alone. Poisoned food would have been a danger to all, and also would have raised immediate suspicions, particularly if one of the children had been taken ill. And we ourselves had partaken of the food and watched carefully to make sure that Wagner partook of nothing that the rest did not. After an initial hour of investigation, Holmes returned.

"If Wagner is not ingesting the poison," said Holmes, "then he is either inhaling it or receiving it through his skin. After examining the kitchen I went directly to his study. It was not a large room, but it was filled with the many things of a long life. Books and musical scores lined the walls. There was an upright piano at which he composed, and a large desk.

"The desk immediately caught my eye, for there were the things with which Wagner worked on a daily basis: his pens, rulers, and paper. Of the latter, there were two piles, an enormous one of blank music paper except for the lines and staves which he had drawn in himself; the other, slightly smaller, on the top of which had been written in Wagner's own hand:

> *Die Sieger, Ein Buddhistische Buhnenfestspiel in Drei Akten von Richard Wagner. Zu Meine Geliebte Savitri gewidmet*; that is, *The Victors. A Buddhist Music Drama in Four Acts by Richard Wagner. Dedicated to my beloved Savitri.*

"The latter appeared to be a work that Wagner had just finished, of which the world knew nothing as yet. I could see that it was a voluminous score and appeared to be complete, including the full orchestral parts. The 'Savitri' of the dedication was not otherwise identified."

The only other object of note on his desk, said Holmes, was a curious wooden box about ten inches square, with doors on one side. On opening them, a rather crude figure of the Buddha appeared. On each side of the figure was a small terra cotta cup, each filled with a grey-black powder. A third cup stored behind the figure contained an oily liquid. It was out of these powders, mixed together with the oil, that Holmes surmised that Wagner made his special inks. He took samples of each of the powders, leaving the oil till later.

Holmes had examined the study not a moment too soon, for just as he finished, we heard a shout from the Wagners' bedroom. I disappeared into my room, watching from my door as Wagner appeared suddenly in the hall, staggering, shaking, sobbing with fear. Cosima was close by him. Liszt suddenly appeared from the shadows where he had been keeping watch.

"He has not slept well. He has been pursued all night by nightmares and hallucinations," said she to her father.

Liszt helped to calm the shaking composer. They led him to a small sitting room off the hall. In a moment, Liszt appeared at our rooms.

"He needs your attention," he said.

Holmes and I followed Liszt into the sitting room. Wagner had stopped shivering and appeared calmer. I felt his pulse, which was quite rapid and irregular, and listened to his heart and chest. I gave him a light bromide with water. In a few moments he seemed improved. He insisted that he be allowed to dress and meet everyone for a very early breakfast.

"My dreams have become fearful over the last year," said Wagner, as Holmes and I sat with him. A few moments later, as the dawn came up, he had recovered sufficiently to discuss what had happened.

"And they maintain their reality into a wakeful state, so that I am unable to shake the mysterious phantoms that I see. Forgive me for sharing such intimate perceptions with you. In sleep, I was beckoned by Kundry, who told me to follow her into the forest. As I did so, she turned into a malevolent ogress, who began tearing at my flesh. It was at this point that I began to cry out, to push her away. I awoke, but she remained, now in the room beside the bed. Only the forest had disappeared. As Cosima responded to my terror, she left, and I staggered into the hall. What lies behind such nightmares I do not know. Dr. Watson, if you have any medical advice, I shall be grateful to receive it."

"Herr Wagner, I should like to examine you briefly this morning. But, as to my immediate advice, I would counsel you to stop all work, particularly composing, and not to enter your study for one week. You will begin to see improvement immediately."

"You ask what no one has asked before: the impossible. How can I sit with the music running through my head unrecorded?"

"Herr Wagner, if you do as I say, you will enjoy both physical and mental improvement immediately. Otherwise, there will be further deterioration in your condition, and your hallucinations will only grow worse."

"Perhaps, Herr Doktor Watson, I can use my influence to prevail upon my husband to take your advice," interjected Cosima.

"If you insist, my beloved, then I shall do it."

Holmes and I followed Wagner to his chambers, where we made a thorough physical examination. Holmes took minute pieces, without Wagner's being aware, of his hair and fingernails, both so brittle that samples were easily taken. The chief areas of concern were the irregular action of the heart, and his enlarged abdomen, which was due to swollen organs, in particular the liver and spleen. In addition, Wagner suffered from a meteorism that had forced the chest cavity to contract, a motion that had a further deleterious affect on his heart.

We left Herr Wagner, having administered another sedative, and brought the samples to my room, where Holmes, the better chemist by far, spent the day with some modest chemical equipment he had brought from London and a few necessary chemist's tools from a shop near Piazza San Marco. The tests of Wagner's hair and nails showed that heavy doses of arsenic had now passed throughout his body. We then tested the samples of ink powders that Holmes had taken from Wagner's desk. The powders were each a different poison: arsenic, belladonna, curare, and, finally, meranic acid, a deadly poison that also creates severe hallucinations, extracted from a rare fungus and used, to the best of my knowledge, by veterinarians to kill mercifully sick and dying animals. It was used only in Switzerland, where the fungus was readily available. And so, we had ascertained, beyond a doubt, that Wagner was not naturally ill but made ill by a set of chemicals, each of which contributed to his strange and numerous symptoms.

Holmes communicated our findings to Liszt immediately. "We must find the source of the ink powders," he said, "and we shall have our culprit."

Following Holmes's wishes, Liszt made quiet inquiries among the servants, and learned that the packages of ink arrived regularly from Germany, from a firm in Dresden. Wagner had given the servants instructions that the packages were to be sent wherever he was, and, as in all things, his instructions had been followed to the letter. The firm was known as E. Windisch and Company, and had been recommended by Wagner's brother-in-law, Hermann Brockhaus, a professor of Oriental languages at Leipzig.

"Monsieur Liszt," said Holmes, "I believe that our work here is now done. We must go to Dresden to find the poisoner. We cannot delay."

"You are right, but you have been here for only a few days. I do not want to reveal anything to the Wagners unless we feel that his condition will improve. Do not forget the ostensible purpose of your visit. The poisoner will have no suspicions as yet. Delay your departure for a few days."

It was by then the twelfth February, if memory serves, and we spent the afternoon with the children, who took us to Piazza San Marco to see the church and the Doge's palace. Liszt and the Wagners remained at home. After the brief tour, the children were content playing with the great flocks of pigeons in the square. Holmes and I sat there, as so many have, contemplating the proportions of this most beautiful of piazzas.

It was about four o'clock when one of the servants appeared to tell us to remain there, for a special concert of Wagner's music to be held in the piazza had been hastily arranged, and the Wagners were on their way. A military band began assembling in the square, and Holmes and I raced to the canal with the children. In a very short time a gondola appeared bearing Franz Liszt and the Wagners. Wagner looked resplendent in his black beret and velvet jacket.

"Come, join us, my dear friends. The concert was announced only a few hours ago without my knowledge. I hope it is better than the one last March in Sicily," said the composer as he alighted onto the pier, his breath coming in short gasps.

We sat with the Wagners in front of the Doge's palace. The band was hardly an orchestra, but a Venetian brass ensemble. They had chosen selections from *Rienzi*, *Tannhäuser*, and the prelude to the third act of Lohengrin, all of which they played rather well.

Wagner was deeply moved. The last pieces were Wotan's Farewell from *Götterdämmerung*, and the overture to *Parsifal*, which, despite the absence of strings, was orchestrated in such a way that the Master was pleased. At the end of the performance, following his lead, all applauded the band warmly. After greeting the conductor, a Signor Torelli, and the members of the band, they returned home.

At supper, Wagner discoursed about many things, including some statements of Bismarck, which he considered wise, and about *Undine*, the famous novel by La Motte Fouqué, as a suitable subject for a music drama. He had read it as a child and had so covered his copy with blotches of ink in reading it that, when confronted by his angry father, he quickly invented a clever excuse. He blamed the blotting on the dark child of a Moorish merchant, who lived nearby. He said that the black boy had cut himself and drops of his dark blood had stained the book. In a final discourse, he compared Undine to Kundry and to other heroines, then rose and announced that he would retire early since he had slept little the night before.

In the morning, Wagner let it be known that he would not breakfast with the family, but that he would meet everyone at lunch. In a brief meeting in which I administered another sedative to him, he told us that he would enter his study only briefly but would not stay. Holmes admonished him, saying that above all he must write nothing. It was a sunny morning, and we went for a long stroll in the city.

It was probably just after the hour of noon that Wagner must have rung the warning bell that was near his desk. Frau Wagner rushed to him, only to find that he was barely conscious. Because we were absent, a local doctor was summoned. When we returned, Joukovsky informed me that Wagner's condition had taken a grave turn. We sat with the chilren for a moment, but before I could see him, the doctor appeared and informed us that Herr Wagner had expired a few minutes before. He had suffered a massive hear attack, but had not suffered greatly. At the end, his face, we were told, was filled with peace and nobility. Frau Wagner had held him in her arms in his last minutes. She announced through the doctor that she would remain with her husband and would not appear until his body was to be moved for burial at Wahnfried, their home in Germany.

On the following morning, the remains of Herr Wagner were brought by gondola to the railroad station. The bearers of his coffin were Joukovsky, Holmes and I, and several Venetian young men, who claimed to be disciples of the great musician. Frau Wagner, attired and veiled in black, rode with her husband and the children. Joukovsky, Liszt, and Holmes and I followed in a separate boat.

The news of Wagner's death spread rapidly and the Venetians had come out in great numbers. At the station, Holmes and I bade farewell to the family. We watched as the mournful group boarded the early-morning train for Germany. Our own left several hours later, and we had time to visit the attending physician, Dr. Vattimo, and read the report that he had prepared: all of it was consistent with our diagnosis. Wagner's diseases—Bright's disease, erysipelas, swollen liver, and a gradually failing heart were all consistent with the slow, methodical poisoning that eventually overpowered him. Clever, and most vengeful, for he suffered constant pain and discomfort while alive.

Holmes had surmised that the poison had been delivered mainly through Wagner's fingers, by the ink that he used. Stored in powdered form, the composer mixed it religiously every morning and spent long hours ruling his music paper. He would then write for several hours. By the evening he would be saturated with small quantities; unable to sleep, he would pace about, then fall into a sleep of terrible dreams. The dosage was precise, and Holmes judged that the poisoning occurred intermittently at first, then regularly over two years. The murder was committed not only by one who hated him, but one who knew poisons and knew them well.

There was only one clue: the ink company in Dresden, And so, later that very day, having wired our plans to Liszt and asking him to join us in Dresden, Holmes and I boarded a train for Germany.

The trip was uneventful, but by coincidence we shared the compartment with someone who had arrived in Venice with the specific purpose of visiting Wagner. She was a Mrs. Burrell, a woman from Philadelphia, who described herself as one of Wagner's American disciples. She was one of many American visitors, mainly female, who came in along stream to meet the Master, as they referred to him. He never refused to see them. She had come to invite Wagner to New York and Philadelphia to conduct performances of his own operas. She also had arrived too late.

Mrs. Burrell was a vivacious and intelligent woman of about twenty-five who had lived in Germany when she was a child. Her father was an American doctor who had served as Wagner's physician before his return many years before to America. She had never met the Wagners, for she was a mere infant when her parents left for America, but a letter from her father had elicited a reply saying that his daughter was welcome at any time. This fact increased her disappointment at the composer's death. She now planned to write a biography of Wagner and to invite two of his close associates, Anton Seidl and Hans von Bülow, to America. She had a long list of people she was going to visit, in Leipzig and Dresden, prepared for her by her father, as well as letters of introduction from the leading conductors of America.

We descended at Munich, bade farewell to Mrs. Burrell, and boarded a train for Leipzig. There we stayed for a day with the Brockhauses, to whom Liszt had provided an introduction. The Brockhauses themselves were busy preparing to leave for Bayreuth and the funeral. Ottilie Brockhaus, Wagner's sister, tearfully questioned me closely about her brother's last days, for she was the closest to him, and he had spent many hours in the quiet, rich, contentment of their home. Hermann, her husband, a large fat man, was a celebrated scholar of Sanskrit, and it was through him that Richard Wagner obtained many of the Buddhist texts that he had learned of in his reading Schopenhauer. Like many professors, Brockhaus liked to talk, and he and Holmes engaged in long dialogue about innumerable things pertaining to the composer. Holmes informed him in detail of Wagner's last days, and Brockhaus expanded on his experience of Wagner, his difficult ways, and his creative genius. Holmes noted that Wagner took his own work so seriously that he used special inks that he himself prepared for the writing of his texts and scores.

"Yes," Brockhaus answered, "Richard was particularly careful in the preparation of his scores. Because his music is so difficult technically, not only for singers but for the orchestra as well, he made his scores models of clarity in order to minimize the number of possible errors before they went to the publisher. It was upon my recommendation that Richard came to use the firm E. Windisch. The firm is owned by the father of one of my students, and they were always prompt in serving him, I gather. We of course use their inks in the books published by our family's company."

"For some projects of my own, I should like to consult the Windisches. I was deeply impressed with the Wagner scores. Perhaps you could inform Herr Windisch that I should like to meet him," said Holmes.

"Easily done, Herr Holmes. I shall give you a letter and send a wire to him today. Because of your interest in Wagner, you may also want to meet one of his employees, Nathalie Planer. She has been in Windisch's employ for several years now. She is the younger sister of Minna, Richard Wagner's first wife. Although she and Richard have been out of touch for many years, she would, I am sure, appreciate hearing from you about your visit during his last days."

I saw that Holmes could barely contain his excitement in hearing Brockhaus's last words. Casually spoken, they may have delivered a significant clew to the solution of the mystery. No one, not even Liszt, had ever mentioned the name of Nathalie Planer to him. With Brockhaus's letters, we left by train for Dresden the following morning, where we arrived just before noon. From the station we went directly to the Hotel Metropole, a small inn recommended by Brockhaus, and then walked directly to the firm of E. Windisch. Herr Windisch received us warmly.

"The world has lost its greatest composer," he said, "and we mourn for his family and for the world."

"You are right, Herr Windisch. The loss is irreparable. I gather that you have working for you a relative of Wagner's through his first marriage, one Fräulein Nathalie Planer."

"She is no longer with the firm, Dr. Watson. She became ill several months ago, and took leave. She has not returned, and I have not seen her."

Windisch gave us her last known address, which he said lay at the other end of town. We took our leave and went directly in search of her. There, in a dilapidated rooming house, we asked the owner to direct us to her. We were led to the third floor. The proprietress knocked on a door at the end of the hall.

The door opened and an old woman appeared.

"What do you want?" she asked curtly.

"I come from the house of Richard Wagner," said Holmes moving forward to the door. "He is dead."

The name made her start, and she immediately let us in. As soon as we entered we realized that we had walked into a small shrine to the dead composer. His portraits and photographs were everywhere, and his scores and libretti were among the few books that lined the walls.

The old woman was dressed in rags. Her room was cold, and her wrists were wrapped tightly in an effort to keep warm. Her feet were bare and swollen. She moved slowly, and I saw immediately that she was very ill. Her hand shook as she motioned him to a chair. Holmes spoke to her bluntly.

"Fräulein Planer, I shall not hide my purpose in seeking you out. My name is Sherlock Holmes. That surely means nothing to you. I am, however, a consulting detective. My colleague, Dr. Watson, and I have been engaged by a client to investigate the decline in health and now death of the composer Herr Richard Wagner. I have reason to believe that you are responsible for his death by poison gradually administered to him."

Holmes uttered the accusation with the utmost conviction.

There was but a momentary surprise on her face. She sighed and looked down at the floor and remained silent for a time. When she began speaking, she made no attempt to deny Holmes's accusation.

"You are correct," she said proudly. "I am, but only in an earthly sense, responsible for the death of that monster, for it is the work of God whose agent I am. You cannot know the happiness I felt when I learned of his death. He is now mine."

Her eyes narrowed at first as she spoke, then a smile formed on her lips.

"Fräulein Planer," said Holmes, "I cannot condone your actions, but at the same I am neither a representative of the police nor am I a German citizen. I am the only one who suspects that Herr Wagner did not die of a heart attack brought on by natural causes. I would encourage you, therefore, to tell me what reason you had to kill him. As to your punishment, that will come from another than I."

"You will hear my story and understand. I do not fear punishment, and I stand ready to receive it. It is perhaps an evil act that I have performed, but one out of which only good can come. Let me start at the very beginning, for the circumstances of my birth are directly related. I believe, with the Buddhists, that birth is the result of circumstances of which we can know nothing when we come into this world and that our life is a journey in profound ignorance. You may not know that my mother was Christine Wilhelmine Planer, called Minna, a woman who had the misfortune to become Richard Wagner's first wife. Wagner, however, was not my father. Long before she met Wagner, Minna, at the age of fifteen, worked in a common working-class liquor shop. Extremely beautiful and in the first bloom of youth, she was seduced one night by a drunken soldier. I was the result of that liaison. To this day, I do not know who my father was. Because of her deep shame, Minna raised me as her younger sister, and her parents also maintained this version of who I was. Most people still believe I am her sister.

"Minna met Wagner several years later, and before they were married she told him her story and the truth about me. He was the only one who knew. He was so infatuated with Minna's beauty that he did not care what her past was, for he said that he loved only her, and insisted that they marry, which they did. I lived most of my early years with them.

"As I grew up, Wagner was kind and gentle at times, but more often distant and aloof, and he often treated me indifferently, never harshly, despite the stormy relationship with Minna. I, myself, of course, had a very difficult time with her, who, while calling me her sister, treated me naturally as her daughter. I could do nothing without her permission, and she never let me out of her sight. I felt stifled by her. Several times she left, taking me with her. When we returned, there would be peace for a few days, then the bickering would break out again. Wagner himself often left on tour for his music, and I was left with my sister alone, who browbeat me constantly. She loved me deeply, I knew, but so stifled did I feel that I ran away twice, only to be found at the home of friends and returned to her. Though I loved her, I wanted to hurt her.

"The stormy relationship between Wagner and Minna gradually grew worse, and on several occasions became almost violent. At these times, I would retire to my room in fright. One morning, when I was fifteen, an argument broke out before lunch, and Minna, without even packing a bag, ran out of the house. She did not return for two weeks. Wagner went after her. He searched everywhere and was gone for two days. I was alone for the first time in my life. When he returned he was in despair. Minna had disappeared without a trace. He did not know whether she was alive or dead. Two days after his return, word arrived through a friend that Minna was alive but despondent and that she had no intention of returning soon. She wanted me to join her immediately at her secret location. Having tasted freedom for the first time in my life, I adamantly refused. Wagner argued heatedly with me that I should go to stay with Minna, that he had his work and had to travel, that he could not be responsible for me, and that I belonged with Minna. I quietly refused.

"On several nights, just after I had prepared dinner, we talked about Minna. Both of us found her so difficult. He looked at me and said tearfully that their marriage was a mistake, that they were not meant to be together, and that his true love was for someone else."

A look of the greatest pain consumed her face at this point. She stared directly at Holmes, as if answering his accusation.

"It was during this period," she said, "when we were alone together that Richard Wagner seduced me. He told me first the story that he had heard of ancient India that concerned a young maiden by the name of Prakriti and a man of fame by the name of Ananda. Prakriti and Ananda loved one another, but their love was not meant to be consummated in their lifetime. They were prevented by the girl's mother and by the Buddha himself, who compelled Ananda to keep his vow of celibacy. Richard told me that he had decided to write an opera based on the story, that it was to be the crowning achievement of his career. Then he introduced me to the doctrine of rebirth or karma, metempsychosis, as he called it, and explained how he felt that he was the reincarnation of Ananda and that I was Prakriti, the Chandala maiden. He told me too of the distinction between the pain of this world, Sansara, as the Indians call it, and Nirvana, the Annihilation of the individual soul into the Absolute.

"So overcome was I by his passionate eloquence that I succumbed rapidly to his advances, and for a few weeks we were happy together. Richard said now that I was his inspiration for this Buddhist opera, and that I was his everything. Indeed, he began quoting to me from one of his favorite Indian books, the Upanishads: *tat tvam asi*, he said over and over to me in Sanskrit, 'That thou art,' my All. He rapidly sketched out the opera and read it to me. He called it *The Victors*, and began calling me Savitri, another name of the Indian maid. I was overwhelmed.

"We decided, at Richard's suggestion, to keep our relationship a secret. This would protect our love until he could divorce Minna and we could live the rest of our lives together. I agreed, and could think only of following him and being with him forever.

"In a short time, however, everything came to an end. Minna, realising that I would not go to her, came to fetch me. Upon her arrival, Richard, rather than being at all harsh with her, welcomed her warmly. I suddenly found myself pushed aside. I became hurt and angry. Richard insisted that I was being foolish and misinterpreting his actions, that we would gain nothing in the long run by alienating Minna. Reassured, I kept my own counsel.

"Two weeks after Minna's return, Richard announced that he had been invited to London to conduct a performance of *Rienzi* at Covent Garden and then of *Lohengrin* in Paris. He did not know exactly how long he would be gone, but that I should not worry. He said that I would join him at the first moment after he had settled in England, and that he would send for me, that he would ask a friend to take me to him. He would then write to Minna and explain the situation, and that she should grant him a divorce.

"The day he left, my heart sank. Already fearful, I could only wait. I never saw him again. A month went by. I received two notes, saying that all was well, that he loved me, but that the rehearsals had taken all his time, and that it would perhaps be better if I met him after he arrived in Paris.

"Another month passed. To my consternation, I learned that I was now carrying his child. I despaired, for I had heard nothing for weeks from Richard. I wrote him a passionate letter in secret to his Paris address. I explained my condition to him. I received no reply. Two weeks later, my letter was returned to me from France, unopened and unread.

"One night, missing him so much, I decided to enter his room. There, surrounded by his books, his clothes, and his other possessions, I sat at his desk, looking out the window at the stars. The full moon lit the room. I began to weep. I cried as a child who had grown too quickly into adulthood. In retrospect, I realise how heinous his crimes were, for I was indeed a mere child.

"I reached instinctively into the top drawer of his desk for something with which to dry my eyes, when I saw a letter in Richard's handwriting. It was addressed to a Frau Wesendonck, the wife of a family friend. I shall never forget the words that he addressed to her: 'You are my Savitri, and I your Ananda! Forever, we shall be together. Happy Savitri! You may now follow your lover everywhere, be around him and with him constantly ! Happy Ananda! She is now close to you, you have won her, never to lose her. You are my All, and I yours.'

"Stunned by this evidence of his betrayal, my heart suddenly became as cold as ice. I vowed revenge. I returned to my room to spend the rest of a sleepless night plotting the slow cruel death of Richard Wagner.

"In the morning, I decided that I would tell all that had happened to Minna, for I believed that, whatever her faults, she truly loved me. My trust was not misplaced. Minna at first was dismayed by my revelations, but in the end she was relieved. She now realized that she could no longer remain the wife of Richard Wagner. It was then, in the kitchen of that small house, that she told me the truth, that I was not her younger sister, but her own daughter. It was then that I learned her terrible secret. Relieved by the truth, we embraced for the first time as mother and daughter. That morning, we packed our things, notified the landlord that what remained belonged to Herr Wagner, and left. Minna was careful to take all of Richard Wagner's letters and documents with her, including the letter that I had found to Frau Wesendonck. We went to her father's house, where we remained until the child was born. During this time, Minna divulged nothing of my secret to anyone. Indeed, you and your companion are the first, Mr. Holmes, to know. She used the letter to Frau Wesendonck to mark publicly her break with Wagner. Of my condition, Wagner never knew anything. Only my grandmother and Minna were aware that I was to give birth.

"The child was a girl, and Minna convinced me to give her up for adoption. She had known for many years an American doctor by the name of Jenkins, who had been many years resident in Dresden. He had originally served in the American consulate, and then, because he loved Germany so much, decided to remain in a private capacity for several years after he left government service. He and his wife were childless. Minna, without naming the father, explained the situation that, since her own health was not that good and her parents were now old and indigent, it would be best if he could help find a home. He decided on the spot to take the child in adoption himself, and to return with her to America where he and his wife would raise her as his own. He insisted that I remain under his care during and after the pregnancy, and he assisted at the birth. Except for the kindness shown by this American gentleman and his wife, I do not think that I could have lived through those few months. He also gave us a sizable sum of money, which Minna invested. Though the income was not great, it was enough for us to live frugally.

"Minna's parents died within a few months of each other, and Minna herself was in poor health. It was shortly after their death that Minna learned from friends that Wagner had secretly taken up with Cosima, the wife of his friend Hans von Bülow. She must still have harbored some love towards Wagner, for she took this news very badly; for her it appeared to be a particularly heavy blow. I have no doubt that Wagner's latest treachery hastened her death. I watched her through her last illness and was with her when she died. As soon as he learned of Minna's death, Wagner announced his intention to marry Cosima, by whom he had already fathered one child and with whom he was expecting a second. Cosima asked her husband for a divorce, and the disconsolate Hans von Bülow could only acquiesce bitterly in a situation that was already a fait accompli. The only dissenting voice came from her father, Franz Liszt, who made his feelings known quite clearly to Cosima that he regarded their liaison and approaching marriage with the greatest apprehension.

"As her heir, I inherited all of Minna's property, including all the letters and documents that she had accumulated through the years with Richard Wagner. It is a substantial collection, one that I have read through carefully. It is a catalogue of treachery, of vicious dishonesty to his friends and acquaintances, but mostly to the women who crossed his path.

In going through these things, I found a box marked with the word "Poisons. From the apothecary Obrist." I learned from Minna's notes that several years before, when their dog Peps lay in his death agony, Wagner had been given some strong poisons by Obrist, an apothecary who had inherited a large number of poisons from a retiring apothecary in Zurich. They were to be used to put a merciful end to the dog's agony. The dog died before Wagner returned, and the poisons were never used.

"Here, then, I had my tools. There were over a dozen vials, each marked with a different poison. There was also a small pamphlet inside which explained their effects, both long and short term, and how they could be administered medically. I knew nothing of such things, and since I wished to proceed slowly and deliberately, I took a position in the shop of an apothecary in Dresden, where I apprenticed, learning all there was to learn of medicines as well as poisons and how to measure them out. I became quite expert within a few months. I now knew which ones could be absorbed through the skin, which ones could be inhaled, and which ones could be most effective through ingestion.

"The only question that remained was how they could be delivered to him effectively and without harm to anyone else. I wished to have him suffer, to make him sick with a variety of ailments before he died, but I harbored no hatred for anyone else. For Cosima, his latest Savitri, his most beloved Isolde, I had nothing but pity, for she was given the worst in this vale of Sansara.

"It was only fitting that, in my quest for the means by which to poison him, Wagner himself should come to my aid. Having heard nothing from him since the notes he sent from London, not even a word acknowledging the death of Minna, I received one morning a letter from him, written in Lucerne and dated 27 November 1868. It was characteristic of him that it mentioned nothing of our relationship, nor his long marriage to Minna. He wanted something, and went directly to the point:

> I have a favour to ask you today which I have kept on forgetting until now. Among the objects which remained in Minna's household in Dresden, and which were all transferred to her at her request, is a present which Countess d'Agoult gave me and which only negligence could have persuaded Minna to regard as one of her possessions. It is a small Chinese Buddha, a kind of gilt idol, enclosed in a small casket of black wood, the doors of which used to open to reveal the small statue inside. God knows what Minna did with this piece: at all events, it was not right of her if she gave it away. May I ask you to endeavor to obtain the return of this piece for me: if the present owner is indelicate enough not to return this keepsake at once, in return for the above declaration, I am ultimately willing to pay whatever compensation may be necessary to ensure its return.

"I found the piece in one of Minna's trunks marked RW. It had not been given away, for Minna had been scrupulous about Wagner's things. How fitting! In triumph, like some divine object, I held up this piece of cheap Oriental junk to the sky, contemplating its sacred nature, knowing that this idol would be the first vehicle of my revenge. That night, using the poisons that my mother had preserved, and protecting myself with the face masks and garments of the apothecary, I carefully covered the idol with a dust that was easily absorbed through the skin and could easily be inhaled. It was my own formula made from the poisons for his dog Peps. I wrapped it carefully and sent it to Wagner marked: "Richard Wagner. Personal. To be opened only by him." Inside I put a note: '*tat tvam asi.*' I left it unsigned. The piece arrived at Tribschen, the Wagners' home, on 16 January 1869. A week later, a notice appeared in the Dresden newspapers that Herr Wagner had been taken ill with what appeared to be erysipelas and mysterious spasms of the legs that had forced him to cancel his conducting engagements indefinitely. My plan was working. The first dose was a success. But how to continue on a regular basis, until the end?

"I finally found the way. This time, however, it was Minna who led me to the solution. In her diaries, she mentioned that Wagner spent hours preparing his music paper for his notations, that he refused to have anyone draw even the lines of the staff for him. When he could not compose, when he felt the music blocked, he would spend long hours ruling large sheets of paper in preparation for when the music rushed into his head. He had to have complete control over this aspect of his artistic life and he insisted that no one else do it for him. He experimented with a variety of pens and pencils, even finding a new kind of pencil whose lead, when mixed with water, became indelible. Finally, he had chosen a special ink made only in Dresden by a small firm called Windisch and

Company, suggested to him by his brother-in-law Hermann Brockhaus. The Brockhaus Publishing Firm used the inks of this firm in their best publications. The recommendation was enough for Wagner, and he had used only these inks in the score of the Ring, *Tristan*, and now *Parsifal*. He spent hours mixing the inks carefully. What better vehicle could there be than these dusts and chemicals, ones that he insisted no one else touch? Again, how fitting, for I would be poisoning not only him, but the physical expression of the music itself. The more he wrote, the sicker he would become, for I was not anxious that he should die quickly.

"By recommendation of the apothecary for whom I worked, I was apprenticed at Windisch and Company as one who mixed the inks and had them dispatched to select customers. Because I was known to have a family relation with him—I was still known as his wife's sister—Wagner's orders to the firm were quickly put in my personal charge. His instructions to Herr Windisch were characteristically precise and firm: two packages per month to arrive on the tenth and twentieth, no matter where he was. It became part of my task to know his travels and whereabouts. This was done through one of the domestic servants whom Wagner instructed to notify Windisch of his plans. I myself was never in direct communication with Wagner, nor did he nor anyone in his household know that I was employed at Windisch and Company. And so, my task began. I experimented at first—"

"Strychnine, belladonna, and arsenic are obvious, but there are others," Holmes interjected.

"There are several others, including curare, and, of course, for the last six months, the deadliest, a mixture of curare and sugar of lead."

"Well done, Frau Planer, the last explains the sweet taste of the ink that he mentioned to me."

"Indeed, I made it known in special instructions that the ink was even safe for him to drink in small quantities. I knew that he would drink it, because he was one of those individuals who could not resist chemicals of any kind."

At that moment, Holmes realised that on the morning of his death, Wagner, feeling better for the first time in many days, attributed his well-being to what was indeed killing him, and probably took a small drink made from the latest shipment, the shipment of 10 February 1883, a final drink that caused his death.

"Frau Planer," said Holmes grimly "I am not here to judge your actions, nor to report your account to anyone but my client."

"It is all immaterial to me," she said firmly, "for I have not acted against Wagner alone, but that he and I should enter a new life. You see, Richard and I are bound together by birth and rebirth. He is my Ananda and I his Savitri. I do not intend to live much beyond today. Over the last few months I have been giving myself the same poisons that I gave him, and I shall soon join him. . . . free from Sansara, in Nirvana!"

At this moment, Nathalie Planer, the bitter old woman, became transfigured. A strange light appeared in her eyes and she gazed into a far distance that was not contained by the walls of her small room, a trance, induced only in part, by the poisons, probably the belladonna.

We decided not to question her further. Holmes examined the room quickly. My eye was immediately caught by the photograph of a young girl on the wall, one aged about fifteen. Judging by the resemblance to her parents, I knew that it must be of her daughter by Richard Wagner. As we left, I glanced out the window, and noticed that a cab had just drawn up to the entrance of the house. Alighting from it was Mrs. Burrell of Philadelphia. We left unseen.

The following evening Holmes explained all to Liszt, who had arrived from Bayreuth after the burial at Wahnfried. He listened in rapt attention to Holmes's account of the deeds of Richard Wagner and of the revenge of Nathalie Planer.

"How strange a tale, Monsieur Holmes. I assure you I knew nothing of this. Nathalie Planer was a mere child when I met her, and I saw her but once. Wagner never mentioned her to me."

"We must leave Nathalie to her fate, to her karma, as she would put it," Holmes replied, "and keep the story to ourselves. It would do no good at this point to reveal it."

"*Così si fa il contrapasso*, Monsieur Holmes. I do not understand Buddhist doctrine. It is one of the things that has separated me from my daughter. I remain a firm Christian, and my authority for retribution remains the Christian doctrine so beautifully enunciated by Dante. Cosima knows nothing of Wagner's relation with Frau Planer, of course, and I wish to keep all of this from her. She has sworn never to appear in public again. I saw her only briefly, and I still feel that she may try to take her own life. I must tell you that Cosima once entered a 'nirvana' suicide pact with a friend, Karl Ritter. They were both unhappy for different reasons, she because of her marriage to von Bülow, he . . . well, he for his own reasons. They decided to drown themselves together in a nearby lake. Luckily, they were talked out of it."

"All the more reason for us to remain silent."

"Yes, let us keep it to ourselves."

We said our farewells, and in two days Holmes and I were back in London.

"Remarkable," said I as we sat in our living room. "The more I think about it the more remarkable a story it becomes. Who would have thought—"

"And it is not quite finished, Watson. Here," said Holmes, holding out a letter.

Dear Mr. Holmes,

I write you because you and I are among the very few who share the same knowledge. I spoke with Nathalie Planer shortly after you did.

You can understand how surprised I was to find my own picture as a young girl hanging in her room. When she saw me, she broke down in tears, and she told me everything, including her intention to kill herself.

Luckily, I was able to dissuade her. She has decided that it is more important for her to continue to live since I wanted it so, but her health is seriously impaired, and she may not live long. I spent several weeks with her, trying to live with the idea of my real parentage. Upon my return to Philadelphia, my American parents confirmed the fact that Nathalie Planer was my real mother. They still do not know who my father was, and I have let it remain so for the time being. Nathalie entrusted to me all of the documents that she had concerning Richard Wagner. These were left to her by her sister, Minna, Wagner's first wife. I hope to employ these in a biography concerning the early life of Richard Wagner, my father. If it is ever printed, I shall send you a copy.

As a token of gratitude, I include a photograph of you, Dr. Watson, Franz Liszt, and Richard Wagner standing in front of the Palazzo Vendramin.

Sincerely,
(Mrs.) Mary Burrell

As I glanced up, I saw that Holmes had already buried himself in the day's agony column. I stared at the photograph for a time, wondering how long it would take the young lady to write the life of Wagner.

THE CASE OF THE TWO BOHÈMES

In the winter of 1899, Mr. Sherlock Holmes and I found ourselves still happily ensconced in our flat in Rome but compelled to endure a fortnight of snow-filled days; indeed, an unexpected blizzard so bitterly cold that it threatened to reverse our long-held convictions concerning the respective merits of cold, foggy London as opposed to sunny Rome. The meager silver light of these short December days in the dead of winter faded quickly into the dark Roman night, and the usually animated city fell silent and still by early evening, as if uninhabited.

"Just remember, old fellow, that in London they talk of heat stroke or even sunstroke on days such as these," said my friend with unusually good humour.

"Quite right, but I shall not move until our landlady recognises how cold her establishment is, and that one of her boarders is about to expire from cold stroke," I replied.

Indeed, our landlady, la signora Manfredini, had done nothing, once we had moved in, to alleviate our sufferings, despite our increasingly vociferous remonstrances. Windows throughout her large establishment remained broken, letting in freezing drafts of icy-cold air. The fireplace, after two days of intense labour on our part, produced only a few sputters and then settled into permanent inactivity. Blocked by countless swallows and their nests, which I had tried in vain to dislodge with the point of my umbrella, the chimney merely produced a dark grey smoke that finally forced us to open the windows, thereby augmenting the long unrelenting chill that blew in and destroyed what was left of our thoroughly diminished comfort.

In addition to her refusal to hear our pleas, La Signora, as we referred to her, took the outlandish action of storing the remaining firewood and kindling in a locked valise which she attempted to hide behind the kitchen stove. When she realised that Holmes could open the valise easily, she hid it in her bedroom, leading us to throw the broken legs of an old chair into the remaining embers of our dwindling fire.

Despite our failure, Holmes kept searching the long halls of the Manfredini residence for things to burn in the hope that he would eventually succeed. I myself moved less and less within our quarters, covering myself with the musty moth-eaten blankets provided to us. They were our only refuge until by chance Holmes found in one of the dark corners of the flat an old metal bucket filled with chunks of coal and kindling with which he produced a small fire.

"My gratitude knows no bounds, Holmes. I doubt that I would have survived the last few minutes without your serendipitous find."

"We are almost warm in this room now, dear Watson, and, with any luck at all, the icy rain and snow will soon abate, and we will again go about our business without frozen fingers and toes. The city appears to be iced over, like some strange glacier. We are not missing anything by staying inside."

I was about to agree, when there was a knock at the door. Without waiting for one of us to open, in strode our strange and wondrous landlady, attired in a way most odd even for her, and seemingly impervious to the cold. Her hair was covered in a thick white towel and her face glistened with some brownish oil. The rest of her was covered in a heavy green robe from which large puddles of water dripped onto the floor around her feet.

"*Mi dispiace, signori,*" she said sternly, "but I need the bucket for my bath, to heat the water."

"*Purtroppo,*" said I, "we need it as well. And may I point out to La Signora that the bucket has not been used in months," I replied brusquely.

I could see that my words angered her, but she did not press us further. She walked away, her robe still dripping, and entered her quarters.

"We have won a small battle, old fellow," said Holmes, "but not the war." He looked at his watch and said, "Dear Watson, in light of our difficulties and the approaching evening, I propose that I pay a visit to the local grog shop to buy some wine and brandy—and some cheese and bread. The salumeria on Via Spontini may still be open. If all goes well, we should be pleasantly comatose in a few minutes and asleep when the hour strikes eight. *Che pensi*?"

"Good idea, old fellow, and buy enough for friend Gabriel and company. It will be Christmas in just a week and I invited them over for a drink this evening." Holmes left, and I fell almost immediately into a doze. Through it, however, I heard our doorbell ring several times. I got up and, throwing the dusty blankets onto the floor, I opened our door to find Gabriel and friends standing there. We greeted each other warmly, and they rushed in and put their bundles down on the table. They were frozen over with snow and ice but recovered a bit in front of our fire. Holmes returned shortly after their arrival. Among his purchases was a hot soup that we consumed in great gulps. We had now enough wine and food for a sumptuous evening, and the mood changed markedly.

These three young friends had come into our lives in Rome because Holmes had wisely decided that he would need a number of allies comparable to the Baker Street Irregulars in London. Instead of the awkward word *irregolari*, he dubbed them I Soliti Ignoti, "the usual suspects," and so far they had been of the greatest help to him in his investigations. The three of them were in their early twenties and had lived most of their lives in the streets with only intermittent contact with their families. Curiously enough, each bore the name of an archangel: Gabriel, Michael, and Raffael.

It was just about half past ten that evening when our companions invited us to continue our merry-making at the Café Momus, a popular establishment near Piazza Cavour.

Holmes agreed to go and said that he would follow in a few minutes. I declined, however, having decided to retire. True to his word, Holmes left after about a quarter of an hour.

Alone, but now warm, I decided to read for a while. I was therefore surprised when I heard the doorbell ring again. By now, it was close to midnight. "*Chi è la?*" I asked. It was a woman's voice that I heard.

"Please, *vi prego*, an old man has fallen in the snow and I cannot carry him alone. He is very ill. I need your help. I am your neighbor."

I opened at once. A young woman, no more than twenty, stood there soaked with rain and snow. I recognized her as the young woman Lucia, who sold paper flowers on the corner of Via Palestrina. I stopped only to put on my shoes and my overcoat and to collect a few blankets.

"Where is he?"

"Follow me," she said, "I am afraid that he will be trampled by a buggy passing in the night."

We fairly flew down the stairs, and once on the street I saw a diminutive figure sitting in the snow, motionless. I put my arms around him and dragged him into our courtyard, out of the icy winds. He was alive but barely. I removed his coat and wrapped him in one of the dry blankets.

"We shall need help in carrying him up the stairs."

I tried once more to get him to stand, but to no avail. I suddenly saw Holmes's most welcome figure emerge from out of the blizzard.

"Hallo, Watson, I'm afraid that I find the Café Momus a bore. And what are you up to?" said the familiar voice.

"Holmes! Thank God you're here. The poor devil is at death's door. No time to waste. Let's carry him up the stairs, if we can. He can barely walk, and his toes may be frost-bitten."

"We can, Watson. Never say die. Come on, old fellow, help me scoop him up. And walk close by in case I lose my balance. Ah, he's heavier than I thought." Holmes handed over a newly acquired bottle of brandy to the flower girl to hold. In no time at all he had the old man up the stairs and seated on our couch. He was a short man, but stout, heavier than one would have anticipated, and more torso than legs.

Holmes and I removed his wet clothing and again threw blankets around him. A few drops of brandy to his lips and he began to revive. I called for the young woman to heat the soup that was left for her father, when I noticed that without a word she was gone, the bottle of brandy placed on the floor near the door.

"She left as we put down our charge on the couch, Watson. Perhaps she will return. Well, we have enough to feed the old man, if he survives his ordeal."

"How odd, Holmes. She has disappered and left him to us, complete strangers."

"I am from Paris," said our frozen guest in a weak voice. "She saw me slip on the ice and tried to help me up, I was too heavy. I shall always be grateful to her and to you gentlemen."

"Do not concern yourself, Mr.—"

"Murger, Henri Murger of Paris. I am here to meet with Mr. Sherlock Homes who, if I am not mistaken, may live in this very building."

"He does indeed live here," said Holmes. "I know him well and will take you to him. But first, a short sleep for all of us. It is very late and we would all benefit by some rest. Monsieur Murger, please make yourself comfortable on the couch and we will see you in the morning," said Holmes.

We left our guest in our sitting room, and I soon heard his rhythmic breathing through the partially open door. I wondered what had befallen the flower girl. It was she with whom our Gabriel had become enamoured. She, however, while she claimed to love him as well, was often seen with other, richer men. Gabriel was deeply concerned because she was ill with pneumonia but still tried to sell her flowers even in the snow.

Holmes was the first up in the morning, and I heard him as he made our tea and breakfast. Murger was sound asleep still at eight.

"Watson," said he as he handed me a cup of tea, "I was unable to tell you last night that I am expecting two clients in just a few moments. The rain and snow have stopped and so I assume that they will not be detained. To talk with them in Murger's presence, for reasons that I shall make clearer later, would be most awkward. And so I will use the kitchen. Our landlady is already gone for the day and will not return until late. We must be grateful for small things. Ah, there is the bell. Watson, please direct them to the kitchen where I shall hear their difficulties to them and feed them *un po' di mascarpone e una tazza di caffè*."

Holmes had told me nothing of Murger or of his two clients. I was in the dark but did as he asked. Two elegant Italian gentlemen were already at our door.

"*Prego, Dottore, noi cerchiamo* Sherlock Holmes. Are you by any chance the famous Dr. Watson?"

"I am. And who shall I say is here?"

"Messrs. Puccini and Leoncavallo."

I did not recognize their names, but led them to the kitchen where Holmes was sitting, reading the local newspaper. Holmes rose as they introduced themselves.

"Mr. Holmes," said the taller of the two men, "*sono Puccini Giacomo e vi presento Leoncavallo Ruggiero.*"

"*Molto lieto. Vi prego,* please have some cheese and coffee. It is all that I have to offer you."

The two men sat down at the old green table. I moved my chair closer so that I could hear what transpired. Puccini spoke first. He was a somewhat stout man, tall, impeccably tailored, his face carrying what appeared to be a permanent look of disdain that made him somewhat unpleasant to look at.

"You perhaps, Mr. Holmes, have heard the news or perhaps rumours concerning me and my friend, Ruggiero, who so kindly accompanied me here in order to explain his side of our problem."

"Indeed, Signore, I spend much of my time at Piazza del Popolo, where one learns much by slowly sipping one's *caffè latte*. One of you might describe your problem once again for the benefit of my colleague, the good Dr. Watson."

"Let me then begin," said Leoncavallo with a nod from Puccini. Taller than Puccini and more handsome, Leoncavallo carried some of the signs of his native southern Italy. His speech, though impeccable grammatically, bore the telltale sounds of his native Naples.

"Briefly, Signor Holmes, the story begins in this way, perhaps in one of the hobbies that Giacomo and I share," he began, "which is a love of old books and old musical scores."

"*Davvero*," said Puccini quietly.

"I am afraid that I share the vice with you both," said Holmes.

"It was no more than a few months ago," continued Leoncavallo, "that I was standing in Largo Borghese, only a few minutes' walk from here, wondering where I would find a suitable libretto for my next opera. My *Pagliacci* had been a great success, and I was under great public pressure to produce a sequel. I could think of nothing that produced even the slightest enthusiasm on my part. I stood as if glued to the street when it occurred to me that the stalls of old books and prints staring at me might contain some hitherto unknown jewel that would serve me. And so I began to look through the stalls. In an instant, my eyes fell on something called *Scènes de la vie de bohème*, a book that took as its theme the life of poets and artists in Montmartre. I took it home with me and read it through. Divided into scenes as it was, it looked like an ideal text out of which a series of operatic tableaux could be easily constructed. I was so happy with my find that the melodies for the new opera began running through my head. I rushed to the house of my librettist and told him of my good luck. Perusing the book, he thought it most suitable, and suggested that we make an immediate announcement of our intention to write an opera entitled *La Bohème*. I then wrote immediately to the author Murger's publisher but received no reply. They appeared to have closed. And I had no way of finding Murger."

"Perhaps I may inject my account here," said Puccini. "I was in Paris when Ruggiero was here in Rome. Almost to the day on which he found the book here in Italy I found it in Paris along the Seine. I then tried to find Murger, but it was difficult to trace him, and I did not succeed. The book had been written almost fifty years before, and his fate was unknown. I sent a letter to his publisher but I too received no reply. I assumed that he was dead. Upon my return to Italy, I showed the book to Giacosa and Illica, my two chief librettists, and they both thought it would be an excellent vehicle for a new opera. Unaware of Ruggiero's announcement—I was at my home in Lucca—we announced our intention to write an opera based on Murger's text. It was then that the argument began. When I heard through a journalist friend that Ruggiero intended to use the same text, I replied good-naturedly, 'Good, now there will be two.' I meant nothing mean or critical, but always ready to report a quarrel, the press twisted my remark and Ruggiero responded strongly."

"Word of Giacomo's intention," said Leoncavallo, "and what was twisted by the press into a highly provocative remark, turned our plans into a public argument. In the end, Giacomo and I, who had always been on the best of terms, met secretly at the home of a friend and tried to resolve the argument privately. We agreed that the first thing that should be done would be to maintain a salutary silence for a time, and then to see if Murger were still alive, and perhaps write an opera together. Could we do it? In any case, we agreed that neither of us would begin our work on *La Bohème* until all problems, both legal and ethical, had suitable solutions and our mutual agreement."

"It was at this very moment, my dear Signor Holmes," said Puccini, "that something extraordinary began to happen that has brought us to you. I was here in Rome at the Albergo Panteone, about to leave for Lucca, when Leoncavallo came to see me at the hotel. He was in a considerable state of excitement and accused me of abusing our friendship and of abrogating our agreement. Why? Because he had just received a package by courier containing the initial pages of a manuscript of *La Bohème*, purporting to be written by me. I looked at the manuscript and could scarcely believe what was in front of me: in what seemed to be my own hand were the first ten pages of *La Bohème* almost exactly as I might have written it. I of course had written nothing.

"Just at that moment," continued Puccini, "a courier arrived at the hotel and presented me with a package in which there was a manuscript labeled *La Bohème da Ruggiero Leoncavallo*. I handed it to Ruggiero and he gasped. His handwriting, his melodies, his plot—all was there in front of us. And then, as if to mock us, a note addressed to both of us was delivered by the hotel maid: dated a week ago, it said simply: *Davvero, ce ne saranno due . . . o tre . . . o quattro!*"

"Indeed, there will be two or three or four *La Bohèmes*, if I interpret the note accurately," said Holmes. "And presumably you have continued to receive, each of you, further portions of the other's opera?'

"Yes, we are almost halfway through each version. All of our attempts to find the strange genius who began this have led to nought. He obviously has managed to obtain access to our ateliers, how and through whom we have no idea. And why has he chosen to do this? What is the motive?"

"But most importantly, *cari signori*," I interjected, "it is not that this scoundrel gained access to your ateliers. Indeed, neither of you has begun to write, so that if your agreement holds, there is nothing in your ateliers for him to use. The physical accoutrements, the paper and ink and other things, are easily available, but the musical insights—they are another matter. If he is working on his own, then we must admit that we are dealing with an incredible musical genius, one who can read your future musical thoughts from what you have already published."

"Brilliantly put, Watson. I must say that I am impressed by your logic. Because of its great achievements in painting and sculpture, Italy is no stranger to artistic forgery. It is not surprising therefore that fraud has finally moved to the field of music," said Holmes.

"We come to you, Signor Holmes, not only because of your international reputation, but also on the recommendation of two people who know you well: Grimaldi, of the Roman police, and Lombroso, who speaks in the most glowing terms of your abilities. Signor Holmes, you must find Murger, to see if he agrees to having his book transformed into opera. If he does not agree, or is dead, then we will abandon our projects. And who is writing these versions of *La Bohème*. And why?"

"I accept, dear *amici*, with pleasure. Please leave the two *Bohèmes* with me and I shall examine them closely for any clews they might provide about the identity of the author. In the meantime, keep strangers away from your notes and manuscripts. Remember that a good musician can easily mimic the work of another, but this appears to go far beyond mere mimicry. As soon as I have some results, I shall notify you."

"Many thanks, and *arrivederla*, Signor Holmes."

"Well, Watson, we have our work cut out for us. Where is Murger?"

"He is drinking his morning tea," said I.

Holmes followed me into the sitting room. There sat Henri Murger, much refreshed and in rather good spirits, considering his ordeal. He smiled and thanked us profusely for our help the night before.

"*Messieurs, merci de nouveau.* I assume you are Mr. Holmes and you Dr. Watson."

Holmes nodded and assured our guest that we were happy to have saved him from the cold and that he should feel free to stay with us as long as he was in Rome. "Monsieur Murger, right now I need some information from you."

"Tell me and I shall answer as best I can."

"M. Murger, what I have to ask concerns your novel *Scènes de la vie de bohème*, a book that you published many years ago, in 1848. Is that correct?"

"Yes, Monsieur. The book was a failure and I forgot about it until recently when two Italian composers of opera, Leoncavallo and Puccini, wrote me asking if I would acquiesce in their writing an opera based on my work. The letters were mi Unfortunately, someone else preceded them and offered me a large sum for the rights, which I have accepted."

"And who is that, may I ask?"

"Monsieur Holmes, that is the difficult part. I do not know who he is, or where he is, except that he lives here in Rome, but not permanently. His home is in Foggia, nearer to Naples. He asked me to meet him tomorrow outside the Rome Opera house. And so, I shall."

"Good, Monsieur Murger. One other question. Who indeed was the young woman who helped you?"

"*De nouveau*, I cannot say exactly. Yesterday, I left my hotel early hoping that I would find you—I have your address from Louis Frobin of the *Sûreté de Paris*—but the snow was so high that I barely managed to reach your quarters. I saw the young woman you mention selling paper flowers in the snow. It was the first time that I had seen her. When I fell in the snow she tried to lift me. I must have fainted. I still heard her say that she knew was my daughter, but my only daughter lives in Paris and so the young woman is at best confused."

"And why were you searching for me, Monsieur Murger?"

"I am an old man, Monsieur Holmes, with many needs. I learned that you were in Rome and I thought that you could accompany me to the meeting with the composers of *La Bohème*. But perhaps the case does not amuse you, Monsieur Holmes?"

"*Au contraire*, Monsieur Murger, it does amuse me and I have already spoken to the two composers. Please continue to rest here. Watson and I have some work to do." Murger nodded, closed his eyes, and was soon overtaken by the fatigue induced by the events of the previous night.

Holmes paced back and forth, almost silently, as he considered his next move. "The young woman, Watson, she is part of this story, though I am not sure as yet how she fits. Right now, she is merely part of the locale. Come, the sun is shining. Let us inform our *Soliti Ignoti* of what has transpired and enlist their aid in finding the woman. Our own Gabriele is said to be enamoured of her. Last night, she arrived at the Café Momus dressed in the most expensive attire and accompanied by a rich merchant from the north, possibly England or Germany. *Era in carrozza vestita come una regina.*"

We found our archangels in their den, a small flat on Via Muzio Clementi. We were in luck. They told us that they knew the young woman and that she had been surviving in the cellar of the Café Momus. Gabriele, in fact, said that he had just seen her as she ventured forth with her paper flowers that morning. She was starved and he gave her some coins with which she bought some bread. She thanked him and said that a great patron of hers had arrived in Italy and was going to take care of her as soon as he arrived in Rome. Then she would repay him. Holmes asked that Gabriele take us to the young woman, and we followed him as he walked quickly toward the Café Momus.

The café was closed, and Gabriele took us to a narrow alley that went to the back. There we saw a broken window through which Gabriele called to the young woman. There was no answer. "She is not here," said Gabriel.

"I must enter," said Holmes.

"Very well," said Gabriele, "we shall stand guard as you break the law."

Holmes climbed through the window. I watched as he searched the room. He later told me that the articles stored there were the pathetic possessions of someone close to abject poverty: a few tattered shawls, a bonnet, a soft muff, some worn-out shoes, and a thin blanket. There were no clothes that fit the description of those of the night before. As to the rest, there was no bed, only a dirt floor. There was only one piece of furniture, an old chair on top of which was a note, recently written, that read in its entirety:

> *Amore, arrivo oggi a Roma. Sono solo, senza P. Incontriamoci al più presto possibile. Sarò all'incrocio di Via Margutta e Via Babuino verso le dodici domani. R.*

"The note is dated yesterday, Watson, and it is now eleven thirty. If we hurry, we shall watch as our young lady meets her *padrone*."

We walked quickly down Via Condotti to Piazza di Spagna. The sun was hot and the snow was transformed into sparkling-clear rivulets that met at the central fountain. The Roman air was as clear as it had ever been. We sat at the Café Margutta, each of us with a large *granità di mandorle* in front of us.

"No one so far," said Holmes as he glanced down Via Margutta.

"Here she comes, Holmes, dressed in her rags. And there from Via Babuino, her *padrone*, no doubt."

He was a tall, thin gentleman, dressed in a long, light blue coat with velvet trim. His hair was blond, and he wore a long moustache and a goatee which gave his face the form of an almost perfect triangle. A look of recognition passed over Holmes's face, but he said nothing.

The couple embraced after running towards each other. The man wrapped her in a shawl and hailed a cab. Holmes and I followed them briefly at a safe distance. Their driver went down the Corso, through Piazza Venezia, to the gate of the Villa Orsini, where they left their cab and continued on foot into the villa.

"We won't follow them for now," said Holmes. "Come, Watson. The musical aspects of the case now thrust themselves on us. Let us return to Monsieur Murger and our quarters."

Murger was still asleep on the couch when we arrived. Holmes moved quietly to his bookshelves where he kept his collection of musical scores.

"You will see now, Watson, the value of my collection of opera scores, at least for a first assault on the problem of the two *Bohèmes*." I helped him carry the most recently acquired scores from the bottom of an old almirah where he kept them in a large pile.

"Here we have, Watson, all of the major operas of the last decade or so, in both orchestral and piano scores. And here are the two delivered to Puccini and Leoncavallo. We remove as well their own operas from the pile, leaving us with the composers whose work is well known to the public and among whom we may find the culprit. The composers are Boito, Catalani, Cilea, Mascagni, Zandonai, and Giordano. We have twenty scores here, all of which I intend to read through rapidly to find the author of the two fraudulent ones."

"Holmes, I flatter myself even if I say that I am musically illiterate, but I have no idea what you are looking for. What indeed *are* you looking for? These are only so many names, none of which is known outside Italy," said I, with the full intention of annoying him.

"Very simple, my dear fellow. You are letting your concern over your admittedly tin ear detract from your reason, and reason always wins in the end. In the realm of art and music, it is reason that rules, and the rules that operate are those of observation and deduction, as they do everywhere Let us see if I can cast some light on the present problem. You agree, initially at least, that the culprit—what shall we call him, this ingenious rogue who can mimic, forge even, the art of Italy's greatest composers? Let us call him Cagliostro, after the great charlatan—must be a composer in his own right, one of great talent at least, schooled in all the musical disciplines: harmony, counterpoint, and orchestration. In this case, he must also have the ability to compose his own libretti, or he must have one who is complicit in his misdeeds, shall we say."

I decided to flaunt my knowledge, meager as it was, and use some of the oddments about music that I had collected by questioning him. "But only one composer has written his own libretti and that was the German Richard Wagner."

"Indeed, old boy, but you noticed quickly that I have omitted all composers who are not Italian."

"And why is that? Surely they would be competent."

"Competent is an excellent term to describe what might be the work of someone foreign to Italy who attempted to forge an Italian opera. The attempt would fail miserably. The scaffolding would be there but not the individual creative impulse. It would be the equivalent of a Rembrandt trying to be a Michelangelo. It would be immediately discovered. Despite their abilities, composers such as Massenet, Bizet, Charpentier, even Wagner, could not pull it off. Their individual 'sound' would give any one of them away. Also, there would be little motive, whereas among the Italians one could predict without exaggeration a certain rivalry, shall we say?"

"But Holmes, what about the similarity of some of Dvořák's *Rusalka* to Puccini's *La Rondine*? Isn't there an aria—Doretta's, I believe—that comes close to being a copy by Puccini of Dvořák's melody?"

"You astonish me, old boy, you have been listening and learning. You raise a valid point, however. The answer is simple: It is the use of the piano as an orchestral instrument that marks this similarity, nothing more."

Holmes was silent for a moment, and I thought that he might wish to be alone when he said, "I thank you, old fellow, for your questions. Please note once more that I have excluded Verdi from the list, though musically he is as qualified as the others. But he is old and unconcerned with other people's work. Leave me now, for I have precious little time to consider this problem before we go to meet its creator."

Holmes was soon lost in his scrutiny of the scores piled in front of him. Every so often he would stand up from his work and pace through our sitting room, but he said nothing. It was only after about five hours of intense effort that he said, "I am getting close, Watson, and I am pretty sure that I have identified the culprit. And I know his motive. Let me work a little longer and I will test my solution on you."

I watched him as he took a last few notes. "Come, Watson, and listen to my solution to this musical puzzle. My method has been simplicity itself: to find in the *Bohème* forgeries and in the forger's own published opera music, as well as in the compositions of the other leading composers, similar musical usages of such rare occurrence that the forger himself unwittingly might have allowed them to appear in the stolen music. In some instances he may have baited his hook consciously in order to tease and mislead, thereby throwing the investigator off the track. Now, as I expected, that no such rarities occur in the works of Catalani, Cilea, Mascagni, or Zandonai is no surprise, since the caliber of their work is far below that of Puccini and Leoncavallo. I must say that I am surprised that Mascagni is out on the first round. While his music is pleasant, it shows no élan, and beyond *Cavalleri*a there is only *Iris*, of which there is little to be said."

"Who then are left? I must say that I can barely keep their names straight."

"Don't bother, Watson. Follow my reasoning, not the names of the composers. What I want, dear fellow, is your critique of the argument. Shall I go on?"

"Please do, Holmes."

"If I am correct, the remaining composers are still under consideration: Boito, Ponchielli, and Giordano. In my judgement, these three are the equal of Puccini and Leoncavallo. Their output is small, but the quality is high. In the coming years, the works of the first group will disappear from the stage, their main arias being the only portion to be widely remembered. Boito, Ponchielli, and Giordano, however, will be performed increasingly."

"I say, Holmes, I am still troubled by the absence of the greatest of all operatic composers, to wit, Giuseppe Verdi. Surely, he deserves a place in your reasoning."

"Thank you, dear Watson. No doubt, he deserves a place on historical grounds, but the old man is now an eighty-year-old Orpheus hard at work on *Falstaff*, his greatest masterpiece. His transition to a late style has evoked much talk, particularly his use of orchestral textures reminiscent of the *verismo* school. More to the point, he has never had any interest in the rivalries of composers. Quite the contrary not even Wagner troubled him in the least."

I detected a pinch of pomposity in Holmes's tone and said no more. "Sorry, old boy," he said. "I am sure my enthusiasm is a bit difficult to take, but hear me out."

"I am listening with the greatest interest."

"Good. We may dispose of Boito immediately. He is now working as a librettist for Verdi. He has no time for the machinations of other composers. That leaves two finalists: Ponchielli and Giordano. Despite the greatness of some of his music, Amilcare Ponchielli is uneven as a composer, and his chief work, *La Gioconda*, is marred by deep dramatic faults, the notorious "Dance of the Hours" being the most reprehensible. That leaves Umberto Giordano, a native of the city of Foggia and perhaps Italy's greatest operatic composer of the present generation. A brilliant melodist, orchestrator, and dramatist, his opera *Andrea Chenier* is the high point of all the scores I have examined."

"I must say, Holmes, that my ignorance is profound in his respect: I have never heard his name before."

"You will hear it more and more. Lombroso knows him well and so it should be easy to find him. I think there is someone at the door. Probably a courier with a message from Lombroso with Giordano's address."

I took the message from the courier and handed it to Holmes.

> Via Orlando di Lasso 45, interno 12. È a casa proprio addesso. Lombroso

"Come, Watson, let us go and meet Umberto Giordano. Let us see if my reasoning proves correct."

I perused a map of Rome that Holmes had tacked to the back of our front door. "It is nearby," I said, "just off Via Palestrina. It is no more than a ten-minute walk."

The walk was indeed a short one, for Via Orlando di Lasso crossed Via Palestrina only two streets north of our residence. Interno 12 was on the first floor. The door opened as soon as Holmes rang the bell.

"Signor Giordano?" asked Holmes.

"*Son' io*," replied Giordano with a grin.

"*Ma io non son la mamma morta*," replied Holmes with a broad smile.

"Certamente no. Infatti, io aspettavo il famoso nemico del male umano, il Signor Sherlock Holmes. Credo, se non mi sbaglio, sia

lui chi sta in fronte a me. E Lei, dovrebbe essere il famoso dottore Watson. Dunque avanti, signori, entrate senza lasciar indietro la speranza."

I beg the reader's indulgence here, for he can quickly see from the above that the converstion between Giordano and Holmes went far over my head with its witticisms, its references to Dante and other poets, and its plays on words. I sat silently with a bemused expression on my face, waiting for Holmes to come to the point. It was Giordano who first spoke with reference to the reason for our visit.

"I calculated that you would arrive precisely when you did. Shall we speak now in all candor, Mr. Holmes, with reference to the two *Bohèmes*?"

"Indeed we must, and as quickly as possible."

"I assume you compared the works of Puccini and Leoncavallo to mine?"

"Indeed, I did. And I found what I was looking for: in Act III of *Andrea Chenier*, just before the aria "Nemico della Patria," there are two modulations to the key of A minor preceded by two mournful notes played by the bassoon that only Puccini and Leoncavallo would be capable writing aside from you. And furthermore, dear Giordano, in your version of Puccini's *La Bohème*, the same rare chord appears. Perhaps we should give it a name—say, the Chenier inversion. And it has led me directly to you."

"Indeed," said Giordano with a broad smile. "Please tell my friends, Leoncavallo and Puccini, that I have made my point. They may have Murger's *La Bohème*, but impress upon them that I have been angered by *Pagliacci and Tosca*, both of which have large elements of my work embedded in them."

"I assume, then," said Holmes, "that you are the gentleman who was to meet Murger."

"I am, and I told Murger that I was no longer interested in *La Bohème*. My next opera will be *Fedora*."

"Ah," said Holmes, "the novel of Sardou."

"Indeed," said Giordano, "I hope you will come to the opening."

"*Ma certo*," said Holmes, and we left.

"Well," said I as we walked toward Piazza Venezia, "what now? You have made peace in the world of Italian opera, an opera buffa in itself. A remarkable achievement."

"Thank you, dear fellow."

Holmes maintained his silence as we walked home. As we approached Piazza Venezia, he stopped suddenly and sat down.

"Have you a pen on you, Watson?"

I pulled out my notebook and pen and gave them to him. He scribbled out a short note, and we resumed our walk home. As we approached the gate of the Villa Orsini, Holmes stopped and handed the note to the guard.

"Watson, it is high time to think about a glass of frascati and a light lunch."

"Indeed," said I.

We took a cab to Campo dei Fior, where we lunched sumptuously. We arrived at our quarters at three. Both of us were overcome by the meal. Holmes relaxed with a cigar and I rolled myself a cigarette. I was about to doze when there was a knock at the door and Holmes rushed to open it. It was a courier with a note in answer to his delivered to the Villa Orsini.

"Watson," said Holmes, "forgive me, but I neglected to tell you that we shall have guests tonight. My note delivered to the guard at the Villa Orsini has received a prompt and positive response. It is Friday, is it not? This note from Raffaele says that he would bring Lucia and her *padrone* here for a light supper. So enamoured is the *padrone* of our flower girl that he is ready to cast her in a minor role in his new music drama. This will at least hide her for a time from his wife, who I gather is terribly jealous."

Holmes turned towards me, a wide grin over his face.

"Who is this mysterious *padrone*? Do you know?" I asked.

"Yes, I am convinced that he is a musical figure of the greatest accomplishment. He is also a well-known aficionado of the card game scat. I gather that he plays with his friends every Friday. By the bye, Watson, what will you entitle this story when you finally write it out? 'The Case of the Two *Bohèmes*'?"

"No, Holmes, I shall call it "The Man in the Blue Coat." He can only be Richard Strauss in this instance."

"Good, Watson. He barely appears in the story, remains without a name, yet he is essential to the plot and insures something rare in the world of opera: a happy ending."

"Very good," said I.

There was a second loud knock at the door. I opened it this time to find our landlady standing there in the black attire of a butler. Held high overhead was a tray bearing a steaming teapot and a fresh loaf of bread. In her left hand was a white envelope, which I was sure contained the rent bill.

"*Monsieur est servi,*" said la Signora.

"*Capriccio,*" said I.

"Good," said Holmes. "My compliments, dear Watson. You have learned much on our voyage in Italy."

Our landlady left our tea near the window and, with a flourish, disappeared through the door.

THE CASE OF THE VERMILION FACE

also known as The Sins of Cardinal Corelli

It was, if I remember correctly, the seventh of April, 1903, a grey, wet London morning, on which I heard Holmes moving about quietly in our sitting room. When I entered, I found him halfway through breakfast. He was seated in his favourite armchair, staring into the rising flames of the fire he had just prepared. Over his lap he had placed a heavy Afghan blanket, on top of which sat a tray with our teapot and bread and butter.

"Good morning, dear Watson," he said jovially. "I trust that you slept well. The tea is still drinkable. I shall pour it for you. And here, the paper is quite dull. I am already finished with it. There is only the short notice once again of Cardinal Corelli's disappearance, more official and complete this time, however."

I caught a note of deprecation in his voice as he uttered the last sentence, as if he were trying to make light of his interest in the case of the Italian cardinal. I said nothing as he brought my tea and then went to his desk and began to rifle through his papers. I read the following account in the morning *Times*:

> In a brief notice this morning, *L'Osservatore Romano*, the official organ of the Church of Rome, officially announced the sudden disappearance of Archangelo Cardinal Corelli, Secretary of State of the Church, and, after the Pope himself, the most powerful prelate in the Roman hierarchy. The Cardinal disappeared two days ago on Good Friday and has not been seen or heard from since. The Osservatore goes on to say that, although it cannot verify his present whereabouts, it is most probable that the Cardinal is safe and has taken time from his busy schedule to enter a retreat. This has been his wont, the Roman paper noted, since his accession to the Cardinalate, and should be no cause for alarm.
>
> Despite the *Osservatore*'s attempt to calm public fears, the concern for the Cardinal's whereabouts is rendered even more acute by the Pope's growing frailty and ill health. It is generally conceded that the present pope, Leo XIII, is nearing the end of his reign and that, at least until his disappearance, Corelli was favored to succeed him. Still relatively young—barely fifty, according to Church officials—the Cardinal is distinguished by the

> power of his intellect and his deep piety. It is he who is said to have penned the encyclicals *De Rerum Novarum* and *Ejus Mentor*, and to have shepherded through the Church the doctrine of the Immaculate Conception, promulgated by Leo in 1878.

I put the paper down. Holmes turned and said, "Well, what do you think, Watson, a bit of an embarrassment, eh?"

"Most interesting, Holmes. Either they know more than they are willing to reveal, or they are honestly baffled as to his whereabouts. Indeed, the case has the elements of a major scandal. Who knows? A chance meeting at a village church with a beautiful parishioner, and a prince of the church succumbs. Then he is done in by a vengeful husband or lover," said I.

"Not bad, Watson, though your proposal presents a rather banal solution," said he with a smile.

"Banality is a powerful force in our lives," said I with mock seriousness. "Perhaps I should phrase it differently, my dear Holmes. Italy, shall we say, often presents us with the stereotype of melodrama. *Cavalleria* and *Pagliacci* are by no means abstractions."

"You have spent too many nights at Covent Garden, dear Watson. We should not give much credence to these peasant tales, though they have a certain psychological reality to them. Italy abounds in crimes of passion, but in this it differs little from other countries. One can cite innumerable cases here in London. That of John Greenacre comes to mind immediately. And it is true that the strictures on those devoted to the ascetic life are far more onerous than those that apply to ordinary mortals. But it is rash to speculate at this early juncture. If the crisis continues and the mystery of the Cardinal's disappearance is not solved one way or another, then the matter may fall into the hands of the Roman police. There are some good minds there: Manzoni is one. He played a major role in the case of Lusoni's daughter. But the best is Grimaldi—"

Holmes stopped talking in the middle of his sentence, his eye caught by something on his desk, and he said no more. It was only after several days passed that the matter intruded upon us once again. We were seated in the morning at our desks when there was a sudden but familiar knock at the door, and Mrs. Hudson announced the arrival of a gentleman from Rome, one Padre Antonio Gasparri.

The person who appeared before us was a young priest of the Church, a thin, almost frail man, who I should judge not to have passed his thirtieth birthday. He was dressed entirely in black, which made his pallor even more dramatic. He had a small, sharp beak of a nose upon which his spectacles were precariously suspended. Despite their thickness, they did not hide his most distinguishing feature, his eyes, dark orbs that radiated an intense light once he began to speak.

"You are Mr. Holmes?" he enquired, addressing my friend in English.

"I am, indeed, and this is my trusted colleague, Dr. Watson. You may speak before him as you would before me. I assume that you come on the grave matter that now concerns the Church."

"I do," said the priest. "I assume you are familiar with the public accounts. I wish to inform you that I come directly from the Pope and with his full authority. Our Holy Father knows that he does not have long to live, and that he has little time remaining to him on this earth. Corelli and he are as one person, and the Cardinal's disappearance has only made the Pope's last days even more difficult. I have come on the Pontiff's behalf to ask your aid in solving the mystery of what has befallen Cardinal Corelli."

He handed Holmes a sealed note. "Mr. Holmes, this is a letter directly from the Holy Father to you asking for your assistance in the matter." Holmes read it quickly.

"But what of Manzoni and Grimaldi? Surely, they would be of the greatest help."

"For reasons of state, Mr. Holmes, we would prefer that the Italian police stay out of the matter. Since there is no final evidence as yet that the Cardinal has left the *Città Vaticana* or that a crime has been committed on Italian soil, there is no reason for any intervention by the Italian police. And of course we wish to have a solution that is privately presented to us before it is made public."

"You realize that the solution may have rather unpalatable aspects to it, difficult for the Church, and that I cannot but present the whole truth?"

"The Church has no problem with the truth, Mr. Holmes. The rumours now floating through Italy are probably worse than anything that has happened in actuality. What the Church and Our Holy Father wish for is a thorough and dispassionate investigation. And, if there is no crime, your promise of secrecy."

"I accede to your wishes, provided that any version of what has transpired is submitted to me for comment before it is made public."

"I agree," said the priest. "Then you will help us?"

"Most assuredly. The general circumstances are most interesting, a case with few precedents. I can recall only the case of the Bishop of Liverpool over a century ago, and of course the infamous case of the Reverend Phineas Roberts of Massachusetts. Unfortunately, a solution similar to theirs would bring little benefit to the Church. The Bishop turned out to be a philanderer and Phineas Roberts a notorious poisoner of orphans."

There was silence for a few moments. The priest remained calm, but his expression betrayed his fear at what Holmes might uncover.

"I have one last request," said Holmes, "and that is that I have full access to all persons associated closely with the Cardinal, including the Pope himself if necessary, and to the Cardinal's quarters and his place of work."

"I can agree to all of your stipulations, Mr. Holmes," said the priest. "With regard to the Pope, there are certain restrictions. Before my departure, our Holy Father expressed clearly his fervent wish to meet with you and to give you every aid in your investigation. He is, however, increasingly weak and no one knows how long he will live. Here his doctors will have a say in the matter."

"I see no difficulty," Holmes responded. "I should like to visit the Pope immediately upon my arrival. But tell me yourself what you can of the Cardinal and anything that might enlighten us as to his fate."

"I myself," said the priest, "have known him for only three years. He is a man of the greatest intellect and piety who has seen his entire life as service to the Church. A person of regular habits, he sleeps little, however, always retiring at ten, and rising at three or four in the morning to work. He always took simple meals prepared by his housemaid, Suor Angelica, and ventured forth from the Vatican only to say Mass at the cathedral of *San Paolo Fuori le Mura*, his own parish."

"What of his family?"

"Little if anything at all is known with certainty, for his early years were spent in a foundling home in Naples. Because of his intelligence, he was taken by the head of the home and placed with a wealthy friend, who gave the boy every advantage. At some early point in his life, the Pope met him and was so impressed that he brought the boy to live at the Vatican. It became clear as he grew that he had a vocation, and he entered the monastery in Monte Cassino. There, before he was twenty, he became known for his theological and philosophical lectures and disputations. Among the Dominicans, he was regarded as another St. Thomas. He came to the attention of the Archbishop of Naples, who brought him back to the city. Shortly thereafter, he was called to Rome as secretary to the Pope, where his rise in the Church was rapid. Four years ago, he was appointed secretary of state, a post he kept until his disappearance."

"A most interesting account, but there is little unusual except for his meteoric rise, shall we say. Surely, there must be more?"

"Only one personal indulgence, which I noticed. Perhaps once every fortnight, he would don the attire of a common priest and after dark leave the Vatican and venture into the life of the common people. In this guise, he was known as Padre Giovanni, for he never identified himself to those he met, though he made no elaborate attempt to hide it. He was by no means always alone when he did this. On several occasions, he invited me to go along."

"And what, pray tell, did you do on these occasions?"

"We walked through the old parts of the city, talking of sin and morality, crossing into Trastevere and then walking back along the Tiber. At about eight, we would part company and he would go alone to a small *osteria* that he enjoyed and have a simple meal and a glass of wine. This was as close to self indulgence that the Cardinal ever came. In this osteria he said that he joked with the proprietor and his wife, and many times they would prepare special foods for him. He loved the *cucina contadina* that he had as a child. And of course, his identity was unknown to the proprietor and his wife."

"And no one survives from his family?"

"No one. He has Suor Angelica and myself, that is all. We are his family," said the priest softly.

"My dear Padre, I shall be most happy to help in any way I can. I shall leave for Rome the day after tomorrow. And I should like Dr. Watson to accompany me."

"I shall cable Rome of your acquiescence. In anticipation of your acceptance, we have arranged lodging for you not far from the Vatican. My deepest thanks to you, and the prayers of the Holy Father for your mission."

The priest bowed and Holmes showed him to the door.

"Well, Watson, what do you make of it?" Holmes asked when the priest had departed.

"A most interesting case, dear Holmes. I shall accompany you with the greatest pleasure. Luckily, Redfern will cover my practise."

"Good, Watson, then let us ready ourselves for the trip. I shall wire Inspector Grimaldi of the Roman police of our assignment and arrival. I trust he will meet us and let us know what he can."

Two days later, we were joyfully on our way to Rome. It was my first trip to Italy since those melancholic and unhappy days when I thought Holmes to be dead. This time we were together as we had been so often in the past.

"The note from Gasparri indicates that we will be staying in a *pensione* near the Spanish Steps. On Via Gregoriana, also near the Café Greco, where we may take our meals. We shall be staying in one of the most beautiful parts of the city, courtesy of the Pope himself, I gather. The Curia seems to be less sanguine about our visit."

We arrived on schedule at the train station and took a cab to Via Gregoriana. At the very end, just above the Spanish Steps, lay our *pensione*. Our rooms were large, and the sun poured through the windows. I felt immediate relief from the effects of a long journey.

"Not bad, Holmes," I said as I looked out from our new quarters.

"A good change from London, Watson. Now rest for a few moments while I record some notes, and we shall be off to the café, a favorite of old Goethe."

It was but a five-minute walk to the café, down the steps to the piazza and then into Via Condotti. Holmes chose a table far in the back, well away from the eyes and ears of the small crowd that began to enter the café.

"Since I know your taste, Watson, let me order for both of us."

"Thank you, Holmes. My Italian is most rusty, almost gone. And I find the few words of Pushto that remain in my head, the relics of my days in Afghanistan, curiously rising to my lips, stopping words of any other language from issuing."

Holmes smiled. "A rather common experience, Watson. Languages struggle for supremacy in the brain. In yours, where English reigns unopposed, the remnants of a language studied twenty years ago in Candahar vie with the more recently acquired Italian. No matter, I trust that your Italian will recover and that your French will come back. The latter is most useful here, particularly with church officials and the Roman police."

Holmes poured the white wine that he had ordered into my glass and then filled his own."You will remember that the Cardinal disappeared on Good Friday. Next week is Whitsunday, which will mark fifty days since he is gone."

"A long time . . ."

"Indeed," said Holmes, "and I fear that it may be impossible to trace him. Still, one hopes. Ah, here comes Grimaldi."

Grimaldi was not a totally unknown figure to me. He had kindly provided help during the period in which Holmes was supposedly gone from this world. He was a slender but powerful man, of average height, who wore the clothes of an Italian gentleman, including the fedora, which covered his almost completely bald head.

"*Benvenuti a Roma*," he said jovially as he sat down with us.

Holmes poured him a glass of wine and immediately began his questioning.

"What have you learned, *ispettore*, even though the problem is beyond your authority?"

"It falls without our authority of course, but we must be prepared. So as far as we can, we have begun our own study of the case."

Sipping his wine, Grimaldi informed us of what he had learned. When the Cardinal did not appear on Good Friday, he said, the housemaid Suor Angelica notified her superiors, who informed the Pope and the Curia. An inquiry was begun, though his rooms were not entered for several days in honour of the long-standing church practise that a cardinal's private domain remain untouched until his death. On the fourth day of his disappearance, his room was unlocked and only Suor Angelica was allowed to enter. She returned saying that the Cardinal was not there, dead or alive. The room was sealed and has remained closed since. After many days, when the Cardinal had neither appeared nor communicated with anyone, the Roman Curia issued the brief statement that we had read in the London papers. The Curia, however, was far more concerned than the brief announcement would indicate. As the youngest and most brilliant of the Italian Cardinalate, Corelli was an ardent spokesman for reform in the Church. This was well known. Unfortunately, he had been frustrated in his efforts by the rest of the Curia—all in their late seventies—and an indecisive and failing pontiff. Because of the disagreements, there had been a concerted effort by the Curia to remove him from his powerful position, but his favored position with the Pope, whom he had known since his youth, could not be broken, and he remained at his post, frustrated but dogged in his attempts to outwit the aged hierarchy that opposed him.

"The Curia, under their leader Cardinal Spontini," Grimaldi continued, "are apparently elated at their stroke of good luck and would be most happy if Corelli were never to return. Spontini made the suggestion that Corelli be removed from his position as Secretary of State until his fate had been determined. Again the Pope refused. It was then that he notified the papal nuncio in London that the services of Sherlock Holmes should be enlisted and ordered Gasparri to England to present the case. In this way, the Pope thwarted any investigation by the Curia itself or the involvement of the Roman police. Since Italian unification in 1872, the Pope has closed himself up in the Vatican and has refused to have anything to do with the Italian government.

"So much for the Curia for now," said Grimaldi, "though I must say they bear watching. As to those who know the Cardinal best, I have spoken to his housemaid. She had little to contribute. She is from the south of Italy, from Cilento, and has worked in the Church since she was a child and for Corelli since he became a cardinal. She corroborated the notion of a man who sought to know the people. On those occasions when he visited places in town, he would return by ten, work at his desk until midnight, and sleep until six, when she brought him his simple breakfast. On the night before his disappearance, she said that he had gone out at seven and that she had turned down his bed at nine thirty. The following morning she knocked on his door but there was no answer. She waited, and then, when no response was forthcoming, she opened the door to find the room empty and the bed not slept in. She notified her superiors, who went directly to the Pope. His room was sealed and she has sat at his door waiting for his return. *Ma, amici*, I am going on and on and you have a meeting with *Il Papa* himself."

Grimaldi went ahead of us to hail a cab and we were soon on our way. It was not long before we were rushing through the lanes in front of St. Peter's. Alert to our impending arrival, the Swiss Guard at the side entrance led us through the grand halls to the inner quarters of the Vatican, and we were ushered into a small audience chamber.

The Pope sat near a window through which sunlight flooded the room. He was dressed in the plain clothes of a priest. Pale and unsteady on his feet, he nevertheless motioned calmly with his hand for us to sit in the chairs in front of him. He spoke in French in a soft but clear voice. He dispensed with all ecclesiastical ceremony.

"I begin by welcoming you to Rome," he said. "You will have our full support in your investigation. You must find Cardinal Corelli at once or learn what has happened to him. He paused for a moment and then said sadly, "He is like a son to me. *Messieurs, je vous implore . . .*"

"Tell us, Your Holiness, what you can of the cardinal."

"I met him when he was a small boy of nine. His family had been killed years before in an earthquake in Casamicciola on the island of Ischia. The boy was found wandering alone in the ruins in a state of confusion and amnesia. He was brought to an orphanage, where he recovered his strength, but not his earliest memories. He did not speak until he was seven. As he grew, he became known for the excellence of his studies. I saw him first at the orphanage. Recognizing the light of Divine Inspiration in him, I brought him here to be raised. Then I sent him to Monte Cassino for study. Upon his return, he became my assistant. Four years ago I made him cardinal, the youngest in the Church, and he became Secretary of State. Until his disappearance, I assumed that he would follow me as Pope. But who is to say now?"

"Who are his enemies?" asked Holmes coolly.

"Some of the Curia dislike him, but 'enemies' is a harsh word. The members of the Curia, all worthy men and filled with ambition, found his quick rise in the Church disturbing. I do not think anyone would harm him, though they might try to destroy his reputation, or put him in an embarrassing situation. His conduct has been impeccable. I know his habits: he rises at four every morning to say mass, then breakfasts, and works on Church business until nine, when he goes through the day's agenda with me."

"Who served him and tended to his needs?"

"Suor Angelica, a nun who comes from the same orphanage as he, though she is somewhat older. She is devoted to him and you may question her at length. She is the only one to have visited his quarters at the time of his disappearance."

"Have his rooms been examined by anyone?"

"No," replied the Pope. "As soon as the Cardinal's absence became known to me, I had his quarters closed with my seal. You can be sure that no one has entered except for a visit by Suor Angelica when the Cardinal first disappeared."

"Then I should like to begin with a talk with Suor Angelica and a visit to the Cardinal's rooms."

The Pope rang. A young priest appeared who was told to take us first to Suor Angelica and then to the Cardinal's quarters.

"Report to me as often as you wish," said the Pope, and we left.

We followed the young priest down a long corridor. When we reached its end, the priest asked us to wait. He knocked at a wooden door, and there appeared a nun, of perhaps some fifty years of age, dressed in a white habit. She was introduced to us as Suor Angelica. Despite her age, she was quite youthful, even beautiful in appearance. When she saw us, she grew shy, saying only that she had served the Cardinal since his arrival in Rome, and that she knew nothing of his disappearance. Her eyes teared over as she spoke. Holmes calmed her and asked that she come with us to his room.

When we arrived at the door, the young priest knelt and broke the papal seal. We entered the Cardinal's room. Suor Angelica waited outside, overcome with emotion. A strong breeze blew through an open window through which one could see the great line of statues of the saints that adorns the colonnade of St. Peter's.

At first glance there was nothing unusual or disturbing. In its simplicity the room was in marked contrast to the sumptuous halls of the Vatican. A large almirah containing the Cardinal's priestly habits stood against one wall. A small table served as a writing desk, upon which there lay a missal. Near one corner of the desk rested a rosary and a ring, presumably that of the Cardinalate. A simple cot against the opposite wall served as the Cardinal's bed. Above it was a large crucifix nailed to the wall, so large that it dominated the room and broke its quiet proportions. The face of Christ appeared as if it had been smeared with some kind of vermilion substance that had trickled down, and gave the image an unforgettable blood-drenched appearance. It was the only disquieting article in the room.

"The tranquil room of a man of the Church," I said to him.

"But one in which there are all the signs of a struggle."

I was a bit taken aback by Holmes's remark, since I saw nothing of a struggle. I went towards the window into the fluttering curtains and turned to watch as he stared at the crucifix. Over and over he walked up to it, then stepped back.

"As usual, you see but do not observe. Note, my dear Watson, the crucifix is a recent addition to the room. On the wall behind it one can make out the outline of something else that came before it, a painting, no doubt. Do you see? Here there is no soot from the candles."

He moved the crucifix slightly, revealing a jagged hole in the plaster.

"A nail, now gone, held the picture in place."

With his forefinger he touched the plaster behind the crucifix and what appeared to be long scratches in the plaster below. Talking more to himself than to me, he said, "Note again the rectangle of clean whitewash that is revealed by the picture's absence. And note, too, the clumsiness of the person taking the picture down, causing these striations. Most interesting, Watson. Now if we just follow those lines down and move the bed—hah!"

There, lying next to the bed, its front to the wall, was what appeared to be a small painting. Holmes turned it over. It was a picture of the Virgin Mary, the front of the frame badly scratched in its slide down the wall.

"The picture, Watson, preceded the crucifix on the wall. It is interesting that Suor Angelica said nothing of this."

"But what is the significance, Holmes? Perhaps the Cardinal decided to change—"

"Nonsense, Watson. This was a man who led the most regular of lives. Devoted to Mary, having written the encyclical on the Immaculate Conception, he would not have let her picture remain on the floor behind a bed. No, something else is afoot here."

Holmes sat with the picture of the Virgin, closely scrutinising it. "Spanish in origin, probably late fifteenth century. A label on the back reads Casamicciola, the town where the Cardinal's family were killed in the earthquake. This is, then, whatever else, the only tangible connection we know of to his family."

Holmes took a rule from his pocket and measured the distance from the surface of the bed to the nail holding the crucifix. "The Cardinal is reportedly a tall man. He or someone else hung the picture. But it was removed and the crucifix placed there by a different person."

Holmes then went to the writing desk and examined the rosary.

"It is broken, Watson, in three places. And the ring is badly bent out of shape. Look at the marks on the table, as if someone had pressed it into the surface in great anger. And finally, Watson, look at the crucifix on the rosary."

The crucifix was some four inches in length, of pure silver.

"Note the face, Watson."

"It is bright crimson."

"Yes, indeed, dear Watson, and now let us open the missal to the marked page. We shall surely come upon something of interest." He handed me the missal.

"*Vexilla Regis prodeunt inferni,*" I read. "The banners of the King of Hell go forward."

"Brilliant, Watson, if I say so myself. Your Latin is still serviceable. The lines are from a famous Easter hymn, but I think slightly changed. Remind me, Watson. A copy of *The Inferno* may be useful. Well, dear fellow, we do not know where the Cardinal is, but I venture to predict that beneath the quiet revelations found in this small room, one tranquil on the surface, there is a great struggle, a fight for a man's soul as well as the soul of the Church itself. Let us speak to Suor Angelica before we leave."

The nun entered slowly, fearful at first, but became more calm as Holmes gently questioned her.

"Suor Angelica, when you were here last, was this crucifix on the wall?"

"No," she said simply.

"Then who put it there?"

"I do not know," she replied.

"And the picture?"

"The picture has been on the wall since the Cardinal came to Rome. He has always had it. I know that because I gave it to him."

"And when was that?"

The nun paused, as if to help her recollection.

"I have worked here at the Vatican since the Cardinal came here. But I have known him since our childhood. I was nine years old and he was five when we met. We shared the terrible event of the earthquake at Casamicciola. At the time his family was visiting. I was born there. When the disaster hit, I was standing near them on a high cliff. The cliff crumbled beneath us. His family was buried and the two of us were thrown towards the beach. I was unhurt, but Arco, for that is what we called him, had a bad blow to the head and was bleeding profusely. I baptized him, thinking that he would die, and ran for help. He was brought to an orphanage and saved by the nurse there. None of his family survived. His parents and younger sister disappeared forever. The picture I found near where they were staying. The Virgin has been with him since that time."

"Suor Angelica, when you were last in this room, which way was the picture facing?"

The nun hesitated for a moment and said, "The Virgin was facing the wall. The Cardinal's habit was to turn the picture to the wall on Ash Wednesday and leave it that way until Easter morning. When I asked him why he did that, he said that he did not know."

"Have you told anyone else what you have told us?"

Suor Angelica avoided Holmes's eyes as she groped for words.

"I may have mentioned it in passing to Padre Roberto, Cardinal Spontini's secretary."

"Thank you, Suora, we shall leave now."

Holmes rang, and the young priest returned. Holmes asked that the room be once again sealed and that no one be allowed to enter.

"Most interesting, Watson," he said as we returned to our quarters.

"But Holmes, I must say that all the small things you saw hardly amount to a grand conflict," said I as we entered our rooms.

"As I have said in the past, Watson, you see but you do not observe. The room, despite its tranquil ambience, has all the signs of conflict. The crucifix I take as a warning to the Cardinal, the broken rosary and bent ring may have been his angry reaction to the invasion of his private chambers. But now, to further the investigation, we must look elsewhere."

We sat for a time in almost complete silence. Holmes was deep in thought and paid little heed to my questions. There was a sudden knock at the door. Signora Piperno, our landlady, stood there.

"There is a message for Signor Holmes," she said, "from Inspector Grimaldi."

Holmes took it from her and we read:

Dear Holmes,
The body of a dead priest has been retrieved from the Tiber.
It is that of the Cardinal. Come at once.
Grimaldi

We left without pause, hailed a cab, and went directly to Grimaldi's office in the Palace of Justice. Grimaldi greeted us and then reported on the discovery.

"Last night, towards dark," he said, "a young boy fishing in the river noticed a hat near the river's edge, not far from Castel Sant'Angelo. He tried to retrieve it with his line and only realized when he pulled that his hook was firmly fixed to the head of a corpse. He informed a *carabiniere* standing nearby, who called for help, and the body was brought here. It is badly decomposed, but it is undoubtedly that of the Cardinal. Cardinal Spontini, the acting chief of the Curia, has made a positive identification and has informed the Pope."

"And the cause of death?" asked Holmes.

"Suicide by drowning. A despondent Cardinal killed himself for reasons that are still not certain, but highly probable. In his hand he clutched a note in a woman's hand. The note is illegible, but the woman's name, Maria Teresa, can be read at the bottom. This is, of course, that name of the woman he has been associated with in rumours among the populace."

Grimaldi handed Holmes a folder in which the note had been placed. Holmes examined it carefully. A smile broke on his face.

"May we examine the body?" he asked.

"Of course," said Grimaldi. "Come, the morgue is at the end of the hall."

"There will be no autopsy," he said, "without the Church's permission. We have yet to perform a complete examination, but we shall supply you with a copy once it is performed."

Grimaldi motioned to the attendant. A drawer was pulled out to reveal the body. It was that of a man in his mid-fifties, dressed in the black habit of a common priest. We watched as the attendant stripped the body of its clothes. The slender but well-muscled body of a man in the prime of life was revealed. There were no wounds on the body.

Holmes made his own examination, carefully observing the head and hands and then the chest and feet. He turned the face upwards. Badly deteriorated, it had been smeared with vermilion. Holmes looked at me but said nothing.

"Please come, Watson, I have seen enough. Signor Grimaldi, *vi ringrazio*. We shall be in touch."

Once on the street, Holmes grinned.

"Most interesting, Watson. What did you make of it?"

"A tragedy, the most popular of cardinals dead in his prime."

"No, Watson, not at all. That is not the body of a cardinal. If the Cardinal is dead, his corpse is yet to be discovered. This is a ruse, clever but not clever enough."

He paused for a moment in thought and then said, "Or perhaps clever and rather bold, even impertinent. The vermilion face . . . we must find its meaning. Something in memory . . ."

"But Holmes, how do you know it is not the Cardinal?"

"Forgive me, Watson. I should have asked you to examine the corpse as well. We would have benefited from your opinion, but I doubt that it would have differed substantially from mine. The hands alone would tell you, Watson. They are the hands of a workman, a mason probably. The rough skin is not the result of the Tiber's waters but of a lifetime of heavy work. The scarred nails filled with stone dust and mortar were so part of the man that they survived a long bath in the Tiber. Poor fellow, he did not die of drowning in the Tiber but of a fall. I detected multiple fractures of the ribs, and a bad concussion that probably killed him. And one more thing."

"And what is that?" I asked.

"Grimaldi knows as well as we do that this is not the body of Cardinal Corelli."

I was completely perplexed by this statement.

"But why the further ruse?

"Ah," said Holmes, "Grimaldi is an old tiger, clever and tenacious. He has joined the fray. He knows, as do all Italians, that the Church is first a human institution, and that it runs on human principles, however much those who run it would have it otherwise. The long reign of Leo the Thirteenth is now drawing to a close, and we are witnessing the first signs of the struggle for power. It has already begun. Indeed, it began with the disappearance of Cardinal Corelli. It will end only when a new pope is elected. These men will do anything to control the Papacy. And all of Italy."

Holmes looked at his watch. "By now, Watson, Grimaldi will have announced the news from the *Palazzo della Giustizia*. Rome will be filled with it. It is therefore time for us to pay a call on Cardinal Spontini, a most jubilant prelate at this moment, but one destined for an inevitable fall."

As we entered the Vatican, we were directed to Spontini's office. Suor Angelica was there. She had been crying, for she had just received the news of the death of Cardinal Corelli. Spontini led her out as we entered.

"Let her not go far," said Holmes.

"As you wish, Mr. Holmes." He told Suor Angelica to remain and closed the door. As he returned to his seat I observed him. A short but elegant man with silver hair, he was what I would have thought the great French cardinals looked like. This one resembled, if anything, an Italianate Richelieu.

"The terrible news is upon us, and I have just informed the Holy Father, who was distraught when I told him," said he.

"Indeed," said Holmes, "we have just come from the morgue."

"I too visited and of course identified the body."

Holmes was silent for a moment. His face was without expression when he began to speak.

"A mistake, indeed perhaps a grave one on your part, Your Excellency, for as you well know the body is not that of

Cardinal Corelli. You, a prince of church, have committed a false identification at the *Palazzo della Giustizia* . . . Grimaldi's trap, I think."

The Cardinal showed no emotion.

"I made an honest identification." he said firmly.

"*La sua posizione, caro mio*," said Holmes bitingly, "*è ancora più gravissima*. For not only did you willfully and most falsely identify the corpse, you had it put there to float in the Tiber."

Spontini grew angry. "Be careful, Mr. Holmes, you are speaking to a prince of the Church," said he.

Holmes ignored his remark and continued.

"I noticed, *caro principe*, upon our first visit here that scaffolding had been raised on the east side of this building. In talking to the masons, I learned that one of them, one Francesco Sarubbi, fell to his death two weeks ago. He was buried in a local potters' field since he had apparently no family. A talk with the custodian at the cemetery confirmed that the body was exhumed by orders from the Vatican, from the head of the *Propaganda Fide*, a position that only you hold, if I am not mistaken. It is the body of the poor Sarubbi that lies in the morgue."

"*Basta con queste bugie*," said Spontini.

"But there is more, far more. You are also the head of a long-banned cell within the *Propaganda Fide* known as *La Faccia Vermiglia*, the Vermilion Face, if you will. Its purpose is the purification of the clergy of the Church. It has its origins in the twelfth century, perhaps as early as the Inferno of Dante, in which the vermilion face of Satan chews for all eternity the body of the betrayer, Judas Iscariot. And so, dear Cardinal, in addition to your official labours, you searched for a heretic or worse among your colleagues. To your profound pleasure you found that the man you hated the most, Corelli, was even worse than a heretic."

"A Jew," said Spontini with clenched teeth. "It was my Christian duty to fight his presence and to stop him from becoming the next Pope. I am determined to drive him from the Church. He is a *converso,* who turns the Virgin Mary's picture to the wall. I have given him ample warning. He hides, however, waiting to return."

"I suspected as much as soon as I discovered myself the picture of the Virgin Mary, its face to the wall and replaced by a hideously disfigured crucifix. All of this was perpetrated to warn Corelli that he could not remain in the Church, let alone in a high place, unless you approved."

The Cardinal turned ashen as Holmes spoke, forcefully and with the greatest disdain.

"What is your price?" asked the Cardinal.

"I have none. Your fate lies with the Pope. My suggestion would be, however, that you resign from the Cardinalate and that you lead the rest of your life as a penitent. And of course, neither Cardinal Corelli nor your reluctant mistress, Suor Angelica, is to be harmed in any way."

I myself was shocked at the latest revelation. Holmes rose, went to the door, and brought in the nun.

"It is through you," said Holmes to the cringing woman, "that Spontini learned of the picture. It is through you that he was able to enter the Cardinal's room and plant the crucifix with the vermilion face on the wall, the sign that Christ himself had been transformed into the betrayer, the Jew, Judas Iscariot. You may tell us in your own words why you did these things."

Suor Angelica looked at the Cardinal with loathing.

"Many good lives have been ruined by this man and his evil ambitions. I am merely one among them. For years he pursued me—since my arrival, in truth. Always Corelli protected me. We were like brother and sister."

Spontini tried to stop her, but Holmes intervened.

"It all began on Ash Wednesday of this year. I had gone to Saint Paul's for Corelli to hear my confession. When I was through, I knelt in a pew not far from the confessional to say my prayers. It was then that I noticed a beautiful woman, possibly an Austrian by her beautiful clothes, enter the confessional. She was the last to give a confession. She stayed a long time, but when she came out she said no prayers, but waited for the Cardinal to come forth. They left together."

She paused to regain her composure.

"I suddenly felt myself seized by an overpowering jealousy. I raced back to the Vatican. I found the Cardinal Corelli already in his room at his desk. I asked him who the woman was. He was taken aback by my question, but in his gentle way he smiled and said, "Just a woman who wanted to talk to me."

"He then went over to his bed and turned the Virgin's picture to the wall."

"I left without a word. The turning of the picture I had seen many times before, but this time I took as a dircct affront, since I had given it to him. In my anger I went to this man and told him of the woman and the painting. Because I had described her as an *austrica*, he laughingly gave her the name of Maria Teresa, which his agents spread through the city. For a brief moment I found solace in his arms. From then on my life became a living hell, with this man threatening me at every turn unless I told him of all of Corelli's activities.

"On the night of this past Holy Thursday, Spontini and I entered the Cardinal's room and hung the crucifix on the wall. Spontini applied vermilion to the crucifix and marked the satanic verses in the missal on the desk. Corelli returned. I heard him shout in anger at what he saw in his room. The following morning he left, never to be seen alive again."

"I shall report to the Pope immediately," said Holmes. "I shall be lenient with you, Suor Angelica."

At eight o'clock that evening, a priest dressed in black was seen to enter an *osteria* near Piazza Rinaldi. The *osteria* was run by a family from Salerno. The priest, known as Padre Giovanni, was on good terms with the proprietor, Signor Barca, and served as the family priest, performing baptisms and other sacraments for the family. Signora Barca went out of her way to prepare his favorite foods.

The priest seemed troubled this evening. Signor Barca brought him a liter of his favorite wine. The priest sipped it slowly, but none of his humour or affability came forward. He smiled wanly and sat as if waiting.

Holmes and I were the next to enter. Holmes looked at the priest, smiled at him, and we took our seats at an appropriate distance. Except for the two of us and the priest the *osteria* was empty, for it was still an early hour to sup by Roman standards.

The priest paid little attention to us but stood up as a woman entered. He greeted her warmly. They smiled at each other and began speaking in German. They ate quickly and left.

Holmes and I followed them discreetly and watched as they stopped at a door near the Porta d'Ottavia. As they prepared to enter, Holmes approached them.

"*Scusi,*" said Holmes, "I would like a word with you."

"*Dica,*" said the priest.

"Cardinal Corelli, the Pope has asked me to ascertain your whereabouts and your safety. My name is Sherlock Holmes and this is my friend, Dr. Watson."

Visibly taken aback, the Cardinal motioned us through the door.

"I know who you are. I knew that you would eventually find me. This is my long-lost sister, Maria Teresa," said the priest.

We climbed to the first floor, where we entered a small flat which, judging by its sparse furniture and general shabbiness, looked more like a way station than a residence.

"These have been my quarters since I left the Vatican on Good Friday. Tell me, Mr. Holmes, I have heard recent rumours of my death and the discovery of my body floating in the Tiber. Is it so? All arranged by Spontini, of course, as a warning to me not to return."

"Quite right, Your Excellency. I can assure you, however, that Spontini is well taken care of. The Pope has removed him from the Cardinalate and assigned him to work in a poor house in Isernia, a fitting coda to a misspent career in the Church. But tell me, how did you come to this decision to leave the Vatican, as if you left the Church itself?"

The Cardinal's sister spoke.

"I am to blame," she said in English, "for much of the disturbance to my brother. I am his older sister and in that terrible earthquake in which we lost our parents and two other brothers, I was also presumed to be dead. I was found wandering in a daze and brought to an orphanage in Benevento, where I was raised. I had no idea that my brother had survived nor he that I had. When I was thirteen, I was traced by relatives and brought to Vienna, where they had moved from Italy. I was raised there in good circumstances but always hopeful that, as I had, one or more of my brothers had survived. Then not long ago, I saw a picture of Cardinal Corelli in a Viennese newspaper. His resemblance to my youngest brother was astonishing. I thought long and hard about trying to see him. You see, we were a Jewish family, and he a prince of the Church. I decided, however, that I had to know the truth. I came to Rome and went to St. Paul's to offer my confession to the Cardinal. It was the only place where I could meet him secretly. I entered as any parishioner, frightened but hopeful of what I might learn. In a few minutes, we had established our relationship beyond a doubt. You can imagine with what joy we discovered each other after so many years. My brother accompanied me to this place and returned to the Vatican. It was Ash Wednesday."

"There," said the Cardinal, "as I was about to turn the Virgin's picture to the wall, an action which I had done without thinking all my life, Suor Angelica entered. She was distraught, and I knew it was over my sister, about whom she had made erroneous assumptions. I tried to calm her without telling her anything, for I was afraid Spontini would learn of my Jewish ancestry and use it against me.

"On Good Friday, I returned to my room after hearing confessions to find that my quarters had been entered. The Christ with the vermilion face had been hung above my bed. Its message was not lost on me. I became angered. I threw my ring onto the table, tried to crush it in my hand, and tore my rosary in pieces. My missal had been opened to the lines from an Easter hymn of praise to the Lord, but they had been tampered with so that they brought to mind Satan and his chewing of Judas Iscariot, the great Jewish betrayer. I left in anger and did not know whether I would ever return. I knew I could not fight Spontini, for he had his evil ambitions that drove him forward. I chose to live here in the ghetto with my sister. Free from the cares of the Church for the first time in my life, I began to debate whether or not I should leave. I still have not decided."

"The Pope was gratified to learn that you were alive and well," said Holmes.

"I shall speak to him in the morning," said the Cardinal.

We took our leave and returned to our quarters.

"Well, Holmes, what do you think he will do?" I asked.

"I do not speculate, Watson. Either way, it is a difficult decision."

A few days later, it was announced that Cardinal Corelli had decided to remain in his position in the Church. The news was greeted with joy by the people of Rome.

Not long after, Pope Leo XIII succumbed to old age and ill health. The world waited for the wisp of white smoke from the Vatican that would indicate that a new pope had been chosen. It came after three days. The new Pope greeted the crowds in St. Peter's Square.

To his great relief, Cardinal Corelli was not elected.

THE CASE OF ISADORA PERSANO

"You are quite right, dear Watson, it is an absurd doctrine."

As he had so many times in the past, Holmes had read my inner thoughts as I sat relaxed in my chair. He did this so regularly now that I was no longer taken by surprise. At times I thought I had begun to comprehend how he did it. In this case, however, I was taken aback, for he had appeared to be sound asleep on the couch.

"As usual, Holmes, you are quite apropos. But how did you deduce my thoughts this time? I thought that you were asleep."

He lay there motionless, his eyes closed, as if he were still well into his nap. He sat up, and lit a cigarette.

"I was, Watson, at least until a few minutes ago. Again, it is child's play if one pays attention to details. If I recall, two nights ago you were reading Bishop Berkeley's famous essay on tar water and its benefits, correct?"

"Indeed, I was."

"The volume which you were reading also contains, if I am not mistaken, Berkeley's essay on perception. Since the volume is arranged chronologically, I noted before my nap that you had reached this essay by where you had placed your bookmark. I was certain that you were then reading the good bishop's remarks on the notion that 'to be is to be perceived,' 'esse est percipi' in Latin, and the old weary problem of whether or not something exists if no one perceives it."

"Quite right. He makes a convincing case for it."

"Berkeley is quite clever. You awakened me, however, with your sigh of frustration when you loudly opened and closed your desk drawer repeatedly, hoping to catch a change in its contents, perhaps something amiss not only in your drawer but in the universe. Your sigh of frustration only underlined to me your lack of belief in the notion. The bishop had raised a clever but silly point, clever because it is difficult to refute outright, silly because it matters not in the least."

"I am not totally convinced that he is wrong."

"My dear doctor, what the good bishop is talking about is not whether someone removed an object or it fell into a dark corner, but that the object simply dropped out of existence because there was no perceiver. But the world of nature, Watson, has two characteristics that the good bishop may have forgotten: it does not forget, and it does not forgive. A miscalculation in favour of the good bishop's theory could prove disastrous. And so, dear Watson, you may rest assured that whatever is in your desk drawer right now will be there all night, tomorrow, and perhaps forever, if we can fathom such a term, whether or not you or I or a third person observes it."

We continued our conversation that evening through a late supper, branching off into Holmes's ideas of perception, hallucinations, mirages, and what inevitably makes the ordinary person quite gullible, willing to believe anything.

"It is not just the average person, Watson. Take the great Lombroso himself, one of the great minds of Europe, taken in by this tawdry medium, Isadora Persano."

Holmes had mentioned La Persano, as she was known, on previous occasions, and indeed it was through Professor Cesare Lombroso that the name of this now famous lady first came to the attention of my friend. As the reader may know, Lombroso had become interested in spiritualism in his later years, and he and Holmes were often allied in their relentless exposure of those cases that involved fraud and chicanery. Holmes, of course, was of the opinion that all cases of reported spiritualism were by their very nature fraudulent. In this way, he differed from Lombroso, who felt more and more that there were realms of supernatural experience that went beyond the conventional and therefore were without the ability of science to explain them. In following assiduously one of the cases that had come to him in recent months, Lombroso had heard the name of Isadora Persano, a medium whose powers had begun to spread her fame beyond the confines of her native city, Naples. He then participated in several séances with her and became convinced that of all the mediums that he had met, she was by far the most gifted. Perhaps the most telling episode was how she brought the spirit of Lombroso's own mother to one of her séances. In every detail of speech and family history, according to Lombroso, La Persano was absolutely accurate. Lombroso told Holmes that he had come away from the séance emotionally overwhelmed by his conversation with his mother, who had died three years before. So taken was he with the abilities of this young medium that he refused even to listen to Holmes's irrefutable explanations.

"For reasons of his own, Watson," said Holmes to me that evening, "Lombroso wants to believe this nonsense."

"The woman must be extremely clever," I said.

Holmes smiled. "And quite beautiful, judging from Lombroso's hymns of praise. I am sure," he continued, "that if I investigated I would find that some old family records were closely studied and relatives of Lombroso were carefully interviewed and paid off handsomely by Persano's agents. No medium I know in Europe or England exists without a large group of paid supporters. In this, the mediums resemble the divas of the opera. Couple this with the inevitable dimming of one's memory over time—Lombroso would be no exception to this and we have a most convincing and cunning course of fraudulence. But how to persuade Lombroso, who is already abandoning his scientific career for these pernicious forms of skullduggery?"

Our discussion ended there for the time being, and I heard little more of Isadora Persano at the time. A week later, I left for England to attend to business, leaving Holmes alone with two cases that he wished to complete before his own return to London.

My return to England had been occasioned by letters received from lawyers of a deceased uncle of mine who wished to discuss some points of law before his estate could be finally disbursed. They thought a face-to-face meeting necessary since my signature would be required on a new sheaf of papers the case had generated. I confess that I knew nothing of this uncle, Mr. Peter Tomkins by name, but the terms of the estate were so favourable to me that I deemed it would be foolish of me to ignore the communications from his lawyers. And so, a few days after my arrival in London I found myself seated in our quarters on Baker Street, before Mr. Charles Herriot, a rather rotund and prosperous-looking gentleman, the senior partner in the distinguished firm of Combs and Herriot.

"I hope that I haven't inconvenienced you in asking you to return to London, but there are some aspects of the Tomkins estate that warrant discussion. In fact, Dr. Watson, your uncle's will stipulates that certain portions of it be communicated to you orally."

"I understand," said I. "I take it that my inheritance is still intact, however."

"Indeed, as far as I can see it is, though it may be smaller than we had previously calculated. But let me leave that for the end of our conversation."

The conversations went on for several hours and I was touched by the care that Mr. Herriot displayed with regard to the substantial estate I was about to inherit. It was but a week after I had arrived in England that an urgent telegram from Holmes asked that I return to Italy at once. His message read in part:

You will recall the name of Isadora Persano. Her influence has grown, and I have decided to stop her. Some of her supporters are well placed and will try to do me in. Already the Roman press is on the attack. Will need your help. Come at once.

Holmes

I did not relish the sudden return journey, but I could not ignore my friend's entreaty. And so once again, putting my practise into the hands of two trusted colleagues, I left for Rome, arriving three days later. Holmes was at the station to greet me.

"Just in time, dear Watson, for we leave for Florence in the early morning." Holmes appeared excited. As the cab took us to our lodgings, he related the latest developments.

"Lombroso is making a fool of himself, and I am almost powerless to stop him, but I must try. Last week I attended a séance with him at La Persano's. She began by explaining one of Lombroso's dreams. So accurate was she that he almost fainted on the spot. He said that it was as if he had been invaded by the woman and that she knew his most intimate thoughts, things that he had confided to no one. She is most clever, and so are her mentors. She has now challenged me to expose her in one more séance. It is to take place in Florence tomorrow night. I will then be asked to prove her a fraud. I suspect that I shall be severely restricted in my investigations."

"Little do they know what they are up against," said I.

"My blushes, dear fellow," said he with his usual chuckle.

The morning train was on time. Lombroso greeted us at the station. He was a tall man, now stooped and hunched after so many years of reading and research. He appeared elated to see us.

"I am happy that both of you have come," he said in French, anticipating my difficulty with Italian.

"Have you overcome your disbelief as yet?" he asked, directing his question to Holmes.

"No, I am merely interested in how she does it," Holmes replied. "And to convince Professor Lombroso of the charlatanry of la signora Persano."

"You are mistaken, *mon ami*, she is a true medium, able, I am convinced, to communicate directly with the spirit world. But come, we have about an hour's journey before the meeting."

We entered a waiting coach and began our trip west towards Pisa.

"We will go to Fiesole, where the meetings will take place, in a villa of the Medici."

"Splendid," said Holmes. "And who else will be there to hold hands around the table?" he asked sardonically.

Lombroso smiled. "Even you will be impressed, Holmes. There is a contingent of three from Oxford—the well-known physicist, Professor Oliver Lodge; the Indian thinker B. K. Mallik, and his companion, Winifred Lewis; the writer Arthur Conan Doyle, someone not unknown to you, I trust; and, finally, Madame Blavatsky, the president of the Theosophical Society."

"Ah," said Holmes, with a smile, "*I Soliti Ignoti*, the usual suspects."

He looked directly at Lombroso as he continued.

"Dear Professor Lodge has moved in recent years from true if narrow problems of physics to the drivel of theosophy. Hence I am not at all surprised at his attendance. Mallik is a charlatan, a lucky refugee from Calcutta, who lives off the labours of a few innocent but impressionable females, among whom my friend Winifred is one; he specializes in the writing of great tomes with pretentious titles, the most recent being a never-ending treatise entitled "The Towering Wave." As to my friend Doyle, he has lost his judgement, poor fellow, and as to La Blavatsky, she is the only new character in the bunch. She brings with her the tawdriest of reputations."

"I am sure there will be others, perhaps some surprises," said Lombroso not without some pique at Holmes's sardonic remarks.

The good professor then explained that the villa where the séances were to take place was built by Lorenzo de' Medici himself and that it had been in the Medici family for generations. Towards the end of the eighteenth century it had begun to deteriorate badly, and the family finally sold it to the Gozzoli family, who found it more than they could bear. They in turn sold it to an American millionairess who had moved to Italy after the death of her husband. She came from a wealthy family from New York, the Macphersons, and had married an Italian nobleman, one Marchese dei Arrighi, a member of the Italian parliament. The death of her first husband had led La Macpherson to spiritualism and its accompanying experimentation, and she had been one of the first to support Isadora Persano in her work.

"I assume that the Marchese is complaisant with his wife's interests in her former husband," said Holmes wryly.

I could see that Lombroso was increasingly annoyed with Holmes. He said nothing more.

When we arrived, we were immediately led to a great hall bright with candlelight.

"Note the coming darkness, Watson. The darker the better for our adversaries." He pronounced the last word with a soft chuckle. We took our seats together.

Professor Lodge spoke first.

"I welcome you, both sceptic and believer, to this historic meeting. All of you, with the exceptions of Mr. Holmes and Dr. Watson, believe in the reality of the spiritual world and our undeniable abilities to make contact with those of our loved ones who are now there. What make these contacts possible are the extraordinary abilities of the young woman who sits next to Madame Blavatsky. I refer of course to Isadora Persano, the great medium from Naples. We are ready to begin. Are there any other observations to be made?"

Mme. Blavatsky immediately stood up. "It is," she said in her deep voice, "a matter of sorrow as well as anger that the great traditions of spirituality represented by most of us here have to suffer the infantile skepticism of the world's so-called greatest detective, but he has gone too far in his criticisms of me. Perhaps we should have disallowed his presence and not attempted this contest, but if he stays, I hope that this experience may change his mind. I hope too that he will judge impartially what is about to transpire in this room."

Holmes answered immediately. "Dear Madam, I am here at the invitation of Professor Lombroso. I understand that he is chairman of your committee. And so I shall stay unless he asks me to leave. As to my severe criticism, it has not been answered by any one of you satisfactorily. Let me add that I am here to be shown the veracity of your experiences. You believe that the world contains a spiritual aspect. I must say to you all that I sincerely hope you are correct and I am wrong. Unfortunately, I must remain unconvinced until you demonstrate clearly this young woman's powers."

Conan Doyle rose and said, "We have in this young woman from Naples the most convincing example of spiritualism that I have come across in my long researches into the subject. Holmes may be skeptical, but I know him to be among the most fair-minded of men. And I must say that he has uncovered a good deal of spiritual charlatanry over the years. My feeling is that Holmes should restate his position after the séance and in the discussions that normally follow."

"Good, a very strong point, my dear Doyle," said Professor Lodge.

"Shall we begin then?"

Doyle proposed a brief toast, and we took each other's hands. No one closed his eyes. Isadora Persano let out a deep groan of pain, her face contorted, her body twisted out of shape. I became suddenly overwhelmed by her monstrous appearance. Holmes was impassive, inscrutable, concentrating on the woman's every move. Then it happened: instead of running from the room I began to laugh uncontrollably and so did the others, a chuckle at first, and then almost a roar.

Isadora gave out an unearthly scream and said, "Someone is coming into me, someone I do not know."

A strange sound came from a box that rested on a nearby table. It was a sound that I had never heard before, like the crackling of flames.

The room became silent and a man's voice came from her throat.

"John, are you there? This is your long-lost uncle, Peter Tomkins. Can you hear me? Your mother and father are standing beside me, waiting to speak to you."

At this moment, I was overcome and I began to sob loudly. While the voice was unknown, the accent was the one that I had grown up with.

"Who the devil are you?" I asked, wiping my eyes, which were now drenched with tears.

"I am your mother's brother. Let your friends know what I have done for you. And tell them why you went to London last week. And be aware of false friends."

I suddenly felt compelled to give in detail a description of my uncle's estate and the monies that he had left to me. I went on, unable to stop the flood of sensations that passed through me.

"Where are you, Peter?" I asked, trying to hold on to my emotions. There was only silence, however.

Isadora slowly resumed her normal shape and walked from the room.

"Are you satisfied?" asked Lodge.

I was about to nod in assent, when I felt Holmes's strong fingers pressing into my arm.

"I am afraid, Professor Lodge, that you will be disappointed with my verdict, but even more so with my explanation. Where shall we start?"

There was a deep silence. Holmes waited for a moment, looking deeply into the eyes of each of the participants.

"First, then, let me begin my explanation. I must say that the small toast we imbibed at Professor Lodge's suggestion contained a very small amount of datura, the Indian drug that causes, in order, hysterical laughter, then tears, then a freedom of the word and the inability to lie. This was supplied by Madame Blavatsky, who first received it from Professor Mallik. Is it not so?"

Malllik stood up and confessed. "But its use here was only to make us all feel relaxed. The séance was not influenced by it."

"Well then, Professor Mallik, do you believe that the voice you heard was that of Dr. Watson's long-lost uncle?"

"Of course I do. Why are you not convinced?"

"I remain unconvinced because my dear friend, John H. Watson, M.D., resident at 221b Baker Street, London, does not have, nor has ever had, an uncle named Peter Tomkins. Nor an uncle by any other name. The voice that you heard is therefore that of someone else."

"But Holmes, what I said about my uncle and his fortune is all true—"

"Indeed, Watson, as far as you are concerned, it is true, but unfortunately it is all false."

Lombroso was now on his feet, shouting at Holmes. My friend waited patiently until the good professor's anger spent itself.

"You demand too much, Holmes. You have seen before your very eyes an experiment as successful as any in your own laboratories. Your closest friend was moved to tears by what he heard. How much more would we have learned had it not been for your unjustified scepticism."

"Professor Lombroso, I ask that you allow me to explain my judgement. You will find in this folder all that you would need to know. The explanation is quite simple: Peter Tomkins does not exist and never has. How do I know that? Because I invented him and supplied the gang that control the Signorina, who is an innocent, with the information for them to use. Please forgive me, dear Watson, for there is no inheritance either. The supposed existence of a large sum of money to be collected by the Palladino gang from your uncle and you was an irresistible lure for them. It is with this promise of ill-gotten gain that they were willing to allow their greatest asset—la signorina here—to participate."

"But the lawyers, Holmes, they were real and quite emphatic about Tomkins. Why, I returned all the way to London to meet Herriot, a partner in the firm."

It was as I uttered the last sentence that I saw the lawyer in Holmes's eyes and the unmistakable look of Mr. Herriot, the advocate I met in London.

"Holmes," I cried, "it was you all along."

"Yes, old fellow. It was the clearest way I could make my point. Should any of you doubt my word, you are welcome to make any inquiries you like at the office of Herriot and Herriot, in Cornwall or London. Since the material of the case is false, the Herriots will have no problem in discussing it at length with anyone around this table. And I am sorry, old boy, that I had you make an extra trip to England, but I had no other way of your hearing the story directly from your lawyers without considerable risk of my plot being found out before our séance here. I see that Madame Blavatsky is trying to get our attention. Let us hear her out."

The leader of the Theosophical Society was visibly angry.

"Clever, Mr. Holmes, but not clever enough. This is another of your outrageous accusations against people of good will. If you cannot believe in the spiritual, then leave it to those of us who see an awakening of mankind in its possibilities. How do I know, Mr. Holmes, that you did not concoct this scheme with the knowledge and cooperation of this man seated beside your closest friend?"

"Permit me, Madam. I have no objection to your attempts to awaken mankind to its spiritual nature. I merely object to the means, which are false and quite frankly faked by an unsavory group of thieves who are using this poor young woman for their own ends. I do not include you in that group, Madam. You are not a criminal, you are merely the gullible minister of her cynical bosses. As to any falsity in my account, you may discuss the matter with Mr. Herriot of Cornwall for evidence of my honesty and goodwill in the matter."

There was a sudden emanation of sound from the wooden box that sat behind us. There was a crackling quality to it as if flames were being fanned by the argument we had just heard. Blavatsky smiled. "You hear, Mr. Holmes, the flames of Hell about to envelop us."

"Not at all, Madam. What you call flames are the static produced by radio waves. The box was shown to me by its inventors, Marconi in Italy and Tesla in New York. I have worked with these gentlemen and indeed am responsible for several improvements in the clarity of reception. You see, Madam, I must keep abreast of new developments in knowledge in order to continue the struggle with human ignorance. You, on the other hand, appear to be content to maintain the old feudal order, of which you are one of the few literate members. It is you, not I, who help to keep mankind in the throes of poverty and unending subservience to those in power."

Mme. Blavatsky took her seat, apparently chastened by Holmes's rhetoric. No one else ventured any comment. Holmes nodded toward the chairman and we parted, leaving the rest of the assembled to their own judgements of what had just happened.

As we walked through the front hall, I heard Lombroso calling to us. As he approached us I could see that he had been quite taken aback by Holmes's performance.

"Well?" said Holmes.

"I believe you now," said Lombroso. "Isadora now admits that she was coached by Nicola Ciocchi, a valet for my father. He knew everything about us, and fed it all to the Palladino gang." He extended his hand and we reciprocated.

"It is almost seven. Let us have dinner together in the Piazza," said I.

"*Benissimo*," said Lombroso. "We shall dine at La Sonnambula, which has the best food in all of Tuscany."

We walked together and gazed at the crowd of people before us and the darkening sky above. The conversation at dinner was mostly about La Persano. Lombroso was excited, for not only did he believe that Holmes was right, but that he himself had thought of a new way of looking at mediums that was worth exploring.

"The whole question, Holmes, is how La Persano and others like her obtain such detailed and minute information concerning the lives of their clients. In my own case, I can see how. We were a household of many people. My parents loved to have guests, we were surrounded as children by servants with whose children we played constantly. Is it not possible, therefore, by as yet some unknown mental power that we absorb much of each other's personalities in addition to what enters our brain through the senses? I do not mean any mystical power but a perspective of the brain itself that enables the individual to recall large parts of the past that were thought to be inaccessible. I hope, my dear Sherlock, that you understand that I am not speaking of what they call in your country channeling."

"My dear Cesare, you choose to walk into fields of knowledge which are fraught with danger. I admire your courage but I am situated within a different set of problems, problems in which the fundamental boundaries have already been set. Some day, dear Cesare, someone will evaluate my work and your work, and find where our results agree and differ. That person," said Holmes with a very broad smile, "might have to be a new kind of medium, a Lombroso medium."

I raised my glass and toasted both of my companions. By the time we departed, the food and drink of La Sonnambula had done their work. I recall only a sound sleep and Holmes knocking on my door, reminding me that we were scheduled to leave for London at once.

"Come along, old boy," he said. "I have a note from our dear friend Lestrade who once again finds himself beyond his depth. Let us have our coffee. If we leave now, we will be in time to assist the poor chap." Holmes handed me a large cup of *caffè latte* and the morning paper.

I wonder what Lestrade is up to now, I thought to myself. In the paper, I saw that a Mr. Peter Tomkins of Sloan Square had been murdered the day before and that Inspector Lestrade had requested that Mr. Sherlock Holmes join the investigation.

"Only the name is the same, old boy, only the name."

I packed my few things and we were off to what my friend often referred to as the "great cesspool" of the British Empire.

A SINGULAR EVENT IN TRANQUEBAR

IT WAS ONE OF THOSE QUIET DAYS ON WHICH SHERLOCK Holmes proclaimed in a loud, determined voice that it was time for him to put his papers in order. By the time he had finished his morning tea, however, he had been diverted to his violin, which he plucked noisily, declaring that it needed new strings. His papers lay silent on his desk, forgotten and unattended, as he took up his bow and began a piece by Paganini.

He played beautifully, but, as was his habit, he played nothing all the way through to its close. The great composers for the romantic violin—Bruch, Tchaikovsky, Beethoven, Mendelssohn, and Brahms—became somehow sewn together into one large musical quilt of excerpts, which had its own peculiar unity. I said nothing, listening to my friend's remarkable playing, when there was a firm knock at the door, one which we both recognized as that of Mrs. Hudson.

"Mr. Holmes, there is someone here to see ya', very persistent, I would say. Why, he's followed me right up. Go on, up ya go."

A middle-aged man, oddly dressed in a green woollen cap and a long black cloak entered our quarters. He removed his hat, and I saw a man who was disheveled, his hair matted and stuck in clumps on his head, his face pasty, dark complected, almost dirty, certainly someone who had not slept in his own bed for several nights. His trousers were muddy and held up by a piece of rope which had been threaded through some crude holes made at the waist. He wore black chupples and thin stockings, also soaked with mud. His eyes were red-rimmed and almost cloudy, a condition that I had often seen in my medical practise as a strong indication of the use of opium. In all, an unhealthy eccentric, I thought to myself, bordering on the deliberately offensive.

"Mr. Holmes, I need you help and wise words. I am afraid that I shall go mad."

"No need of that, Mr. . . . ?"

"McMillan, sir, John McMillan."

Holmes stared at the man as one would stare at a puzzle of oddments, one in which the main elements were missing.

"I see that you have spent a good deal of the last day in Hyde Park . . . and that you were attacked by . . . something that soiled and tore your cloak."

McMillan looked surprised at Holmes's words. "You are most observant, Mr. Holmes. You are quite right," said our guest.

"Let me see," he continued. "You were born in India, lived there until you were perhaps eighteen or nineteen, when you left and settled in England. At some point you lived in Italy, where you served, in your penultimate posting, as assistant to a lady of aristocratic origin, then domiciled in the Abruzzi. The lady had also managed through her personal connections to have you positioned as a low functionary in the office of the consul general for Her Majesty's Government in Naples. Before that, you had no permanent position, but supported yourself by tutoring and by occasional employment as a teacher in a boys' school in Florence. You are now employed as a part-time janitor in Sussex."

"Amazing, sir, you are correct on all points. How did you know?"

"Hardly a mystery, Mr. McMillan. I need not explain the arcane reasoning by which I arrived at all of my conclusions. You may note the following in brief: You are wearing a large rather common school ring which I have seen before worn by students of the Goodstock School in Madras. The graduates are a close-knit group of alumni, and it is not uncommon to see it and rings like it in the pawnshops in London these days. It is given to each student at the time of final matriculation. You have worn the ring for many years without removing it. It has become overly tight on your finger. In addition, your English, though native, bears the characteristic lilt of South Indian languages, the Dravidian so-called; finally, your cap was made in a small village in the Abruzzi, and is rarely worn outside of Italy. It has on its rim the seal that was once commonly given to honorary consuls. But, sir, please tell me and my friend Dr. Watson of your plight. And do sit. I see that you are exhausted by what has happened to you in the last day or so."

"My story, if one can call it that, begins in India, Mr. Holmes, a country which I left thirty years ago, but in a frightening way has come back to haunt me. In any case, let me commence by telling you the needful. I was born in Madras fifty-one years ago, the son of John and Mary McMillan. My father was the editor of the *Madras Observer*, a highly respected newspaper. I was an excellent student, and I won many prizes for my schoolwork. As a reward, my father announced to me one day that, because of his love for India and my successful studies, he proposed that I should take a walking tour of the subcontinent before we settled in England. He offered to pay all my expenses along the way and encouraged me to travel not only with the rich and prosperous people I had been raised with, but with the poor as well, the latter being a means of knowing India which he said was avoided by most of our countrymen, who considered their lives there as a dreary bore.

"I of course jumped at the offer. Imagine, Mr. Holmes, having such an opportunity. I planned my route carefully. I decided to walk along the coast down to Cape Comorin and then up the Western Ghats, making full circles to the great religious sites of the interior. Early on in my trip, something happened which almost stopped me from going on. But I persisted and arrived back in Madras fifteen months after my trip began."

"And what happened early on?"

"It happened in a place scarcely on any map, a small colony called Tranquebar."

"Ah, yes," said Holmes, "there is a Danish fort there and a convent of German nuns—Lutherans, I believe. We captured the fort and the land around it about a century ago."

"You are again quite right, Mr. Holmes. I had been to the village many times in the past because there were also two temples on the beach, both filled with beautiful images carved in the stone but woefully neglected by both the Danes and by us, the English. Sometimes I would sit for hours in the ruins feeling the surf envelope me. Then I would help the fishermen with their nets.

"It was near sunset when I left the fishermen on that fateful night at the start of my long journey. The sea was calm, but there was a strong ominous wind which I thought might quickly turn into a tufan. I decided therefore to stay in the guest room of the nunnery. I took a path which I well knew through the small patch of thick forest that grew around the convent.

"And then, Mr. Holmes and Dr. Watson, it happened: I was grAbbéd from the rear by assailants who forced me to the ground and tied me up with my feet stretched back and tied tightly to my wrists. They gagged me, making it impossible for me to cry out. It was dark and my captors said nothing. All that I could see was that they were naked except for the usual loincloths worn by the local fishermen. I shall never forget the strangest thing about them: their faces glowed a bright yellow in the dark as if they had rubbed some glistening ointment on their faces, something resembling the phosphorescent light of countless June bugs. They spoke not a word, but carried me silently to an obscure place in the wood, dropped me there on my stomach, and disappeared. Their faces seemed to float disembodied in the darkness as they passed into the night.

"I spent the hours before dawn in mortal terror, not only because of the painful position they had put me in but because I was terrified by the thought that I should die there without anyone ever knowing what had happened to me."

Mr. McMillan seemed to shrink as he spoke to us. His breathing became laboured and he almost fell out of his chair. I caught him just as he was about to drop onto the floor.

"Hold him, Holmes; let me listen to his heart."

His heart was beating rapidly but steadily enough and I revived him with some salts.

He sat up and apologized profusely. "I am so sorry, Mr. Holmes, but I am most upset," said our guest.

"Please continue," said Holmes, "I suspect that we are a bit far from the end of our story."

"I writhed all night, trying to extricate myself from the ropes, but I could not. I heard wild beasts moving about and was afraid. Morning finally came. By this time, my wrists were bloodied and my back nearly broken, or so it felt. It must have been just before dawn when I sensed the presence of someone near. It was a nun from the school, dressed in grey and white, her face hidden, who cut my ropes and quickly disappeared into the forest. So great was my relief that I fell into a sleep and only awakened around noon.

"Instead of going to the convent, I went down to the sea and threw myself into its icy depths. The salt water stung my bloodied wrists and feet, but I felt renewed and determined to continue on rather than look back on the incident that now began to seem more like a nightmare than reality.

"I moved on, following the plan that I had laid out for myself, and continued through India. Towards the end of the trip, when I had arrived in Bengal, my father came to meet me and we visited together Puri, the home of the Juggernaut temple and other religious sites. It was in Gauhati in Assam that my father said that he had arranged for me to attend the university in England. I was overjoyed at the prospect. I returned with him to Madras. Shortly thereafter I left for London and a new life.

"I needn't tell you much more of my career, Mr. Holmes. After my studies at the university, I became a teacher at the Overbrook School in Sussex, where I taught for seven years. I was then sent to Italy by the school to tutor English children living in Rome. Returning to London after years as deputy consul, I served for a time as principal of the Grindly School in Horsham.'

"I am still in the dark as to why you are here, Mr. McMillan," said Holmes with a bit of impatience.

Our guest grew pale and visibly sagged in the chair as he fought to continue his story.

"I implore you, gentlemen, to listen to the end," he said with a sob. "I came to London from Horsham three days ago to visit friends. Yesterday, towards evening, just at dusk, I entered Hyde Park on my way to my friends' house, the way I had taken several times during my stay, when I suddenly saw the masked faces of that bitter night in Tranquebar. Fearing that I was hallucinating and about to expire, I sat down on a bench. But there was no doubt now: the creatures came towards me, the same expressions on their strange faces. I became terrified but I could not cry out. Then I must have fainted for I have no memory of what came next. I awoke tied as before and lying in a thick set of trees and brush. I was in an unfamiliar place. I tried to break my bonds but to no avail. At daybreak, I heard someone come. It was a nun, dressed in the grey habit of before, who cut my bonds and disappeared into the bright sunlit dawn. I sat up in what turned out to still be Hyde Park I have been half dazed since I was released."

Holmes looked directly at our guest and said, "Mr. McMillan, your story, highly improbable as it is, is one that has obviously caused you considerable distress, but one that I find of some interest to me, largely because of the rare circumstances in which you have found yourself. I shall take on your case, provided that you leave London and return home immediately and remain there until I visit you. Please leave your address. And do not tell anyone that you have spoken to me about the matter."

"Mr. Holmes, I agree to your stipulations. I shall return to my residence at once and await your visit."

Our guest appeared so weak that he barely could lift himself out of his chair, and I guided him to the door. When he had left, I turned to Holmes, who was peering through the window curtain, watching as our client walked down Baker Street and faded into the crowd.

"What do you think, Watson?

"Almost too bizarre, Holmes, the man may be a congenital liar or someone who suffers from terrible delusions."

"He walked at a fair clip as I watched him and seems to have recovered from his ordeal fairly quickly."

Holmes began his usual pacing. "Interesting, Watson, most interesting. Masked figures. Strange, absurd, and inconsequential, if what you say is true, but there may be more to it. One must first eliminate all impossibilities—and whatever remains must be the solution. In this case, we have a very high degree of improbability, to say the least. Let us think for a moment."

"Surely, Holmes, the man is quite mad, or is telling tall stories. Frankly, I wouldn't waste my time. The only question is why he is taking the bother to engage the world's greatest detective."

"A good question, Watson, to which I have as yet no satisfactory answer, but all in good time. And, by the by, did you notice how quickly he accepted as true my random statements about his life, relying on me to explain his grim circumstances rather than reveal the truth. His story is certainly most incomplete. If it is made up, why did he, for instance, not tell us that the same thing happened to him in Italy? Surely, the masked dancers would have found him there as well if they are located in his brain, and not outside it? Come, Watson, a walk in Hyde Park will do us some good. There are only a few places where McMillan's encounter could have taken place. Let us see what we might find there. My ragged irregulars must have seen the man. Let us speak with them and have a look ourselves."

"Why not?" said I in agreement.

"Keep your eyes open, Watson."

"For what?"

"Anything of a material nature that might have been part of McMillan's—what shall we call it—his meeting, let's say for the moment."

Holmes knew Hyde Park well. He often walked there when he thought through a case. This time, however, the park itself was part of the riddle. We walked away from Oxford Street toward the seediest section, an infamous jungle of urban despair. Here the drunks, the hungry beggars, the down and out and other malingerers tried to survive amidst the hundreds of rumbling pigeons that surrounded them. Holmes stopped for a moment and beckoned to someone at the edge the crowd.

"Hello, Harry," said Holmes. One of the ragged denizens came forward.

"'ello, Mr. 'olmes. This be your sidekick, eh?"

"Indeed, Harry, this is the illustrious Watson, teller of tales and custodian of the Holmesian fables," said Holmes. "Harry, we have a question for you and your friends. Have you seen a man wearing a green woollen hat during the last few days?"

Harry nodded. "Yeah, Mr. 'olmes, you mean McMillan. 'e aint 'ere right now, but we know 'im. Comes often and sleeps under a tree, thet tree in fact. I know 'im pretty well. Strange old toff. Does terrible things, Mr. 'olmes, like today 'e killed a big dog by stranglin' it. Right be'ind thet bush over there. Never saw such a thing before in me 'ole life. We chased 'im out of 'ere after 'e did it. Why, 'e tied up the poor mutt and 'ung 'im from a tree, and then 'e 'elped the rope wid 'is 'ands. 'e's not gonna be allowed 'ere again. 'e's got the boys all riled up, all right."

"Show us the place, Harry. Where is the dog?"

"Still there, Mr. 'olmes, as far as I know. Come along."

We followed our guide to a most neglected part of the park, one where the gardeners had not been for many weeks. Piles of dead leaves, uncut grass, and the smell of rotting flowers produced in me a sickening foreboding. A large, tall oak shaded the place. Around one of its low branches I saw a rope. Below it the body of a dog stiff as death, its eyes staring at us as if still hoping for help. Holmes looked over the ground, sifting through the grass.

"Rather disturbing, wouldn't you say, dear Watson?"

"A criminal act, Holmes; the perpetrator of this cruelty should be punished. But I know of no British law that protects animals in cases such as this."

Holmes was silent for a moment. Then he turned towards us and asked, "Harry, my good fellow,you are sure that this is the work of McMillan?"

"Sure as anythin', Mr. 'olmes. I was 'ere and tried to stop the bloke. The poor dog tore me clothes to shreds, and McMillan, why, 'e was wearin' a fancy cloak, 'e was, and thet cloak is probably no more."

We walked back to Harry's crowd in silence. Holmes passed him a couple of pound notes and we left.

"Knowledge proceeds by contrasts, dear Watson," said my friend as we entered our quarters, "a constant series of revelations between the old and the new. The differences that arise provide much that is fundamental to any criminological solution. But we know only a small portion of what has happened in any particular case, and thus the science of deduction enters the mystery to help make sense of what has transpired while we are elsewhere: a nun, a father, a man in a green cap, a dead dog . . ."

"And the devil dancers," said I with a smile, "and more than one dead dog."

"Yes, Watson old boy. Furthermore, my dear friend, we must look to the absent and the missing in any tale: a parent long deceased, another relation in prison for a long period, one sick in an institution. All of these bear silent witness to the activities of men. In this case, we might well ask: who is McMillan's mother? Is the father the only parent? She is completely absent from the tale, and remains unknown to us. But why the loud presence of one parent and not both? Perhaps McMillan himself does not know why, or even perhaps who she is. Perhaps he is attempting the impossible: to hide his mixed Anglo-Indian blood, of which he is an undeniable example. Who else of importance is hidden, or, better still, hiding?"

Holmes donned his robe, lit his pipe, and continued his train of reasoning.

"Suppose, Watson, that McMillan has told us all he knows in good faith, and that he himself is ignorant of the rest of his own story. Let us suppose that he came to us first to enlist our protection from the ghostly but real devils that have accosted him, in the hope that we could unmask them and free him from their fearful threats. That would indeed mean that what you call the devil dancers are real actors in the story. Bah, so much for abstract principles. We now need some facts."

He walked over to his bookshelves, pulled a large tome out of its place, and began to leaf through it.

"Hah, old boy, here we go. I am reading the entry under the name McMillan in Rupak's *Prominent Persons of South India.* Rupak is generally reliable in cases such as this one. Here we are: "McMillan, Hugh. Editor of *Madras Pioneer*; minister of the Church of Christ Reborn; found dead in his home in Madras in 1878 under suspicious circumstances known only to police. McMillan stAbbéd to death. Mystery remains unsolved."

"Surely, Holmes, this would indicate that there is a painful story different from what he has told us."

"Let us read further, Watson, before we put the pieces of the puzzle together. Now let us look under Tranquebar. This may help. Here we are: 'Tranquebar, a British colony in southern India. Rarely visited. Home to a small convent of nuns, most of whom are Indian by blood. Order of St. Gertrude, an Austrian order with small convents in England and Denmark; headquarters London. 6 Marlborough Rd.' It is always gratifying to find what one is looking for within one's own library. Chosen well, a few volumes organized according to one's chief preoccupations yields wonders. Come, Watson, let us hie ourselves to a nunnery. We are on track."

In a few minutes, Holmes and I were on our way to the convent of St. Gertrude. Hidden from the street by large tall bushes, it did not look imposing until we were well inside the gate. A long brick-lined path led up to an old massive stone mansion. I guessed that it may have been the city residence of the Marlborough clan at some time in its history. The dukes of Marlborough were no longer in evidence, for the place was dilapidated and repellent.

Holmes walked slowly, peering in every direction. I followed him silently. When we reached the entrance, I saw a nun dressed in grey waiting for us. She was short, plump, pink, and pleasant, friendly even—as she greeted us. She appeared to be untouched by the pervasive gloom cast off by the convent itself.

"Forgive me; we have so few visitors here that I am almost speechless. You look as if you mean no harm. May I ask who are you?"

"My name is Holmes, and this my colleague Dr. John Watson. We would like to meet with the mother superior if she is not otherwise engaged."

"May I know the nature of your business?"

"Yes. It concerns a gentleman of Madras by the name of Hugh McMillan."

The nun curtseyed and directed us to a small foyer, where we waited.

The room was unadornedly austere, as we were to find the rest of the building. The nun who had greeted us returned. We followed her down a long corridor at the end of which stood a tall gaunt woman of a deadly pallor, an unearthly white, who, judging from her attire, was the mother superior. We followed her to a large office, where she directed that we sit across from her.

"I am Sister Gertrude, director of the convent. May I know the nature of your visit?" she asked.

"Indeed," said Holmes. "The nature of our inquiry is rather complex. It may even lead us to a request for an exorcism."

"We rarely have such requests. I suspect that your needs would be far better served by speaking with Father Alfred of the Church of the Epiphany, which is located about a mile from here, still on Marlborough Road."

She appeared ready to leave and stood up, whereupon Holmes said, "Please. I have several questions of great importance to my client. Dear Sister, my inquiry concerns a gentleman by the name of Hugh McMillan. I wonder if you knew him in Madras."

"He was my father, I am sorry to say," she said with apparent insouciance.

She paused as if she would say nothing more.

"Who is your client?" she asked suddenly. My brother John, no doubt. Quickly, then, with your questions. I shall answer in the hope that you will go away as in the twinkling of an eye. You must forgive me if I have no interest in my father, my brother, or anyone else from your walk of life."

"Who, then, was your mother? I know nothing of her," said Holmes.

A sudden gush of words came forth.

"My mother was a fine woman of English origin. She married my father because he was handsome and successful. But he was corrupt and fanatical as well.

"Not long after my brother was born, my father took a mistress from the local community. My mother, when she learned of this, tried everything to save her marriage, including having me, her second child. Nothing worked. After my brother's birth, my father became unavailable and they rarely saw each other except for occasional moments of tranquility. In the end, she became a member of this order. She died in the convent in Tranquebar. I was raised by her in the convent, and after her death, as I was old enough to determine my own future, I decided to stay on.

"My brother, John, lived with my father, but in a part of the house made separate by my father's lady friend. It was a very difficult relationship. There were major disputes and there were suspicions later that my father was murdered by his mistress, or perhaps my brother, but no charges were brought. And the little I know of John would lead me to believe that he was incapable of such violent action.

"Mr. Holmes, I am dedicated to the religious life of this order and never knew either of my parents well. The news of my father's demise reached me at the convent in Tranquebar several months after the funeral services, when I was in retreat. John came to visit me before he left Madras, and I have seen him only a few times during these last thirty years, although he has managed to keep nearby me all this time. I should tell you with some embarrassment that I have supported him financially by sending money to an account in Horsham.

"This is a small contemplative order, Mr. Holmes. I chose it because its doctrines gave me peace through meditation. You may be surprised to learn that this is by far the longest conversation I have had with anyone in more than six months. If I seem abrupt it is because I spend every moment possible in retreat. I am not at all interested in the world you live in. We are only seven nuns, all dedicated to a life like that of St. Gertrude."

Holmes remained silent until Sister Gertrude had finished. When he finally spoke it was in a soft voice, all the more persuasive because of its gentleness.

"I trust that you will understand that those of us who are necessarily involved in the world outside this cloister may have undeniable obligations. I have, unfortunately, to pursue my inquiries with you for but a few more moments, however importunate you may find them. I shall endeavor to make them as brief as possible."

"Very well, proceed. But do not be surprised if I leave before you finish."

"Your father was difficult but religious," said Holmes. "I gather that he was also a very cruel man."

Holmes's question seemed to unnerve her, and she remained silent for a time.

"He killed a dog once at his school," she then said quietly. "This made him infamous, especially to those who took the story of the dog as an illustration of God's retribution. And there were many in the congregation. He had found the poor creature rummaging for food, and before the assembled student body he hung the creature as an example of what happens to thieves if the sixth commandment is not kept. I of course was not there, but the poor dog was the subject of discussion for weeks after. My mother was disconsolate, my brother so enraged that he attacked our father with an iron pole, almost killing him as he was pulled away. They parted company and never met again as far as I know. My brother's rebellion seemed to intensify my father's cruelty. From that time onward, Father made it a point to kill a dog publically at the beginning of every school year. I must tell you that the group of English and other foreigners who sent their children to the school approved of his cruel message, some out of religious conviction, others out of pure terror."

"I continued to live at the convent and accepted ordination after three years. One day, I learned of my father's death and my brother's disappearance. One of the nuns, herself a Tamilian from Madras, had overheard some talk about how my father's killers had tortured him before he died. She said that they appeared to be hired men and had tied him the way he had tied up the dogs that he had killed."

"Fortunately for me, we seven nuns moved to Italy in 1899, to a town called Isernia, where we housed ourselves in an old dilapidated monastery inhabited by an old priest and a servant boy from the hills of the Abruzzi. My brother followed me and came to live alone nearby in the village, but I rarely saw him, Two years ago, seven of us were asked by the head of the *Propaganda Fide* to move to London. My brother made his presence known shortly after our arrival here. He continues to follow me."

Sister Gertrude rose, and it was clear to us that she would speak no more. The same pleasant nun who let us in the convent showed us out. As we left, Holmes turned and asked her: "Tell me, where does your gardener throw his rakings and pile up his leaves?"

"Near the greenhouse. Come, I can show you."

She led us quickly to the composting area, where a gardener was at work. His presence reminded her that she was to leave us at the door of the convent, and so she turned quickly, her face even more pink, and entered the convent.

The gardener, a wiry man of middle age, nodded as we approached him.

"I wonder if you might help us," said Holmes. "May I know your name?"

"Judson. 'enry Judson. We don't usually talk to strangers. Fact is we're told not to. But I'm about to leave 'ere anyways. What's on your mind, Mr. . . . ?"

"Holmes, Sherlock Holmes. I am a detective, and this Dr. Watson, my colleague. Tell me, Mr. Judson, in a few weeks London will be in full flower. Will there be any June bugs in this garden?"

"Strange that you should ask thet question, Mr. 'olmes. Yes, there will be, but not so many now. For the last three years, the nuns 'ave ordered me to capture them and to put the lightning jelly in glass jars. Seems they think it is a medicine, good for your aches and pains. Never tried it meself."

"Has anyone ever spent the night in this garden?"

"Yessir, a strange man, friend or maybe a relation of the Sister Gertrude. 'e spent many a night 'ere, even in the cold weather. Sometimes she let 'im in—or one of the others would."

"Did he bury anything here?"

"Yep, I remember one night not so long ago, maybe a month ago, 'e came in, drunk as a Welsh farmer, dug an 'ole over there, put a wooden box in it and buried it right there.

Then wot made me think 'e was crazy was that 'e uncovered the box and took it out of the 'ole. Put the dirt back and left the box at the door. After 'e left, around midnight I guess it was, I 'eard the front door open and one of the sisters reached out and took the box inside. Weird goin's on, I say, too much for a simple bloke like me."

"You have been of great help to us, Mr. Judson, and I hope that you will allow me one last question. Do you know where the gentleman with the green hat lives?"

"Well, Mr. 'olmes, I can say where 'e says 'e lives and thet's in 'orsham. Fulham Road, I think."

We thanked the gardener for his time, and I found myself pondering what Holmes would do next. "It may be a waste of time," he said, "but I want to visit our client in his abode in Horsham. If we leave now, we can be there in two hours."

We took the first train and were in Horsham around one o'clock. Holmes was silent through our trip, keeping to what I could only call a meditative pose. He jumped up with great vigor as soon as we approached the station, and I found myself struggling to keep up with him.

"Where to?" I asked.

"Fulham Road, number forty-one. But let us first talk with the station master."

"You mean the bloke in the green 'at, do ya? I know 'im to see 'im. Can't say I like 'im much. Buys 'is tickets in the mornin'. 'e's part East Indian, I think, dark complected. 'e works for Lord Fitzwilliam. There doin' some plant experiments, but 'e aint 'ere right now. 'e's gone to America, so the queer bloke is 'ere alone."

The station master directed us to Fulham Road. Number 41 was a cottage at the end of the cul de sac. There was a note tacked to the front door which was addressed to Holmes. It read:

Dear Mr. Holmes,

Do enter. I am not here of course, and shall not be again. I shall be elsewhere.

Holmes smiled, but I could see a certain anger in his eyes. The door was locked. Holmes broke the glass, put his hand in, and turned the knob.

What greeted us can only remain indescribable. Every sense, every sensitivity was assaulted by the horror that faced us: dead dogs were everywhere, some stuffed, some hanging on ropes from the ceiling. Overcome by the stench, we raced outside. Holmes broke several windows and the ensuing draft was enough to allow us to re-enter.

"Good Lord, Holmes. What is this?"

"The work of a madman, whatever else it is. Look, mixed with the dogs are some true exotica: a mongoose there, two bandicoots in the corner, a panda . . . and look over there, Watson, look."

My eyes reluctantly followed Holmes outstretched arm to a corner of the room where there were three black masks shining, dancing in the wind. I entered the only other room, which contained a bed and chest of drawers. The walls, however, were covered with masks and wooden crosses hung alternately in neat rows.

"Come, Watson, back to London as fast as we can make it. I suspect that we shall be too late no matter what. McMillan unfortunately has the jump on us."

We almost ran to the station. Holmes barely had time to ask the station master to call the police when our train arrived.

Holmes was silent, but wrought. When he finally spoke, it was with a rueful sigh.

"I should have seen through it all at the very beginning. But I didn't. Perhaps it doesn't matter at this point."

It was about five p.m. when we reached London. Holmes hailed a cab and directed the driver to Hyde Park. There we walked to where Harry had initially taken us, to the dingy end of the park. From a tall pile of moist oak leaves there emerged, perpendicular to the earth, a human leg naked to the knee. The foot wore a white sock and a black chupple, attached to which was a green woollen hat that fluttered every so often like the flag of some faraway country, mysterious and unknown. Holmes gently removed the leaves to reveal the face of John McMillan and that of his sister, Gertrude. Brother and sister were still tied together with ropes, unable to free themselves except for McMillan's one leg. Sister Gertrude clutched a wooden box to her breast. Holmes opened it. It was empty.

Harry found a bobby for us, who reported the deaths to Inspector Hopkins of Scotland Yard. In the morning we read the *Times* accounts of the fire at the convent and of the unidentified corpses in Hyde Park. At the end of each report, without any reference to the other, was written:

Mr. Sherlock Holmes is known to be working on the case.

"As of now, Watson, I regard this as one of my defeats. The man has won or at least played his game well enough for me to call it a draw at best."

"Perhaps we will have a visit from the masked men," said I.

"Quite possibly, but let us not wait for such an eventuality. Watson old boy, reach over to the shelf next to you and hand over the book on peerage in England. I want to know something more of Lord Fitzwilliam."

THE CASE OF THE MISSING LODGER

OF THE MANY FRIENDSHIPS I HAVE BEEN LUCKY ENOUGH to have forged in an increasingly long life, none, with the exception of my relationship with Sherlock Holmes, was ever as strong as my friendship with Dumond Davies. His premature death was the saddest of events for all who knew him.

Davies and I had grown up in the same part of London, attended school and the university together, and finally, commenced the study of medicine at the same time at Edinburgh. It was only in 1878 when I joined our forces in Afghanistan that we were separated. We corresponded fitfully for a time until he informed me that he had met and fallen in love with a young woman of great beauty, who, he was amazed to say, agreed to marry him after the briefest of courtships. More than anything he wished for me to be present at his wedding.

As luck would have it, a Jezail bullet had hit me in the shoulder several weeks before the arrival of his letter, and the necessary papers authorizing my discharge were thus already prepared. I wrote Dumond that if he and his bride-to-be could wait until my release, I would be overjoyed to attend. My wound, though a minor one, suffered in Candahar, was thought by our commanding officer to be of sufficient gravity for me to return to England and rejoin civilian life.

The wedding took place shortly after I arrived in London, just after my initial meetings with Sherlock Holmes. Indeed, learning of my new acquaintance, Dumond and his bride immediately extended an invitation to him. In the coming months and to my great surprise, Holmes and the Davieses became good friends. Their home was often a refuge for the now famed detective during those moments when he was close to the solution of a crime, but was still unsure of his way forward. Dumond would then provide a willing ear for him when I was unavailable because of a medical or other emergency.

It was a terrible moment that particular evening, therefore, when I read Barbara's note imploring us to come as quickly as possible, for Dumond, she thought, had accidentally electrocuted himself while mending a lamp. For a moment on the way, Holmes and I hoped that he could be revived. We knew it to be too late, however, when we heard Barbara's grief-stricken sobs as we entered and saw the look of helplessness on the face of Tanner, the local police doctor, whom I knew quite well and for whom I had the highest respect.

"Too heavy a bolt, I would say, for him to survive," he said quietly. "He must have tripped, and the current from the main went right through him."

Holmes and I took a quick look at the body and nodded to Tanner in reluctant assent. A strong odor of singed cloth and hair permeated the room. We remained with Barbara and their two young daughters through the night until morning. Dumond was buried that afternoon.

It was not long after the death of her husband that Barbara felt the need to take in boarders. Dumond left neither inheritance nor pension, the large house on Lloyd Square being the only substantial asset bequeathed to her. There was no question of selling, for the square was quite rundown, with many of the houses in great need of repair. Only the most optimistic of investors would have considered purchasing any of them. Doing some of the initial work herself and thus balancing her first rental income against the repairs, she made steady progress. The Davies home in time became not unlike that comfortable residence at 221b Baker Street run by Mrs. Hudson, who generously took it upon herself to guide Barbara in the making of a boarding house.

In the days immediately after Dumond's death, we saw Barbara with great frequency, but soon our meetings became rarer, and we kept in touch through Mrs. Hudson, who as a landlady of long experience with peculiar and often penurious tenants had become one of Barbara's close and valued friends. It was indeed through her insistence that Holmes and I found ourselves one morning in Lloyd Square standing in front of the Davies residence, ready to help with what Mrs. Hudson saw as an unusual occurrence, one of which Sherlock Holmes at the very least, she thought, should be made aware.

When the door opened, a smiling Barbara greeted us. She had aged considerably since we saw her last. Her hair had turned almost white and she walked hesitantly before us, slightly bent, trying to hold her head straight. When she spoke, however, she showed considerable strength in her voice, and her face displayed the same vibrant spirit as before.

"Do come in, you two. It has been too long a time."

We sat together over tea and heard the story of what had troubled Mrs. Hudson.

"I don't think it's anything of consequence, but your landlady thinks quite differently. And since she has lived with you two for so long, I feel that she may be right."

"Mrs. Hudson has developed a certain acuity in these matters," said Holmes, "a knack for perceiving irregularities in human affairs that even I at times have overlooked. Indeed, I have come to value her opinions. But let us hear directly from you what has happened."

"Dumond's death, as you know, was a terrible blow to me, and for a time I could barely think," she began. "The world, however, does not stop even at the loss of one's beloved. I found that Dumond had, to add to my sorrow, no money except what he earned as a doctor. There was nothing for me and my two young daughters to live on. I tried to find work, but all my efforts in that direction came to naught. It was at this low point in my life that I thought of taking in boarders. The house, as you know, is large, and when I examined it closely, I found that if I took in a few boarders, I would be able to survive: I could keep the house and feed my daughters and myself. I spoke to Mrs. Hudson about my plans, and she not only approved but helped me over the coming months. When the rooms were ready and Mrs. Hudson had approved the changes, I began interviewing prospective clients. It took me only a week to fill my rooms, and for the first time since Dumond's death I thought I could go on."

Holmes sat back and I could see his eyes running over the room and its contents, noting the stair just beyond the door, the paintings Dumond worked on during his spare moments, the large number of books neatly stored in their shelves.

"A few weeks ago," she continued, "one of my rooms, then given to an American writer from Boston, was vacated, and I promptly advertised in *The Times* for a replacement. I could have rented the room twenty times over, but among the crowd of candidates was a young man, a medical student. His name was Ian Rose. He was an acquaintance of Dumond's at the university, but I only knew him slightly. He was a Scot from Edinburgh, charming and witty, willing and able to pay an advance of six months. He knew my tragic story, since Dumond was among the occasional lecturers in surgery brought in to discuss special topics, in Dumond's case the specialty being the knee.

"Mr. Rose turned out to be an ideal tenant, one considerate of others, neat in his habits, and extraordinarily helpful with my two daughters, whom he often took to the zoo when I was occupied. He kept irregular hours, and often was out for much of the night, but to his credit, he was as quiet as a mouse when he came in, sometimes in the early morning."

"About three weeks ago," she continued. "Mr. Rose came to my office to inform me that he would be returning to Edinburgh for advanced study and that he would soon be vacating his quarters. I was truly sorry to see him leave. I gave a small farewell party for him with his friends in the square, and on the morning of his last day in our house, I had a special breakfast prepared for him. At nine in the morning he came down those stairs with two suitcases. He placed them in the hall and told me that he was going to hail a cab to take him to the train station. We would then say our farewells. I nodded to him and went to my office, thinking that I would hear his familiar knock at my door momentarily. To make the story short, however, he never appeared. The valises were there in the late afternoon, and indeed are still there. I allowed no one to touch them. I called our mutual friends and his teachers at the university. No one had seen him. After two days of frantic searching for clues, I placed an advertisement in the paper and waited. There was no helpful reply, and at that moment I called the police. They were less than considerate, saying that missing persons were the greatest problem of the police in England. Their number had increased dramatically, and they, the police, hopelessly understaffed."

"The rather typical remark of one who finds himself beyond his depth," said Holmes with a smile. "There may be more to this disappearance than meets the eye."

"There is one more point, dear Sherlock, that I must bring to your attention and that is this: one of our neighbors, Mr. McHugh, insists that he ran into Ian Rose as he was entering the station at Russell Square, but it was a very different Ian that he saw, if indeed it was Ian. The man was filthy, dressed in torn rags, his hair and beard unkempt. As soon as he saw Mr. McHugh, he uttered a cry of surprise, turned, and disappeared into the morning crowd."

"Most interesting. Mr. Rose is most probably alive then. And where is Mr. McHugh? May we speak with him?"

"Yes, you may, but first have a look at Ian's flat, and then we shall meet McHugh at his residence across the square."

We followed Barbara up the stairs to the very top of the building. Rose's quarters were very small and barely constituted what might be called a flat. They consisted of two small rooms, each with a small window, one large enough to take a bed, the other slightly smaller. It contained a desk and chair.

"I see that you have had the place cleaned," said Holmes disappointedly. "A pity, since we might have found something of value to our investigation. Still, I shall have a brief look."

I watched as he combed the floor on all fours, taking samples of dust and carpeting, anything that he could fruitfully test under the microscope. When he rose, he looked out one of the windows to the street below. He then examined the window frame and stared for a long time at one of the glass panes, which had some scratches on it. He called me over and asked whether they suggested anything.

"They appear to be curved, almost a circle, as if a round object had been repeatedly pressed and turned against it," said I. "And there appears to be some soot and a bit of wax on the window, somewhat higher up."

"Good, Watson. Now the question arises: what was the object employed and why was it used? Note, old boy, these holes in the window frame, recently filled with putty. There are four holes arranged, if I am correct, into a rough rectangle. Finally, look here, just to their right, a larger hole, about half an inch in diameter and also filled with putty only recently applied, since it appears to be soft, almost fresh. Let me have your pocket knife, Watson."

Holmes extricated most of the putty. The hole went through the wall to the outside.

"Most interesting, Watson," said he pensively, as if he were speaking to himself. There is some dark-colored soil, almost black, mixed in with the putty. Barbara," said Holmes, "do you remember any of this being here before Mr. Rose left?"

"Yes, I forgot to mention to you that . . ." she paused.

"Mr. Rose was an amateur astronomer," said Holmes finishing her sentence.

"Yes," she replied in surprise, "but how on earth did you guess that?"

Holmes smiled. "I never guess. Watson can attest to that. I assume that when Rose first took the room he also took your permission to drill the holes—with the promise that he would do or pay for the necessary repairs. He said that he would need to do so in order to affix a small telescope, the implication being that in some vague sense he was indeed an astronomer."

"You are quite correct. He filled the holes the day before he left. But what significance do they have? They are such a small detail."

"My profession is based on such details, call them trivia if you will, but without them, the solution to many problems would never occur. And since we are only at the beginning of the case, they indeed may still prove to be of no significance whatsoever. The important thing is to observe them, however minute they might seem to be. One more look in this closet. Hello, what have we here? How did I miss that?"

Holmes had now noticed a loose board in the closet floor. He lifted it up and pulled out a small telescope.

"Ah, here we go. Let us see if it fits the holes we find there."

The telescope had attached to it a wire from which a piece of metal about two inches square hung. The holes in it matched precisely those on the window frame. By tightening the wire, the telescope became fixed. Holmes peered through it.

"Interesting, dear Watson, have a look."

I looked through it and saw the upper storey of a house on the corner of Wharton Street.

"Well, Holmes, I must say that I see nothing remarkable. It looks like a house—indeed, the one over there," said I, returning the telescope.

"Well, my dear friends, whatever its purpose, it is not pointed at any known celestial body. The use of the instrument must have been more mundane," said Holmes.

"But why pretend to have such an interest?" I asked.

"We do not know at this point," said Holmes. "Let us leave it for the moment.

"And now, if we may, let us pay a visit to Mr. McHugh."

John McHugh lived directly across the square with his wife, Mary, and their two children. The family occupied a single room on the second floor of a house in almost total decay. Unlike their father, the children were thin and listless. McHugh, however, was a rough-hewn man, stout, unkempt, and out of work. His huge stomach pushed through his shirt where several buttons had popped.

He offered us a glass of ale, but we declined. He seemed incredulous at our refusal and filled his own glass. Mary McHugh, a short gray mouse of a woman, was obviously ill at ease and kept uttering apologies for the disorderly house we had entered. She repeatedly watered two wilted aspidistras in the window as we spoke. The signs of poverty—that peculiar London variety—were everywhere. Much of the furniture was broken and in tatters, and the floor of the sitting room was littered with newspapers and jagged pieces of broken glass. A filthy rug covered much of it. A young kitten sat in front of me chewing on the remains of a small mouse. The kitten was as emaciated as the children. Everything appeared to be sticky with the fingers of the two girls.

McHugh motioned us to sit and Holmes handed our host a paper left on the chair he took.

"This is Mr. Sherlock Holmes and his colleague, Dr. Watson," said Barbara. "They are here to look into the disappearance of Mr. Rose. You claim to have seen him."

McHugh spoke with assurance. "'Twas 'im I tell ya, Mr. 'olmes, no doubt of it. I'd know thet face o' 'is anywheres.

The bloody rascal popped out o' sight as soon as 'e saw me. Poor man, 'e seems to have gone off 'is rocker."

"Quite possibly that is the case," said Holmes. "But tell me, Mr. McHugh, you are a singer, a tenor if I am not mistaken, and have performed at Sadler's Wells on occasion."

"Now 'ow did ya come ta thet conclusion? Mrs. Davies told ya all about me, eh?"

"Quite the contrary; I deduced it. I observed also that Rose owed you a large sum of money for losses at the gambling table, one hundred pounds I would say."

"'ow did you know thet? Even my Mary 'ere don't know thet."

"I am a student of opera, Mr. McHugh, and I heard you on occasion years ago before you ruined your throat with the overindulgence in substances antithetical to the musical stage. Your gambling debts did not help your voice, either. I remember vividly your remarkable rendition of 'Nessun dorma.' As to the gambling, here: this paper, which preceded me in this chair, and which I removed as we sat down, registers the debt. I assume its veracity."

"The money's gone wit 'im, Mr. 'olmes. I 'ope you find 'im, the bloody thief."

"Please tell to me again exactly what you saw, where, and when."

"It was three days ago, Mr. 'olmes, I was goin' to me new job at Simpson's food market. I was mindin' me own business when I saw 'im. It musta bin aroun' six thirty in the mornin'."

McHugh stopped long enough to finish his ale. He wiped his lips on his sleeve.

"It was at Russell Square. It was still dark, I remember. 'e came boundin' off the lift when 'e almost run me down. Then I saw who 'e was and tried to grab 'im but 'e pulled 'imself free and ran off. 'e looked if anythin' very bad, wot wid 'is 'air all shootin' in every direction, and 'is face almos' black wi' dirt. But I recognized 'im I did. No doubt about it. "'Course I dint get me money, the bloody crook . . ."

"Do you remember anything else, anything at all?" asked Holmes finally.

"I do, as a matter of fact. 'e was carryin' a shovel."

"Thank you, Mr. McHugh. Should you remember anything else, please let me know."

Holmes stood up and we left. We returned to Barbara's house. As we entered her sitting room, Holmes said, "Barbara, let us open the valises that Mr. Rose chose not to retrieve."

Holmes brought them into the light. They were locked. Holmes took a pick from his overcoat and opened them.

"How curious, Holmes, why there's nothing here—mirabile dictu—except two pieces of an old shovel, one in each of the valises," said I.

"Interesting. A shovel, the column of which is broken in two so that it is now useless. But it may be no ordinary shovel, Watson. Note the letters stamped on it: C and L. It has been thoroughly cleaned, indeed scrubbed, before it was placed in the valise. I suspect that it broke just before Rose was set to leave and caused him some inconvenience. Most probably it is one like the shovel that McHugh saw."

"But why did he not just throw the shovel into the trash?" I asked.

"I suspect, dear Watson, that when we learn that we shall have found Mr. Rose."

We accompanied Barbara to her door, and then walked south and west to the edge of the square. Holmes stopped for a moment and glanced towards the Davies residence, then turned and looked upwards at the house in front of which we were standing.

"This one is empty, Holmes," said I.

"Yes, indeed. I thought as much. And vacant for a long time. Now, Watson, let us walk down the hill to Kingsway."

We had not gone far down the hill on Wharton Street when Holmes stopped again, this time in front of a small iron gate. It appeared to mark the entrance to no house or yard in particular, but opened upon an unkempt dirt path that went between two houses.

"Come, let us enter," said Holmes.

We found the gate to be unlocked. Holmes closed it after us.

The path turned north and we walked now between two windowless walls that belonged to adjacent houses, one of which I realized was the vacant house we had just seen from the square. We walked to the end of the path, where it opened up into a grassy plot of weeds and trash, mainly pieces of rotted wood interspersed with which there were piles of filthy rags and what looked like the remains of an upholsterer's shop. It was a silent piece of isolation in the very heart of the city, invisible from the street.

"Nothing of interest here," I said.

"Quite the contrary, Watson. This pile of wood and other castoffs may have some connection with the circular marks on the window and the putty-filled holes in Barbara's establishment. But let us continue."

What struck me as an outlandish conjecture on Holmes's part produced a wide smile on my face.

"Holmes, you're going daft, old boy."

As I spoke, Holmes climbed the stairs to the back of the nearest house and turned the knob. The door was unlocked.

"You may be right, but let us see. Remain here while I take a look."

I stood firmly on guard of this unexpected melancholy spot between two houses. Holmes returned very quickly.

"It is all beginning to fit together quite nicely. Come, Watson, we haven't a moment to lose. My only fear is that we will be too late. It is the new moon tonight, and our quarry will want to act in complete darkness."

He pulled at me so strongly that I dared not ask him what he had found. He closed the gate and we continued our walk to the bottom of the hill, where he hailed a cab. When we reached Museum Street, he told the driver to halt and jumped out.

"Watson," he said in almost a whisper, "I must spend a few hours on some questions related to this case. Meet me at home at six this evening. Call Lestrade and have him come. Tell him it is urgent, and both of you bring your revolvers."

I watched as Holmes walked into the museum, and then directed the cabby to Baker Street. I called Lestrade and he arrived immediately.

"What's he up to this time?" he asked as we sat and waited.

"I don't really know," said I, "except that Holmes left me at the museum and seemed somewhat excited, shall we say?"

We were both silent for several minutes as we pondered Holmes's intentions.

"Then he's onto something rather big, I should think."

"Rather big indeed," said Holmes as he came through the front door at that very moment.

"Here, gentlemen, put these rags on and we shall be off."

The rags were an old shirt, torn trousers, and black handkerchiefs to hide our faces. Holmes was wearing the same.

"Gentlemen, let me explain part, at least, of what we are doing dressed this way. A few moments in the museum examining the architectural plans of this square when it was first built in 1820 gave me the clue that I needed. You may recall, Watson, that in the suitcases left behind by Ian Rose there were two parts of a shovel with the letters C and L?"

"I know that one, Mr. Holmes. Any bobby can tell you what that stands for: City of London. Those shovels belong to the city."

"Indeed, Lestrade. And the old plans and maps I found in the museum pull all the clues together."

"Why is that?" I asked.

"I'm afraid that we haven't time for me to explain it all. Let us say only that a number of thieves, gravediggers to be exact, may be on their way to Lloyd Square, as I speak. We must get there before they do. As soon as we arrive, Watson, the two of you go to the cellar of the house we visited and hide in the dark corners far from the door. If I am correct, a group of men will begin to gather. By all means stay out of any light. One of the thieves, their leader, may address the men. As he leaves I shall arrest him. I shall be carrying a large kerosene lamp. When I light it, pull out your revolvers. I shall do the same. At that moment, Lestrade, identify yourself and put the whole group under arrest. If all goes well the men will be caught by surprise and will offer no resistance. If you have to fire, fire into the air. I shall see you in a little while, and I shall share my deductions with you."

We hailed a cab for the square. Lestrade followed me into the house and then into the cellar. We each chose a corner and put the black bandannas over our faces. It was pitch-dark.

In a few minutes we were no longer alone. Several men entered one by one. None noticed us. One stood up and addressed them in a soft but earnest voice.

"Men, I won't waste time on words. We have received the signal. We have to move quickly. You know what we are looking for. There will be a lot of it. When you find it put it in one of these barrels. Remember: we have three hours, no more.

"We have to accomplish our work in that short time. You all know and trust each other. I shall be on guard outside. When I return, we leave. Have to it, lads."

There was a change in the grammar and enunciation, but there was no question that the voice was that of John McHugh, his pot belly almost visible in the shadows.

There was a general commotion, quiet but steady, and then the sound of shovels digging into the earth, followed occasionally by the sound of someone emptying a shovel into one of the containers.

The digging continued steadily into the deep night. Despite the cold outside, the cellar was warm. Sweat poured from us, and we commiserated with some of the other men with grunts and groans.

Then, as he had said he would, Holmes entered the room and lit a large lamp. The men were momentarily blinded by it. Holmes addressed them in a loud firm voice.

"I am sorry to interrupt your excavation, dear gentlemen, but, unfortunately, you have been found engaged in looting an old graveyard, a serious offense under British law. Your leaders have been captured. Men from Scotland Yard are guarding the exit. Please turn and face the wall. Follow the shadow of the man to your right. You will exit now one by one and will be put in temporary custody."

The men obeyed and went out calmly, though I heard some grumblings about the stupidity of the leaders. Lestrade went before me, and I was the last to leave that awful place with its odor of living human sweat mixed with the rot of mildewed bones. As my eyes grew accustomed to the street lights, I saw Ian Rose, the ringleader whose nocturnal scheme it was. He suddenly turned, however, and, pushing the men to the ground, freed himself and ran into the dark cellar. In a flash, Holmes was after him.

"Follow me, my boys, we'll get him," said Lestrade.

From outside I heard the scramble up the stairs.

"Hold your fire, Lestrade, I have him cornered. He can't move unless—"

I heard the noise of window glass shattering. Suddenly, Rose was beside me, on the ground, stunned by his leap through the window. He tried to grab my gun, but I gave him a blow to the head with it, and he fell to the ground. Cuffed now by Lestrade, there was no possibility of escape. We watched as the culprits were led away and then took a cab to Baker Street. Lestrade joined us.

"Well, Holmes, perhaps you should explain. I am completely in the dark . . ." said I as we entered our cab.

"I could use a few details," chimed in Lestrade. "The fact is, Holmes, I don't have any idea of what this is all about."

"It is simplicity itself, but, unfairly, I think I have all the cards, you two no more than two or three. Shall I begin at the beginning?"

"By all means," said I.

"As you will remember, Watson, from our conversations with Barbara Davies, we learned that our suspect Ian Rose was a medical student, but was fairly well heeled since he paid six months in advance. The rent was rather high for such a small place, so we must believe that he wanted that flat for other reasons only known to him. We learned too that he kept irregular hours and sometimes did not return until the early morning. He also was a gambler and had enough money to owe John McHugh about a hundred pounds, a good deal for a student. Already you see and feel, gentlemen, the contradictions in this man Rose. From where does he get his money? He must be more than just a medical student. He may be doing something rather unusual for his earnings."

"And what is that, Holmes?" I asked.

"Something especially out of the ordinary, Watson: grave digging, at first for respectable people bereaved by the loss of a loved one and needing a grave in a cemetery of their choice. Our culprit is greedy, however, and moves up in the chain of chores and their concomitant rewards. He moves from grave digging to grave robbing. Literally by the worst kind of skullduggery, he begins providing cadavers for the university medical students. The university is quite pleased with his supply at first because he makes it a point to remove the freshest examples from what is supposed to be their eternal rest."

"The man is a fiend, Holmes," shouted Lestrade with great disgust.

"But we are only at the beginning. Rose has a problem."

"Not enough cadavers . . ."

"Quite right, Lestrade. He needs a steadier and larger supply of corpses. He hires agents who comb the streets for derelicts and do them in. The number of missing persons in London suddenly increases as the number of agents willing to do this horrible kind of work grows. He has learned through Davies that Lloyd Square was originally owned by a rich merchant, Josiah Lloyd Pepys, who had built in the back of his house a hidden cemetery for rich members of a small sect of religious fanatics known as "The True Brethren of Ekkebu." The sect was founded in America some seventy-five years ago by one Lawrence Oliphant and his chief successor, a Thomas Harris of London, with whom coincidentally I have already come in deadly contact, but that is another story. Pepys convinced the congregation of Ekkebuites to change its wealth into gold bullion and allow the use of his own embalming methods to preserve their bodies for their future life in the heaven of their world spirit, the god Zandonai.

"Rose now has more than he can handle. The doctors have grown suspicious of these strangely embalmed cadavers. Rose needs a confederate, and he enlists our friend McHugh as his colleague in the gruesome work. McHugh, desperate for money, agrees to do the digging and hire help; but they are an unnatural pair. Rose is meticulous and McHugh is not. Rose's use of two small telescopes, for instance, and two candles in windows on the square was timed so that the bobby on duty would be at the far end of the square when Rose entered and exited. McHugh several times failed to put out his candle, causing the bobby to try to open the door. Luckily for them, the bobby does not pursue the matter. The bodies continue to arrive at the medical schools in a steady flow. There is no gold found, however, and despite his investigations that support a contrary conclusion, Rose is convinced that gold is still interred with the bones of the members of the Brotherhood. He cannot relinquish the idea, so attractive to a greedy individual is it. Think of it, gentlemen, the individual fortunes of several hundred dead, conveniently changed into gold bullion, lying there in wait for those willing to take the trouble to dig it up."

'Never heard the likes of it before," said Lestrade. "How did you figure all of this, Holmes? It is still beyond anything of its kind that I have heard of before."

"Rose realizes that he must act immediately. For him, it is all a matter of time. He recruits a few of his cronies to join

McHugh and his group. And he chooses this very night to dig out the cemetery because there is no moon. It is the perfect night. He cannot wait another month. At a meeting behind the Pepys house he explains to the men what is at stake. Most naturally, they are ready and able."

"Let us go back to the suitcases left and not picked up," said I.

"Indeed, Watson. And here the crime committed is far greater than housebreaking. You must change the charge, Lestrade, to include murder in the first degree."

I must say that I was stunned when I heard Holmes's words. And then I realized what he meant.

"Rose, if I am not mistaken, killed Dumond Davies in cold blood. He did this in order to silence him before he brought the cemetery and its contents to public attention. It was indeed Davies who first learned of the strange cemetery and shared what he knew with Rose early in their friendship. Rose became a model of stealth and deceit with Davies, and concluded that he must move quickly. The houses built over the cemetery had been vacant for decades, forgotten by the family, priest, and sect, everyone unaware now of the treasure that lay in that dark chamber, a few feet below the street. Rose had to have it.

"On the day fateful to him, Davies had invited the younger man home to meet his wife. Completely alone with his host, Rose dared not forgo the opportunity. He watched carefully as Davies began to repair an old lamp. Rose looked for a weapon. He saw the shovel in the Davies garden. Dumond was now kneeling on the floor concentrating on putting some wires together. A heavy blow to the back of the head caused Davies to fall forward. A few sparks and it was all over. Rose left unseen with his weapon, fearful that somehow it would be found and traced to him. When he decided to move he cleaned it thoroughly and broke it in two pieces to fit in his valises."

"But why did he not return and take the valises with him?" I asked.

"Here," said Holmes, "I can only conjecture. Perhaps he asked McHugh to retrieve them. Barbara surely would have let him have them."

I looked up as the first silver signs of morning appeared in the sky. I heard someone singing.

"And why did we and Tanner not see the blow to Davies's head?" I asked.

"*Nessun dorma*," said Holmes. "Let no one sleep. Listen."

THE MOUNTAIN OF FEAR

N.B. The reader of the following story will note, as he progresses into the text, a certain inconsistency in style, particularly at the beginning of the second section. Holmes himself pointed it out to me, and I enter a note of explanation here. Although I have used the same technique in other chronicles, particularly in "The Valley of Fear," Holmes has convinced me that a word of comment would not be amiss.

Some time ago, on one of our long journeys between London and Rome, Holmes settled himself quickly in his seat and barely spoke, having immersed himself in a very long novel from which he refused to be distracted.

"My apologies, Watson, but as soon as I finish with this I shall hand it over to you."

It was on the following morning, if I recall correctly, that he read through the final pages and with a flourish, handed me the large tome.

"Here," he said, "is one of the finest novels I have ever read. I recommend it to you with great enthusiasm."

I took the book from him and read on its cover: The Betrothed *by Alessandro Manzoni. I confess that I had never heard of either before. I began reading, and once past the first few pages, I was enthralled by the subject as well as its style. Holmes must have found me tiresome as I marveled constantly at the writer's skill.*

I finished the volume after we reached Rome and could not rid myself of its beauty. In homage to the great writer, I have followed his style in a few places in the following story. I beg the indulgence of the reader of these meager fables for the seeming but unintentional impertinence.

John Watson, M.D.

IT WAS A TIME OF GRAVE CONCERN IN THE HISTORY OF Britain. The year was 1901, the sixty-fourth year of Her Majesty's reign. The Queen lay dying, and the world waited with the greatest apprehension for the announcement, now deemed inevitable, that the longest reign in English history had come to an end. Edward, Prince of Wales, stood by, manfully aware of the awful burden that was about to descend upon his shoulders.

During this period, I had seen little of my friend, Sherlock Holmes. Indeed, the national melancholy seemed to have affected him severely. He offered almost nothing beyond rather curt greetings when we met, and appeared to be completely absorbed, possibly in a case of great importance and intricacy. At least so I judged, for I had lived with him long enough to have become familiar with his most peculiar ways. He was as he had always been, only more so during this period, or so it seemed to me. He came and went at all hours, often in disguise, rarely as himself. On these particular occasions, he had a preference for members of the working class. A carpenter, a housepainter, and several varieties of maid were among the figures that came and went from our quarters, almost on a daily basis.

Once at home, he would sit silently or immerse himself in a strange assortment of books. I noted at the time a number of old tomes strewn across the floor in front of his easy chair: Mackey's *Extraordinary Delusions* and *The Madness of Crowds*, van Noltke's *British Heraldry*, Wright's recent biography of Nana Sahib, Prescott's *History of the Tattoo*, and Lombroso's *After Death—What?*, the latter a most singular choice considering Holmes's strong views on such matters. I must confess that I could make neither head nor tail of this odd assortment, strange even for Holmes' peculiar tastes.

It was towards eleven one night, a cold, rainy one in early January, if memory serves, that the mystery in which Holmes was engrossed began to show the first grim fragments of its still rather shadowy outline. I sat alone in our quarters on Baker Street. Holmes had not appeared for dinner, as he had promised in a rare moment of affability. I supped alone, therefore, and then lit a fire and sat reading, warmed by its flames. I must have dozed off for a time, for I remember being startled awake by the rapid opening and closing of our front door. I jumped up to find an old woman, her hair and clothes dripping from the rain, standing on the threshold, shaking and closing her umbrella.

"Please, Watson, control yourself if you can, and refrain from comment," said a familiar voice. "I am soaked through, and I can assure you that a tight feminine corset stuck to one's middle does nothing to improve one's humour."

My friend must have seen the smile that flickered across my face as he stretched to his full height and tossed the old woman's grey wig onto the floor. There, soaking wet in humble feminine attire that would have befitted our landlady, Mrs. Hudson, stood Sherlock Holmes, the world's greatest detective.

Avoiding my gaze, Holmes retired to his room for a few moments and then returned wearing the heaviest of his woollen robes. At first, he said nothing. He lit his pipe, sat in his easy chair, and stared at the myriad shapes produced by the flames in the fireplace.

"Lestrade should have been here by now," he said absently. "There has been a murder tonight, dear Watson, and our ferret-like friend will be well beyond his depth in trying to solve it."

"And who was murdered?" I asked rather offhandedly.

"Sir Jaswant Singh," he replied firmly. "We shall read of it in the morning papers."

I was taken aback at the news. "Good Lord, Holmes, how terrible. One of the great lights of London Society. How did you learn of it?" I asked.

"I was there, Watson, and called the bobby for help. A man rushed up to him shouting "*Muori!*" and fired at close range. Sir Jaswant was dead as he fell to the sidewalk near his home in Eaton Square. There was little I could do. The bullet was a direct hit to the heart. No doubt the papers will mention an old woman who called the police and who subsequently disappeared. That old woman, as you may surmise from my most recent attire, was your friend. Lestrade most probably has issued orders for her arrest by now."

"And the killer? Did you see him?"

"I did indeed, but I couldn't follow him, having to rush to Sir Jaswant's aid. I have a fair idea of where I may find him. He is quite clearly an Italian, judging from his appearance and language. But it is late, good doctor. Shinwell Johnson and Bobbie Neary, the most resourceful of the Baker Street Irregulars, are on his trail as we speak. There is little to be done before they report. Let us therefore continue our conversation in the morning. The rain has turned to snow, and by now Lestrade may be fast asleep in his bed, waiting for the morning to show his face."

I awoke early the following morning. I had had difficulty falling asleep and felt weary in my bones. The murder of Sir Jaswant had lain heavily on me, and I slept fitfully. As I dressed, I reviewed to myself what little I knew of the great financier. I had known him personally, if not at all well, for we had served together on the boards of several of London's medical charities. Sir Jaswant had become in recent years one of England's most generous philanthropists, the benefactor of hospitals and other institutions. Of his origins, I knew little except the barest facts known to almost everyone. He was reportedly the scion of a Rajpoot family of the United Provinces in India, the son of a petty rajah of a small kingdom near Gwalior. He had arrived in England some twenty years before after a quarrel with his father, and in a short time had seen his small family inheritance grow into a successful banking business. A man possessed of great financial talent as well as considerable personal charm, Sir Jaswant soon came to enjoy the trust of many of London's rich, and his bank, the Anglo-India Bank, Ltd., was at the time of his death second in financial power only to the Bank of England. He was a financial pillar of the Empire, and the symbol of his bank—a simple cross inside a triangle—was now to be seen even in far-flung outposts of the empire, recognized even by children. In recent years, he had become a favorite of the Queen, and a confidant to some of the most illustrious of Britain's leaders. He was a lifelong bachelor until his marriage, a few years before his death, to Marietta, the youngest daughter of Melchior Barony, the shipping magnate, a woman twenty years younger. The marriage was not a happy one, and there was great public gossip as to the reasons, all of which must have been quite painful to Sir Jaswant. There were no children. Sir Jaswant lived in his mansion in Eaton Square, and his wife spent much of her time at their country mansion in Sussex. He traveled extensively on business and spent a good deal of his time in sport and other pastimes.

That is, in brief, what I knew of this quiet and polished gentleman. Shivering from the cold damp, I entered our sitting room to see that Holmes was up and sipping his morning tea. He had already lit the fire and read through the account in *The Times* of the murder.

"Here, Watson is the account in the newspapers. Lestrade did not sleep a wink last night, contrary to my accusation.

Considering what he has done, however, he would have done far better to have slept a full night."

I took the paper and read the following brief account:

> The Times regrets to inform its readers of the death of Sir Jaswant Singh, O.B.E., the well-known banker and philanthropist. His violent death at the hands of assassins unknown has shaken London society, where he was a familiar and beloved figure.
>
> The investigation has been hampered by last night's heavy rains, and the account of the events is perforce incomplete. It is known with reasonable certainty at this juncture that Sir Jaswant was shot fatally at close range shortly after 8 p.m. in Eaton Square as he made his way home after a meeting of the board of the Kensington Orphanage. The assassin escaped into the darkness without being seen. An old woman, still unidentified, discovered the body, and notified the police, who immediately went to the scene. Sir Jaswant was already dead. Inspector Lestrade of Scotland Yard was then called in and, after a preliminary inquiry at the scene of the crime, the inspector ordered Sir Jaswant's remains to be taken to the morgue at Scotland Yard for further examination. He then notified Lady Singh, who, it is reported, is on her way to London. As a precautionary measure, Inspector Lestrade, in the meantime, has detained Mr. Daniel Manin, the reported paramour of Lady Singh, and Mrs. Reeve, the housekeeper at Sir Jaswant's Eaton Square mansion, who, according to the

first bobby to arrive at the scene, bears an extraordinary resemblance to the woman who called to him as she tried to assist the dying man.

It is to be noted also that despite his pagan Hindu origins, Sir Jaswant had some time back formally converted to Christianity, and during his life worshipped regularly in the Anglican faith. Indeed, he explained often that the symbol he had chosen to represent his bank—a cross placed inside a triangle—represented the eternal truth of all religions but especially that of Christianity: the triangle the infinity of God and the Universe, the cross the suffering of Christ and mankind, and the three small lines at the bottom the eternal triads on which the prosperity of mankind rested: the triune god; past, present, future time; and Queen, Crown, and Empire.

On learning of her husband's death, Lady Singh last night described her relations with Sir Jaswant in recent months as distant but cordial. Grief-stricken, she has notified the Prime Minister that she intends to petition the appropriate authorities in order for Sir Jaswant to be interred in Westminster Abbéy in consideration of his great work for the Crown and Empire. His conversion will of course make his burial among the great of England all the more possible.

"Well, Watson, what do you make of it?"

"A most laudatory piece, Holmes, and Lestrade has lost no time in apprehending suspects, shall we say."

Holmes laughed for the first time in weeks. "So he has, but he is, as usual, running up the wrong alley. Poor Mrs. Reeve, that dear old soul. She was nowhere near the scene of the crime. My disguise of course was partly based on her appearance. It should be a busy morning, Watson, and I hope that you will be free to assist me. I was not alone last night. Shinwell and Bobbie were with me, and should report to me soon on what they saw and learned."

As he spoke, there was a knock at the door. Mrs. Hudson handed me two notes, one that announced that Lestrade wished to see Mr. Holmes that very morning at the morgue at Scotland Yard, if at all possible before noon.

"About time, eh, Watson? And the other?"

"Eusebio Ortiz y Vasquez . . ." said I, reading hesitantly from a card.

"Ah," said Holmes with enthusiasm, "Eusebio Vasquez, Chief of Detectives, Santa Fe, Territory of New Mexico, and the finest detective in the Americas. A most welcome surprise. What does he say?"

"That he will call upon you within the hour," I replied.

"Excellent, Watson, excellent. I shall be delighted to see Vasquez again. If possible, we shall have him accompany us to Scotland Yard. We met years ago, in 1885 I think, at the first criminal anthropology conference in Rome. Since then we have met at Montpellier and other places. We find each other's company congenial, and I am anxious for you to meet him. He is one of the great detectives, worth at least fifty Lestrades. He has the sharpest of analytical faculties, enormous physical energy, and deep appreciation of minutiae, which often leads to the solution of a case. A pity that he works in a backwater like New Mexico where his talents are rarely taxed to their fullest and crime is of the most uninteresting kind. What wonders he could work in London. Were he here, we could eliminate Scotland Yard altogether."

"I shall be delighted to meet him, Holmes. I have rarely heard you describe anyone in your profession with such words of praise."

"He has his weaknesses, of course, Watson. We all do. His is a tendency to become obsessed with his failures. While this in itself is not a fault, there is one obsession that he refuses to let go of: the murder of a priest many years ago in the southern New Mexico desert. It was Vasquez himself who found the victim's remains, but he has had no luck in solving the case, and through the years it has distracted him from more important things."

Holmes stopped abruptly. Then he continued: "Let us leave Sir Jaswant for the moment. Watson, on the shelf just behind you are my files on unsolved crimes. If memory serves, the name of the murdered priest found by Vasquez was 'Agostini.' Let us see if I have preserved anything on him."

As he spoke, Holmes pointed to the large scrapbooks in which he had placed innumerable clippings and had recorded in his own hand through the years a variety of strange cases that had received his attention. I handed him the first volume.

"Here we are, Watson. 'Agostini: name of a priest hermit found murdered in southern New Mexico in 1868. He appears to have arrived around 1865 from Italy, just after the American Civil War. Celebrated in northern New Mexico because of alleged miracles and cures performed. Ensconced on top of a mountain near the trading town of Las Vegas, where he practised his austerities and saw his pious visitors. He left suddenly in 1868 without warning to his adoring flock of worshippers and disappeared. He was reported to have been seen in Las Cruces near the Mexican border in the fall of the same year. His remains were found later in a desert cave a few hours' ride by horse from Las Cruces, presumed to be the victim of a robbery. Crime narrated to me many years later in Rome by E. Vasquez, who himself found the priest's remains. I made several suggestions to him, none of which bore fruit. Oddities: priests are rarely killed. When found was wearing a solid gold crucifix attached to a rather odd rosary. Rather inefficient thieves.' "

Holmes closed the scrapbook and reached over me to place it back on the shelf.

"The case is old, Watson, very old, and will remain unsolved in all probability. There is a period of time, say in most cases three months, in which a case must be solved. Otherwise, it becomes stale and difficult, almost hopeless. All depends on the freshness of the clues, and the thoroughness with which they are preserved. My greatest successes have come within twenty-four to thirty-six hours."

"And what is the oldest case that you have solved?" I enjoined.

Holmes thought for but an instant and said: "You have chronicled it yourself, Watson, in the case of the French savant—the case of a murder perpetrated centuries ago. By that standard, Vasquez still has a good chance. Only thirty-some-odd years have passed. We shall see . . . perhaps he has already solved it and is on to some new horror. . . . Hallo, that may be Vasquez now."

The door opened, and Mrs. Hudson led Inspector Vasquez into our sitting room.

"Welcome, Eusebio," said Holmes warmly. He beamed as the two shook hands.

"And this is my trusted friend and chronicler, Dr. Watson."

I extended my hand to the American. "I am most happy to meet you," I said. "Holmes has rarely spoken of any one with such praise as he has of you this morning."

"Praise from such a source is enough to warm you up, even on a morning like this," said Vasquez with a smile that showed his perfect teeth.

"I hope I haven't inconvenienced you by coming so early. You must be preoccupied with the Singh case. I read about it in the paper this morning."

"Not at all, Eusebio, we are delighted to see you. As to the Singh case, well. I am involved in it in several ways, but Lestrade is the chief investigator, as usual. He has sent a request that we join him this morning at the morgue. I trust that you would be able to accompany us."

"Of course," said Vasquez. "I am free, Sherlock, I have retired from official duty and so I have arrived in London my own man. Following your lead, I have become a consulting detective in Santa Fe, no longer attached to the New Mexico police."

"Splendid. My felicitations to you on your new freedom, Eusebio. You must enjoy it to the utmost."

As the two enjoyed their talk, I had the opportunity to observe the American detective. He was a short man, of powerful build, whom I judged to be somewhere in his fifties. His hair was black with a touch of grey at the temples, and he was dressed in what I took to be the uniform of the American West: blue denim shirt and trousers, black leather boots, and a light brown leather coat adorned with tassels everywhere. In his hands, he held a large-brimmed Stetson, which he played with as he talked. His most remarkable feature were his eyes: almost black in color, and piercing with a bright light that spoke of a considerable intelligence behind them.

"And what brings you to London, if I may ask?"

"My obsession, as you have called it in the past," said Vasquez quietly, as if to deny the obsession itself. "Since my retirement, I have been free to devote my time to this unsolved murder. There are new developments and they have led me here."

"All crime leads eventually to London, the great cesspool," said Holmes. "Watson and I are at your disposal, and of course we may call upon Lestrade and Gregson for the facilities of Scotland Yard, should it be necessary."

"Thank you," said Vasquez. "I'll need all the help I can get."

Vasquez spoke with a heavy American accent that betrayed only the slightest trace of his Spanish ancestry. His words had a most pleasant cadence to them, one that I learned later was typical of New Mexican speech.

"Perhaps I should review my tale, if you can bear it once again, Sherlock."

"Of course," said Holmes. "I acquainted the good doctor with the chief facts just before you arrived. But your own account would be most welcome. We have just enough time before we must meet with Lestrade," said Holmes looking at the clock.

Holmes stoked the fire, and our guest began his account. Sensing that we would be there for most of the morning, Mrs. Hudson anticipated our needs and brought in a new pot of tea

"This case has haunted me for over thirty years," he began, "ever since the beginnin' of my career. I had joined the Union Army when I was eighteen and after service for two years, the Civil War ended, and I was discharged. I then joined the New Mexico police and was assigned then to Las Cruces, a growin' town in the south of the territory. Lawlessness was rampant. Gangs of outlaws and Indians—mainly Apaches and Comanches—preyed upon the new settlers who came looking to set up small farms and ranches. I was given an area north of the town to patrol, one that had been recently cleaned out of outlaws by the army from Fort Union. So it was pretty peaceful when I began. I rode all day 'cause I liked to be in the saddle, and I stopped at all the new homesteads, makin' sure that all were happy and content. For three months the work went pretty well. Except for some big family rows, all that I had to contend with was pretty petty.

"One mornin'—must have been now almost thirty years ago—I was ridin' on some land that belonged to a local rancher named Juan Archuleta. Juan was a friend of mine, about my age—we had grown up together—and he had recently set up a small ranch with a few cattle, no more'n a few hundred head. Because some of his cattle had disappeared as soon as he brought them there, he decided to fence them in. But then he found that the fences had been cut in several places and his cattle run off. After talkin' it over with him, I decided to inspect the fences myself. Somebody, it seemed, was up to no good. Maybe I could find out who it was.

"I remember that it was the worst weather that anyone could remember. The old timers, both gringos and Mexicans as well as Indians, couldn't recall a drier spring. It was in fact a drought, the worst in fifty years, they said. There had been no rain for six months, and the melt from the mountain snows was too little to help. It was the month of June, and the water holes and ponds were dryin' up every where. The grass was brown and dead. I remember thinkin' that it looked like winter when everythin' dies, only it was hot, the sun without mercy.

"Anyway, it was about nine in the mornin' when I set out to check Juan's fences. I rode for about two hours into the desert. The fences in several places had indeed been cut, not broken, and I saw the tracks of several horses mixed with those of the cattle. Their trail led far to the west. I followed it for a time, then decided that, rather than follow it alone, I would return for help. We had been told at headquarters that there was a good chance that the Beaumont gang, led by Nick Beaumont and Ronald Kincaid, were up from El Paso and rustlin' all the cattle they could find. Rather than try to take them on alone, I took a shortcut to the southwest back to Las Cruces.

"Then, what happens so often in New Mexico happened. The blue sky suddenly began to disappear and black clouds rolled in on the first cool winds in months. Flashes of lightnin' lit up the whole sky and there was the loudest thunder I ever heard. I decided to head for cover. In the distance I saw a rocky ridge where I thought I might find shelter. I got my horse to run like the wind and lucky for me, for suddenly we were hit, my horse and I, with huge hailstones that fell everywhere just as we reached the ridge, I mean that hail was somethin' else again."

Vasquez stopped for a moment and sipped his tea. "And here, Sherlock, begins the mystery that has been with me since."

"Pray, continue, Eusebio, we are the willing captives of this drama."

"Indeed," said I, mesmerized by our guest and his tale.

"As I approached the ridge, I noticed that it was riddled with small caves, none of which appeared to be very deep but any one sufficient to keep my horse and I out of the storm. I reached the ridge just as the rains poured down on us at their heaviest. I dismounted and led my horse into the nearest cave. We gazed at the rain as it became a torrent, and I thanked the good Lord for this shelter. I sat down near the entrance just out of the rain and took my pistol out of its holster. For I knew from experience that these caves, the likes of which you can find all over New Mexico, often served as dens for a variety of varmints—especially mountain cats, coyotes, and rattlesnakes. I tried to peer into the darkness, but the sky had been too bright and my eyes saw nothin'. I took a drink of water from my flask and held it out in the rain to fill it. As the rain slowed, a cool breeze blew into the cave, and I fell asleep for a time, exhausted by my desperate ride to safety.

"When I awoke, the rains had stopped, and except for a wet spot here or there, you'd never have known that it had rained. They say that water is drier in New Mexico, and maybe it's so, for you would never have known that there had been such a downpour. The sun told me that it was near four o'clock. I turned toward the inside of the cave. It was about twenty feet deep and I could now see to the back of it. I got up and started to explore it. It was then that I saw, in a far corner, the figure of a man on his knees, his hands tied behind his back to a post. I went over and realized that the shape of a man was all that was left. There was nothing there but skull and bones and the clothes that covered them. He had been shot several times through the head. The skeleton wore the black vestments of a priest. From around his neck hung a gold crucifix and there was a silver ring on the fourth finger of the left hand. From the hands hung a rosary. I noted at the time, and will show you at the appropriate moment, that the rosary was a bit peculiar. The beads appeared not to be made out of glass or metal as usual, but out of some sort of seed or small round pieces of wood. The holes in the skull were the only marks of violence on the remains. But despite the lack of distinguishin' marks, I realized that I had come upon the corpse of a person who had long before disappeared and whose whereabouts for several years had been unknown. I knew then that I had found the remains of the Italian ascetic and hermit Giovanni Agostini, once a celebrated figure in New Mexico. He had lived on a mountain called Tecolote and such had been his influence among the local people that they changed its name to Hermit's Peak.

"I left the dead priest where I found him, and returned to report on what I had discovered on my trip. The following day four of us returned to the scene, carefully placed the remains in a rough coffin and returned with them to Las Cruces. An official report, issued after a thorough investigation, declared that indeed Agostini's remains had been finally found. He had been murdered by assailants unknown. His remains were interred in the cemetery at the great cathedral in Albuquerque. People came from everywhere to show their respect.

"It was just after the funeral ceremony that a very well-to-do gentleman came up to me and said that he wished to speak with me about the deceased. We entered the church and sat down in one of the back pews. He introduced himself as Carlos Romero of Las Vegas, New Mexico. He said that he was the person who had originally brought Father Agostini to the southwest. He had met him on a ship that they both had boarded in Marseilles, bound for Baltimore and New York. He spoke good English. He was impressed with the priest, who told him he wished to spend time alone in spiritual practise. He invited him to his home, and the priest accepted. His ranch, called El Porbenir, was near a suitable mountain—he had climbed it himself many times—and it was from his house that the priest had gone to climb the mountain where he had stayed for several years. He became in a short time a popular figure in the area, known as a miracle worker, and the local people began makin' the long climb to where the priest stayed. He had found a cave, where he practised his meditation, and he had learned to live off the plants that he found growin' wild at the summit.

"Romero had to travel often and was busy with his ranchin' business during the first year of the hermit's stay. One day he decided to visit him and found that he was not alone. He had with him an acolyte, who helped him perform mass. The man was extraordinarily short, almost a dwarf, but powerfully built. The man was not from the region, and when Romero spoke to him, in either English or Spanish, he only grunted in reply. The hermit explained that he was dumb, and that he had been abandoned as a child, for the hermit had found him livin' alone atop the mountain. He said that he thought he was an Apache. The man seemed harmless enough, but somethin' in his eyes made Romero uneasy. It was as if he was constantly on guard. And, said Romero, he noted that the man was not truly dumb, for he communicated with the priest in some primitive soundin' language that he had never heard before. He pried no further, preferrin' to maintain a certain distance from the priest. The acolyte certainly did not interfere with the priest's activities in any way and was rarely seen.

"Finally, said Romero, just before the priest left the mountain and disappeared, someone came to El Porbenir lookin' for him. He was a man, well dressed, and in his early forties, who said he was lookin' for the priest. His English was good, but he had a heavy Italian accent. He said that he had come because there was a chance that the priest was a long-lost brother of his, and he wanted to meet him to see for himself. His brother, he said, had a history of mental trouble, and his family had sent him to find him. His brother had boarded a ship in Marseilles bound for America but had never been heard from again. A chance meetin' with one of the passengers on that ship a year later had indicated that a priest had left the ship in the company of a well-known gentleman from northern New Mexico. Upon his arrival in Las Vegas, the Italian had learned of him and the hermit of the mountain. Romero immediately sent word by one of his servants, who returned and said that the priest was gone. Romero himself climbed up to the hermit's cave with the Italian, and found the place abandoned. The followin' day, Romero learned that the priest was seen in Las Vegas, from where he was reported to have headed south on foot. The Italian gentleman thanked Romero for his help and said he would follow the priest to see if he could catch up with him. The Italian never returned to El Porbenir, and the priest was never seen again alive."

Vasquez gulped down his tea and said, "Maybe I should stop there. It's time to go . . ."

"Indeed, it is," said Holmes.

The three of us bundled ourselves against the cold, and hailed a cab that took us to Scotland Yard. We arrived just before twelve at Lestrade's office, where we found the inspector pacing up and down, a smile of triumph on his face. Holmes introduced Vasquez and we sat there as Lestrade began his description of the night's events. As he reached the end, he said, "And so I arrested Manin, the well known and jealous paramour, and the old lady Reeve, the accomplice—"

"You would do well to release them immediately, Lestrade," said Holmes, interrupting him.

I could see Lestrade's face fall. He had been in this position before many times, and Holmes was rarely easy on him.

"And why is that?" he said meekly.

"First, my dear Lestrade, I must inform you that before the murder I was hired by one of the principals to make a certain investigation of the deceased. In pursuing this investigation, I happened to be at the scene of the crime when Sir Jaswant was murdered, though in disguise. I can assure you that the murderer bears no resemblance to Daniel Manin, and you should release him immediately, poor man, he has done nothing to warrant his arrest."

"And the old lady, Mrs. Reeve?"

"Safely home in bed, as she claims."

"Then, pray tell, Mr. Holmes, who was the old lady and where is she now?"

Holmes stood up, "Your humble servant, the old woman, stands before you exposed. Forgive the theatricality, Lestrade, but my disguises are quite good. As to the truth of what I am saying, my friend Watson here can attest to my return home last night not, shall we say, in my usual attire. No, Lestrade, the murderer is sitting here in London, about to leave, if my surmise is correct, and I would ask you to direct your assistant to usher in Mr. Shinwell Johnson as soon as he appears. He will know where the murderer is at this very moment. And now to the morgue."

Lestrade showed a certain pluck at this moment, despite the unassailability of Holmes's arguments. "I suppose I could stop you, Holmes, at this juncture from viewing the body since you are connected to one of the principals. And who is that, may I ask?"

"You could stop me, Lestrade, but I could have the necessary papers within the hour to view the remains. As to my client, it is Lady Singh herself. But more of that in due course."

We rose as a man and followed Lestrade to the morgue. The body of Sir Jaswant Singh lay on a table in front of us. Jones, the forensic pathologist of Scotland Yard, stood by. Holmes motioned me forward.

"Anything unusual, Doctor?"

"It is as you described, Holmes. A direct hit in the center of the chest, destroying the heart. Death instantaneous."

"Quite correct," said Jones. "Here is the bullet, which I extracted."

Holmes took it, examined it and passed it to Vasquez.

"Forty-five caliber, Colt revolver of the most common variety," said he.

Holmes then took to a minute scrutiny of the dead man, pouring over every inch of him, particularly his wrists and ankles.

"Hallo, what have we here?" said Holmes. He was pointing to a rough patch of skin on the man's right wrist. I took a look and saw what appeared to be a series of pin pricks.

"And here," said Holmes, pointing to the left ankle.

"I've seen them many times," said Vasquez. "They're what you get when you remove a tattoo—"

"Precisely," said Holmes. "Jones, a pen please. Thank you. Now, if I simply connect the dots . . ."

Holmes skillfully traced the outline of the old tattoo.

"An odd one," he said, "first the letter A, then the letter I, or so it appears, and then the numeral 3. So much for the wrist. Now the ankle: a triangle with a cross inside, with three marks at the bottom. It is the symbol of the bank. Or very close to it."

Vasquez's face became quite dark with thought. He began to pace.

"Holmes, you know what we have here. These are prisoner brands, tattooed on this man at some time in his life. We've used them in New Mexico. He obviously had them removed . . . to hide his identity."

"Precisely, Eusebio, you are quite right. But note. The wrist marking is a tattoo, the ankle mark is a brand, burnt into his flesh with a hot iron, somewhere in this vast Empire of ours. It may have been the supreme irony of this man's life to employ this common thieves' mark as the symbol of the prosperity of British might throughout the world."

Holmes fell silent for a moment, as if in deep thought.

"It is clear now that Sir Jaswant had a past which he wished to deny," he said. "What that past was we shall soon know, unless I miss my guess. You know, Eusebio, one is sometimes put in the position of Javert . . . the unmasking of a Monsieur Madeleine to find a Jean Valjean."

"With this difference," replied Vasquez. "I suspect that our man here is guilty of far more than the stealin' of a loaf of bread or a pair of silver candlesticks. Tell me, Mr. Jones, what was found on the deceased? Any personal objects, jewelry perhaps?"

"No jewelry, Mr. Vasquez. A few pounds, a pen . . . and this peculiar set of worry beads found round the neck." He handed a string of beads over to Vasquez, whose face showed immediately a frown of recognition.

"Rudraksa," said Holmes from across the room, "the beads of Shiva, a common enough devise in India."

"But not in New Mexico, and yet they are remarkably similar to what I found in the hands of Agostini's corpse. Look . . ."

There was total silence in the room as Vasquez pulled from his pocket a set of beads precisely like the one found on Sir Jaswant.

"Gentlemen," said Holmes grimly, "I sense the shrinking of the world around us, that what appears far away and unrelated is all part of a web, made possible by a new world in which nothing is unrelated and nothing is as it seems. Lestrade, do you have here at the Yard the records of our prisons abroad?

"We do, indeed, Holmes," said the inspector.

"Then let us look up A.I. 3."

"And what may that be?"

"Very simple, Lestrade, and obvious as soon as one directs one's attention to it. A.I., unless I am mistaken, refers to the Andaman Islands and our prison at Port Blair. The numeral "3" means the third prisoner placed there. As you may be aware, the prison in the Andamans was opened shortly after the Mutiny in 1857 as the place where the most dangerous prisoners would be housed. Unless I am again mistaken, Sir Jaswant, or whatever his name was at the time, was placed there shortly after the Mutiny itself, considering the low numeral three. Surely hundreds of prisoners have been housed there by now. Let us see, then, if the records of Port Blair show who he was and when he escaped. Then we shall be more able to piece together his later career, in particular how he arrived."

"In New Mexico," said Vasquez almost inaudibly.

"Precisely," said Holmes, staring at Vasquez meaningfully. "Welcome again, Vasquez. I trust that your long obsession may be approaching its fruitful conclusion."

I must say that at that moment my head was reeling with the quick series of revelations and conclusions that had just presented themselves. Who was Sir Jaswant? I stared at the dead man, his eyes closed now, and wondered what he might have told us had he been so inclined. My confused reverie did not last long, however, for an orderly burst in followed by a frantic Shinwell Johnson.

"Mr. Holmes, sir," said Shinwell breathlessly, "the man you asked us to watch, sir, he's been shot. He's dead. Neary is with him."

We were out of there in a flash. Lestrade ordered an armed guard to clear the way before us. Shinwell rode with the guard and we followed through the narrow streets of Soho. There in a filthy narrow alley was a small boardinghouse, filled with migrants from across the empire and elsewhere. Our man was in a basement room, dead in his bed. He had been shot in the head and, judging from the wound, possibly by a weapon similar to that which had killed Sir Jaswant. Neary had allowed no one in until our arrival.

"I know this man," said Vasquez, "he is the man I followed to London and have been searchin' for. His real name is Angelo Vetri."

He turned to Holmes. "There's one person left to find now, Sherlock."

"The acolyte," said Holmes simply.

"A.I. 4," said Vasquez.

That portion of the Gulf of Salerno that lies between the ancient citadels of Paestum and Agropoli contains, rising above the confines of its narrow shore, a number of uninterrupted rocky cliffs, unassailable were it not for the steep paths worn into the rock by the feet of peasants and animals over countless centuries. No more than the crudest of tracks, these trails are neither for the foolhardy nor the faint of heart. Only the local inhabitants are wont to use them, and many of these, whether fishermen living on the shore or farmers living above the cliffs, prefer to take a more circuitous but less laborious route that leads down a gentle slope north near Torre Greco, the promontory that forms the northern arm of the gulf.

The sea and the cliffs along this coast are among the most beautiful sights of Italy, by common consent a country where natural beauty is everywhere. But few from outside venture into the interior of these southern precincts. The mountainous district above the cliffs, known locally as Cilento, is considered even by more adventurous Italians to be among the wildest and most dangerous parts of the whole peninsula. Here, they say, all is thievery, vendetta, and black magic. The power of the curse, the evil eye, and all the many superstitions of an impoverished and ignorant peasantry reign supreme, in conspiracy with brigands and secret societies. None of Italy's many rulers, neither monarch nor pope, Habsburg nor Bourbon, has ever ventured to penetrate its isolation. Only their minions have entered and quickly left, leaving behind a ravaged and pillaged people, one vilified as well for its active resistance to oppression.

Yet, to the casual visitor courageous enough to confront the reputation of this ancient land, there would appear to be nothing remarkable here, particularly on the bright, unfilled mornings that are common in the southern regions. The life he observed would conform in general to what he might see elsewhere in the Italian peninsula, or in Europe for that matter. The land is tilled by industrious men and boys, their skin made leathery by the heat of the sun. The women, aided by their children, tend the animals and cook the simple meals that sustain the men in their labours.

If there is nothing unusual in the conduct of these people, our observer might still note, were he interested in such things, that the people appeared to be poorer than most. The soil is dry and rocky, the rain insufficient and unpredictable, and the sun relentless. Meals are perforce simple, a *minestra,* or soup, and the local bread, which is as hard and sharp as glass. The houses are of stone, often adjoining each other, and in many cases, attached to the hillsides in order to take advantage of caves and other natural openings in the hills. The people are rough hewn, the men in peasant garb, the women often dressed entirely in black in mourning for the dead.

Hearing their earthy language, our observer would rightly conclude that it is far from the language of Dante, incomprehensible to all but those of the region and the learned philologist. In this language, the people refer to themselves, as well as all other human beings, as *cristiani,* or "Christians," for, there being no other religion within their experience, the name of their own has become a universal appellation. In hard times, however, there is a tendency to remove themselves from this category and designate themselves as *disgraziati,* "fallen from grace," and living in a place where even Christ has chosen not to set foot.

It was towards sunset one evening in July in the year 1865 that our observer would have noticed, should he have bothered to look out to sea, a small boat leave a large fishing vessel farther out in the gulf and move smoothly and almost silently through the calm waters towards the temple at Paestum. Once arrived, three men jumped ashore, bidding good-bye to a fourth, who, as soon as the three had alighted, began his return to the fishing boat.

The three were robust and strong, in their early thirties at most, and resembled each other rather strongly. Indeed, two of them were brothers, Alessandro and Gaetano Vetri, and the third, a first cousin, Giacomo Santucci.

A small shower of rocks from above caused the three men to look up, where they saw at the top of the cliff a young boy motioning to them to climb the ancient stair that descended to the shore. Each carrying a large bundle on his back, the men laboriously climbed the steep cliff and arrived at the top, where the boy motioned to them to follow. In a few minutes, they were ensconced in the house of Francesco Gramsci, a native of Sardinia who had come several years before to Cilento as a schoolmaster. Gramsci greeted the men in a friendly manner and, after his wife served them a simple meal, he began to explain to them the nature of their mission.

The three could not but help stare at Gramsci, for he was a diminutive figure, made even shorter by a severely hunched back which contorted all of his body, making his round head look even larger than it was. Gramsci, however, moved and spoke as if he were oblivious to his physical condition. His voice was deep and resonant, and he spoke with such authority that the listener too soon forgot his physical appearance.

"You are about to go on a long journey," he said gravely, sipping from a glass of wine, "to participate in a mission essential to the formation of the new state of Italy. You have been chosen because of your bravery in action and your loyalty to the cause. As you know, the Neapolitan authorities are not at all kindly disposed to our movement, and will do all that they can to prevent you from succeeding. Should you be apprehended, you must do all that you can to avoid telling them anything. You are hereby advised to take this quick poison should you be caught."

Gramsci handed each man a small vial, which they placed among their belongings.

"Fortunately for you," continued Gramsci, "since most of your mission lies abroad, in America, your chances of avoiding the police are excellent. Now: to explain. You are probably aware that the nationalist movement badly needs money for its army and the latest weaponry. Much of the needed help lies in the pockets of those many Italians who have become rich in America. We have a list of the richest of them living in the cities of New York, Philadelphia, and Chicago. You are to convince them, by any means at your disposal, to contribute to the army fund. The details of your voyage are enclosed in each of these packets. Once you separate, your disguise as a traveler and your route will be unknown to the others. This is for your protection. You will not meet again until you arrive in the United States. Upon your arrival, you will be met and told how you will reunite and coordinate your efforts. Once there, you will be readily safe from the hands of either the Bourbons or the Papacy. But America houses its own hazards and you must be on your guard at all times. You will sleep here tonight, and tomorrow morning, before dawn, you will be taken to the first destination on your voyage. From then on, you will be on your own. Time is of the essence. Follow your instructions closely. They were carefully prepared. Make no mistakes in their execution, for the powers that oppose us are well aware of our financial plight and the possible ways that we might seek to improve it. And their agents and collaborators are everywhere. Please ask now any remaining questions."

The men remained silent, and Gramsci then directed them to their rooms. In the morning, at dawn, they left, each on his own path.

Two of them, Alessandro Vetri and his cousin Giacomo Santucci, left on ships from Italy, one from Naples, the other from Genoa. A third, Gaetano Vetri, the brother of Alessandro, traveled to Marseilles, where, after a wait of three days, he boarded an American steamship bound for New York. His disguise was that of a Catholic priest and his new name was Padre Giovanni Agostini. He was pleased with himself. The character of a priest came easy to him, for he had been an acolyte for many years and had been destined by his family to the seminary. He would have none of it, ran away, and joined Garibaldi's army. He fought all over Italy, knew Garibaldi personally, and had been highly decorated as a soldier. He sat smugly on his berth, alone now, for the other passengers had not yet arrived. *Ben fatto*, he said to himself, well done. He was lost to the world now. Who would have thought that he would finally become a priest?

He fell into a pleasant doze for a few hours. He was awakened suddenly by the motion of the boat. It was leaving. But there were no other passengers in his cabin. Rosary in hand, he opened the door and climbed to the lowest deck. He heard a few passengers on the deck above him, but none where he was. It was dusk. He watched as Marseilles drifted behind into the darkness. He smiled, content with his mission and the adventure that lay before him. He repeated his Hail Marys instinctively, hypnotically, fingering the rosary as if in a trance. So at peace was he for the moment that he was unaware of the figure that had emerged wet and naked from the sea, now behind him, who grAbbéd him with all his strength at the neck, twisting it, killing him instantly. The killer pulled the priest's body into the deep shadows, donned his clothes, and as quickly as he could, threw the naked body overboard. He watched as it disappeared into the wake of the ship. He quickly found the key to the cabin in the right-hand pocket of the priest's frock and went below. The boarding pass found in the same pocket gave him the priest's name. Only one other passenger was to take his place in the same cabin, a well-dressed man who introduced himself subsequently as Mr. Carlos Romero of the town of Las Vegas in the territory of New Mexico and a recent pilgrim to Lourdes. The killer responded with a smile: "I am Padre Giovanni Agostini. I am from Italy."

On the first night on board, as the ship entered Spanish waters as it pressed toward the Strait of Gibraltar, a diminutive figure, naked except for a loin cloth, came forth from the darkness and, bending over, reached for a plate of food that had been left there for him. The man was extremely muscular but small, dark-haired, his skin a kind of yellow that almost glowed in the dark. His eyes had within them the simple look of a child. Hungrily, he stuffed the food into his mouth, gorging, as if his hunger had become almost uncontrollable. When he had finished, he left the plate where he had found it and disappeared into a dark corner of the ship, where he was safe from view, covered by a tarpaulin stored near the lower deck.

If the upright Mr. Romero had harbored any suspicions concerning the priest with whom he shared a cabin, he would have noted that the priest prepared such a plate of food every evening and took it outside and placed it on the deck, usually just after dusk, like food for a dog or cat. Mr. Romero, however, saw nothing out of place and indeed was awed by his cabin mate, for he grown up to have the highest respect for the clergy. The priest, receiving no question from his cabin mate, mumbled some remark in explanation, something about the Christian duty to feed the animals, as did St. Francis, in this case some pelicans that had decided to travel to America with the ship.

It did not take the killer long to learn more about his new identity. The dead man's small valise contained the information that he eventually deciphered. He felt no remorse. For him it was survival that came first. And who worries about killing such a man? he thought as he went through the various articles in the bag. He learned that "Agostini" was an Italian agent instead of a holy man, bound for America in order to raise funds for Garibaldi. His instructions noted that he would be met by agents of the Italian revolution at Baltimore when they docked. And so the killer learned that he would have to leave the ship before they landed. Luckily, he was told that they would be docking in the dark in the early morning.

Except for Mr. Romero, the priest kept his distance from the other passengers. He spoke to no one, pretending to spend most of his time in religious meditation. This impressed Mr. Romero, who was a good, religious man himself. Indeed, so impressed did our New Mexican traveler become with his priestly roommate that he suggested one day shortly before they arrived that the priest journey to New Mexico.

"It is a magnificent place, barren and empty, most of the people are honest and hard working. A few are bad, and they could use another priest or two," said Romero between Hail Marys on his rosary. "Why don't you come?"

The priest explained that he was in spirit a monk, not a priest who served, but a Religious hermit, who practised austerities and wished to do that in a lonely place atop a mountain somewhere. Were there such places in America?

"Well," said Romero, "I got the most beautiful mountain on my land. The locals call it Tecolote. You'll love it. Nobody there. My place is called El Porbenir."

The priest agreed. He told Romero, however, that he had to meet some old friends in Baltimore and that the captain had given him permission to leave early.

The night the ship docked, Agostini, having bid good-bye to Romero, disappeared into the waters of Baltimore Harbor followed closely by his diminutive companion. It was a short swim, and they reached the shore undetected.

The two Italian agents who had come to meet him were surprised to find that Agostini was not there. They did not think to question Romero, but rushed back to their commander to report the disappearance.

As they had arranged, after two months, the priest met Romero in Kansas City, from where they continued their journey together to New Mexico by stage coach. It was a long and arduous trip, for the caravan was often beset by sudden storms and the threat of Indian attacks. When they reached Colorado, reports from Fort Union said that in order to avoid the Apache warriors in the vicinity they should take the northern trail through the mountains and descend into New Mexico through the Raton Pass. There a contingent of the American army would meet them and escort the party to Las Vegas.

The trip through the mountains was uneventful, and as they descended into New Mexico, they were met by Captain Knox of Fort Union and his men, who saw them to their destination.

A few miles out of Las Vegas, Romero pointed to the western horizon.

"Look," he said to the priest, "there is Tecolote, your home."

The priest looked in the direction Romero had indicated. There on the horizon, like some great purple whale, stood the mountain that would be the priest's sanctuary for many years.

That evening we convened at our quarters at Holmes's suggestion. Shinwell Johnson and Bobbie Neary sat on the floor near the door listening to every word. Holmes and I, together with Vasquez and Lestrade, sat in various places in the room. Even Jones, the forensic examiner, was there.

Holmes sat, weighted down by a large tome that Jones had brought from Scotland Yard. It was the volume on prisoners in the Andamans for which Holmes had made a special request. He had spent an hour perusing the appropriate entries. At a certain point, he looked up and said: "Gentlemen, we should begin our discussion, though one of our difficulties is the many points of entry possible from where we might begin. Let me start, however, with what we learn from this heavy tome. At least then I can rid myself of it once we have reviewed the facts."

Holmes opened the volume to its beginning. "I shall briefly summarize its contents rather than read everything to you. The entry we are concerned with primarily is A.I. 3 and, as it turns out, A.I. 4 as a secondary matter. The real name of A.I. 3 is Ranjit, a man born in Motihari, India, in 1840, son of an untouchable worker in the early indigo plantations. From the beginning he seems to have had a religious bent, encouraged by his father, and he planned to devote much of his life to Hindu religious practise. He was raised in the household of the plantation owners, an English family by the name of Blair. The boy was accepted by the family, and he learned to speak English well. One day, when the boy was about fourteen, Mr.

Blair, reacting to the threat of a workman's strike, or hartal as they call it, had several villagers' huts burned, among them that of Ranjit's family. All were lost in the fire, father, mother, and sister. Ranjit left the Blair household, swearing eternal enmity to the British. He became attached to a number of violent revolutionary groups, and in 1857 participated in the Cawnpore massacre, where he personally is said to have killed over ten people. He was caught, tried, and sentenced to life imprisonment at the new jail in Port Blair, Andaman Islands. His behaviour there was initially most cooperative, at least on the surface. One day, eight or nine years after his arrival, he participated in an attack on Lord Mayo, the visiting Vice-Roy. Mayo was killed in the fracas and Ranjit disappeared into the hills, presumably protected by some of the natives, who had no liking for our invasion of their territory. He escaped with an accomplice, A.I. 4, a member of the Santal tribe of Bihar by the name of Sujat, caught also at Cawnpore and again a member of the assassination plot to kill the Vice-Roy."

Holmes stopped at this point and placed the great tome on the floor. "At this point we are on our own, for there is no longer an official record of either of these men. Somehow they must have made their way out of the Andamans to the mainland, probably as stowaways. Then, either by land or by sea, most likely the latter, they arrived in Europe. They chose to escape to America, and here let Inspector Vasquez pick up the thread."

"What I say, of course, is at this moment is based on the available evidence, but may change as we talk. Let us see how far we can go . . ." continued the American detective.

"The two arrive in France, at the port of Marseilles, where one of them, possibly both, sneak aboard an American ship destined for New York and Baltimore. On the ship is one Gaetano Vetri, an Italian revolutionary disguised as a priest, Giovanni Agostini. He is one of three brothers on their way to the United States on different vessels to raise funds for Garibaldi's army. Unfortunately for Garibaldi, Roberto is immediately killed and thrown overboard by Ranjit, who, bein' roughly of the same stature and looks, replaces him immediately and becomes Padre Agostini. It bein' the very beginnin' of the voyage, Agostini is known to none. The number of passengers remains the same, the replacement is unnoticed. Ranjit, of course, is unaware at first that Agostini himself is in disguise. He befriends a wealthy New Mexican returnin' home from a trip to Lourdes and Rome. He is one Carlos Romero, who offers Ranjit sanctuary in a distant place. It is a perfect place to hide for a time, even possibly for ever and to begin a new life without the danger of the British ever findin' him. Agostini goes to New Mexico unaware that he was supposed to meet his brothers and engage in political activities for Italian unification. His companion, Sujat, accompanies him, but is rarely seen. He lurks in the shadows, his master's faithful companion. The survivin' brothers, of course, miss their compatriot and begin an inquiry. It takes them a long time to trace the priest, and they trace him to his lair, now called Hermit's Peak. One of them, Roberto, gets there just as Agostini leaves. He follows him and finally catches up with him in Las Cruces. There Ranjit murders Vetri and does his second impersonation. In disguise as

Roberto, he goes to New York, uses keys in Roberto's clothes to get his money—almost fifty thousand dollars—and decides to create a new identity for himself. He must act quickly since he is only a step ahead of the Italian agents in America. He shaves his head close, removes his beard, and buys the most expensive clothes he can find, goes to London, and begins to move among the great of England. He establishes a new bank with his newly acquired wealth and the help of some interested business men. He is in the clear. No one know who he is. Only one man is looking for him: the third Italian brother, the one who lies dead today in London."

"Or so it all seems," said Holmes.

The discussion that followed lasted late into the evening, but it added nothing more. The guests left around eleven o'clock.

The following morning Lestrade issued a order for the arrest of the accomplice and murderer, Sujat, or A.I. 4, as we called him. He has yet to be apprehended.

Vasquez visited us frequently during his stay, and out of our many conversations a more detailed and correct version of events arose, as well as a deepening friendship between us. When he left, we thought that we had a complete account, which eventually, in written form, Holmes submitted to Lady Singh. Both Lady Singh and Holmes decided to keep the report secret, for Parliament had already decided to allow Sir Jaswant's burial in Westminster. One day after his burial, Britain and the world were stunned to learn of the death of Queen Victoria.

"A bad week for our side," said Holmes with a touch of irony.

"Indeed," said I.

JAICO PUBLISHING HOUSE

Elevate Your Life. Transform Your World.

ESTABLISHED IN 1946, Jaico Publishing House is home to world-transforming authors such as Sri Sri Paramahansa Yogananda, Osho, the Dalai Lama, Sri Sri Ravi Shankar, Sadhguru, Robin Sharma, Deepak Chopra, Jack Canfield, Eknath Easwaran, Devdutt Pattanaik, Khushwant Singh, John Maxwell, Brian Tracy, and Stephen Hawking.

Our late founder Mr. Jaman Shah first established Jaico as a book distribution company. Sensing that independence was around the corner, he aptly named his company Jaico ('Jai' means victory in Hindi). In order to service the significant demand for affordable books in a developing nation, Mr. Shah initiated Jaico's own publications. Jaico was India's first publisher of paperback books in the English language.

While self-help, religion and philosophy, mind/body/spirit, and business titles form the cornerstone of our non-fiction list, we publish an exciting range of travel, current affairs, biography, and popular science books as well. Our renewed focus on popular fiction is evident in our new titles by a host of fresh young talent from India and abroad. Jaico's recently established translations division translates selected English content into nine regional languages.

Jaico distributes its own titles. With its headquarters in Mumbai, Jaico has branches in Ahmedabad, Bangalore, Chennai, Delhi, Hyderabad, and Kolkata.

SINCE 1946